T0116965

Prisoner
of Love

Other Ellora's Cave Anthologies
Available from Pocket Books

The Hottie Next Door
by Shiloh Walker, Elisa Adams, & Ruth D. Kerce

Good Things Come in Threes
by Anya Bast, Jan Springer, & Shiloh Walker

Doing It the Hard Way
by T. J. Michaels, Shiloh Walker, & Madison Hayes

Out of This World Lover
by Shannon Stacey, Summer Devon, & Charlene Teglia

Bad Girls Have More Fun
by Arianna Hart, Ann Vremont, & Jan Springer

On Santa's Naughty List
by Shelby Reed, Lacey Alexander, & Melani Blazer

Asking For It
by Kit Tunstall, Joanna Wylde, & Elisa Adams

A Hot Man Is the Best Revenge
by Shiloh Walker, Beverly Havlir, & Delilah Devlin

Naughty Nights
by Charlene Teglia, Tawny Taylor, & Dawn Ryder

Midnight Treat
by Sally Painter, Margaret L. Carter, & Shelley Munro

Royal Bondage
by Samantha Winston, Delilah Devlin, & Marianne LaCroix

Magical Seduction
by Cathryn Fox, Mandy M. Roth, & Anya Bast

Good Girl Seeks Bad Rider
by Vonna Harper, Lena Matthews, & Ruth D. Kerce

Road Trip to Passion
by Sahara Kelly, Lani Aames, & Vonna Harper

Overtime, Under Him
by N. J. Walters, Susie Charles, & Jan Springer

Getting What She Wants
by Diana Hunter, S.L. Carpenter, & Chris Tanglen

Insatiable
by Sherri L. King, Elizabeth Jewell, & S.L. Carpenter

His Fantasies, Her Dreams
by Sherri L. King, S.L. Carpenter, & Trista Ann Michaels

Master of Secret Desires
by S. L. Carpenter, Elizabeth Jewell, & Tawny Taylor

Bedtime, Playtime
by Jaid Black, Sherri L. King, & Ruth D. Kerce

Hurts So Good
by Gail Faulkner, Lisa Renee Jones, & Sahara Kelly

Lover from Another World
by Rachel Carrington, Elizabeth Jewell, & Shiloh Walker

Fever-Hot Dreams
by Sherri L. King, Jaci Burton, & Samantha Winston

Taming Him
by Kimberly Dean, Summer Devon, & Michelle M. Pillow

All She Wants
by Jaid Black, Dominique Adair, & Shiloh Walker

Prisoner
of Love

JAID BLACK
TAWNY TAYLOR
MICHELLE M. PILLOW

POCKET BOOKS
New York   London   Toronto   Sydney

Pocket Books
A Division of Simon & Schuster, Inc.
1230 Avenue of the Americas
New York, NY 10020

First Pocket Books trade paperback edition September 2009

POCKET and colophon are registered trademarks of Simon & Schuster, Inc.

For information about special discounts for bulk purchases, please contact Simon & Schuster Special Sales at 1-800-456-6798 or business@simonandschuster.com

Designed by Renata Di Biase

Manufactured in the United States of America

10   9   8   7   6   5   4   3   2   1

Library of Congress Cataloging-in-Publication Data
  Black, Jaid.
    Prisoner of love / Jaid Black, Tawny Taylor, Michelle M. Pillow.—1st Pocket Books trade paperback ed.
        p.   cm.—(Ellora's Cave anthologies)
    1. Erotic stories, American. I. Taylor, Tawny. II. Pillow, Michelle M. III. Title.
    PS3602.L285P75 2009
    813'.6—dc22   2008050598

ISBN 978-1-4391-3153-4

Contents

WARLORD

JAID BLACK

Prologue

The Isle of Skye in the Scottish Highlands, 1052 AD

Euan Donald watched dispassionately as the decapitated body of the Hay fell lifelessly at his feet. Blood oozed out from where the laird's severed head had been but moments prior, pooling around him in a river of dark red.

Sheathing his sword, the Donald's dark head came up, his black eyes boring holes into the anxious faces of those Highlanders surrounding him. None would rebel. None would second-guess his decision to execute the Hay chieftain. None would dare.

'Twas not bravado on his part, not even ego. Not really.

'Twas simply the way of things, the territory that came with being the Lord of the Isles, the king of the Highlanders, a god unto himself. Euan's word was law, as it had always been, as had the word of his father, as had the word of his father's father, and so on.

At the age of five and thirty, Euan had been chieftain to the Donalds and Lord of the Isles for over fifteen years. The price of being the master of all he surveyed had been paid in full.

His six-foot-six-inch body was heavy with muscle and riddled with battle scars. The harsh angles of his face were chiseled into a stone-like façade and hinted at no compassion, no mercy for any who would come up against him. His eyes were as black as his hair, calculating pools of obsidian that broached no argument and conveyed no emotion at all.

To come up against the Donald was to die. This fact was one that kinsmen and Outlanders alike understood well.

Today, as he did on most days, Euan wore his plaid of muted blue and green, a large emerald brooch holding the material together at his shoulder. 'Twas a fitting banner for the man who ruled the Highlands with an iron fist and who dwelled on an island many said was close to the heavens themselves, for it was surrounded on all sides and in all views by a formation of impenetrable clouds.

"'Tis done then." Graeme Donald, youngest brother to Euan, nodded toward a bevy of soldiers, indicating 'twas time to remove the Hay's bloodied carcass from the great hall. Turning to scan the nervous faces of the clan chieftains behind him, he waved a hand toward them and bellowed, "Will another amongst ye dare tae steal from the Donald?"

Murmured nays floated throughout the great hall, all eyes shifting from the Hay's remains to Euan's stoic form.

Graeme's upper lip curled wryly. "Weel then, 'tis time tae make merry, aye? Ye came fer a feast and a feast ye shall have."

Oppressive silence filled the chamber for a suspended moment. None were certain what to make of such an odd declaration. They had come for a wedding feast, every last one of them. They had journeyed from the protection of their respective keeps to witness marriage rites betwixt the Lord of the Isles and the first-born daughter of the Hay.

Not a one amongst them had ever fathomed the possibility that Tavish Hay would refuse to deliver the Donald's betrothed to her own wedding. Not a one amongst them would have credited the notion that the Hay would have been daft enough to allow Moira to break her sacred agreement and run off to the northlands with the brother of a Viking jarl.

For that matter, not a one amongst them would have been lack-witted enough to deliver such news to the Donald himself. Nay. They would have run hightail in the opposite direction. But then the Hay had never been renowned for his thinking abilities.

At last the laird of the lesser MacPherson clan broke the uncomfortable spell with a forced chuckle. "I will drink tae that." He lifted his goblet toward Euan. "Tae the Donald," he toasted, "and tae, err . . ." He shifted uncomfortably on his feet, the color in his face heightening. "Tae . . ."

Swallowing roughly, the MacPherson met Euan's black gaze. "Weel . . ." He lifted his goblet higher. "Tae the Donald."

"Tae the Donald."

The others were quick to chime in, all of them lifting their ales and meads in toast to the Lord of the Isles. Graeme's brow shot up, forming a bemused slash over his eyes as he cocked his head to regard his brother.

Euan smiled humorlessly as his dark gaze flicked from Graeme to the men standing behind him. Saying nothing, he stalked toward the dais that had been prepared for him in a slow, methodical stride. The great hall was so silent that each of his footfalls could be heard effortlessly, rushes on the ground or no.

When at last he reached the raised dais, he lifted the goblet that had been prepared for him and turned on his heel to face his rapt audience. Nodding once, he prepared to down the honeyed mead. "Aye," he rumbled, "I will drink tae that."

"What will ye do now, brother?"

Euan lifted a curious brow but said nothing. Standing atop the battlements, he scanned the outside perimeter below their position and absently awaited Graeme's meddling. His youngest sibling was the only one in god's creation who could get away with such. 'Twas mayhap because he had raised him and felt him more a son than a brother.

Graeme waved a hand absently through the air. "Aboot getting wed, aboot siring an heir, aboot—"

"Graeme," Euan said quietly. "I'm no' lackwitted, mon. I ken your meaning."

Graeme nodded. "Then what will ye do?"

Euan shrugged. He had known three wives and had lost all of them to laboring his bairn. Out of all three pregnancies and subsequent fatal deliveries there had been but one survivor, and that was his six-year-old daughter Glynna. After losing so many wives and babes, 'twas nothing really to lose a betrothed.

He turned his head to look at his brother, his facial features reflecting the fact that he had not a care one way or the other. A woman was a woman. Any woman of breeding years would do. "Get another wench tae take Moira's place in the bedsheets."

Graeme chuckled at that. "Mayhap had ye tumbled the Hay's daughter before the wedding she would have shown up."

One dark brow shot up. Euan shook his head slightly and looked away, his gaze flickering back down below the battlements. His hands fisted at his hips, the thick muscles in his arms bulged further in response. "I'm glad she dinna," he said honestly. "Truth be told I think a troll would be better bedsport than Moira."

Graeme grinned. "Ye have seen her before then?"

Euan shook his head. "Nay. But on Michaelmas three years past 'twas said by her own clansmen that she is possessed of an awkward appearance."

"I was no' there. That must have been whilst I still fostered under the MacPherson."

"Aye."

The brothers stood in silence for a long moment, breathing in the crisp night air. 'Twas May so the days were longer now, darkness still not having descended though it was well past the time of the evening meal.

Graeme's chuckle at last broke the silence. "I was thinking . . ."

"Hm?"

"Aboot the Hay."

Euan craned his neck to glance toward his brother. "Aye?"

"He owes ye a bride."

Euan waved that away. "I did no' kill the mon over Moira, though I know 'tis what the other lairds think. I killed him for betraying me. 'Tis a difference." He shrugged his broad shoulders. "Besides, the mon is dead," he rumbled. "His debt has been paid."

"No' really."

Euan sighed. It had been a long day and he was in no mood for conversing let alone for solving riddles. His youngest brother was mayhap lucky that he was able to rein in his temper where he was concerned. "Explain yourself."

Graeme thought to tease him a bit, but relented when he saw his brother's lethal scowl. He sighed. Why couldn't the man learn how to make jest? "As to that, 'tis true the Hay paid the price for helping Moira in her deceit, yet did he no' deliver another bride tae take her place in the bedsheets."

Euan grunted. "'Tis true."

Graeme stood up straighter, his back rigid with determination. "Then mayhap a wee bit o' reivin' might be in order."

"Reivin? Ye want tae go steal some *cattle*?" Euan said the last incredulously. "'Twill no' even the score."

Graeme's face flushed at the criticism for which the Donald felt an uncharacteristic pang of sympathy. He knew that the boy had only been trying to help lighten his black mood. What his sibling seemed unable to understand on his own was that his mood was always like this. After ten and eight years the boy should know that. But he didn't.

Sighing, Euan forced a grin onto his face and ruffled Graeme's hair affectionately. "Ye are just wanting tae prove that ye learned things from the MacPherson more useful than merely how tae bed a wench. Aye, that's what it is I'm thinking."

Graeme chuckled, no longer embarrassed. "Mayhap."

Euan considered the idea more thoroughly before responding. Mayhap his brother was on to something. Not something quite like Graeme had envisioned—he hardly needed more cattle on Skye for the love of the saints—but something vastly more important. He did, after all, need a wench to take to his bed and get her with heir. Besides, as black as his mood had been as of late a bit of thrusting between a wench's legs was an enticement unto itself.

The Donald's black gaze flicked over the castle walls and toward the rock-strewn beach below. 'Twas not so long a boat ride to the mainland. And from there mayhap a sennight's journey to Hay lands at best. "I think," he murmured, "that ye might be right, brother."

Graeme's eyes widened in surprise. "I, uh, I . . . am?"

Euan couldn't help but to grin at the boy's astonishment. 'Twas true he wasn't a man known for changing his mind. Set in his ways he was. "Aye." He nodded, his demeanor growing serious. "We shall depart on the morrow when the sun falls."

Graeme smiled broadly, unable to contain his excitement. 'Twas the first reiving the Lord of the Isles had made him a part of, brother to him or no. 'Twas past the time to prove he was now a man and no longer a boy. "'Twill be a good time, thievin' the Hay's cattle."

Euan shook his head slowly as he met his brother's eager gaze. "'Twill no' be cattle we steal, boy."

Graeme's eyebrows shot up forming an inquisitive dark slash. "The Hay's sheep are sorry I've heard it be told. No' verra wooly at all. Nay, brother. I dinna think their sheep are worth the time."

Euan shrugged. "'Twill no' be sheep we reive either."

"Then what? What will we be reivin'?"

The Donald arched one arrogant black brow. His upper lip curled into a mirthless smile. "Wenches."

Chapter 1

Nairn, Scotland, Present Day

EYES NARROWING, JANET DUVAL'S LIPS PINCHED TOGETHER AS she studied her outfitted form in the inn room's unflattering and depressingly accurate mirror. Nobody had ever accused her of being too skinny, she thought grimly, but lordy did she look pudgy in this number.

Twirling around to get a better look at her backside, she qualified that mental statement a bit. She didn't just look pudgy, she looked downright fat.

She wanted to go on a diet—really she did . . . !—but she knew at the same time that she never would. Janet morosely considered the fact that her body seemed to be at its happiest when she was about twenty pounds heavier than what was considered cosmopolitan back home in the States.

Ah well. C'est la vie.

Unzipping the fashion monstrosity that she was supposed to wear to her business meeting tomorrow, she threw it into a pile on the nearest chair and fished around her suitcases for a comfortable sundress. Janet told herself as she climbed into the cotton, clingy number that nobody at the whiskey distillery cared one way or another how she dressed up for meetings anyway. So long as she showed up tomorrow with a hefty check and purchased a ton of Highlander whiskey for the American-based firm she worked for, they'd all be happy.

After she'd donned the thigh-length, spaghetti strap green sundress, Janet took a speculative look at herself in the mirror and as usual found her attributes lacking. She wasn't gorgeous, she knew, but she oftentimes doubted that she was even remotely passable.

But then, Janet was the sort of female who would need a miracle before she'd realize her worth as a person and as a woman. Where Janet would have called her long, tawny-colored hair unremarkable, others would have noted the sleek beauty of it, not to mention the unruly curls that gave her a sensual, freshly bedded look.

Where Janet would have said her lips were too big and her smile too wide for her face, others would have thought her mouth lushly formed, her smile able to brighten even the blackest of black moods.

Where Janet believed her body to be too fat for a man to get turned on by it, men conversely tended to think of her curves as fleshy and voluptuous, the kind of body a man could cuddle up with on a cold night and love until all hours of the morning.

But Janet Duval never saw that possibility. Never even considered it. Not even once.

Turning away from the mirror, Janet glanced about her private quarters in the local inn until she located her favorite pair of sandals. Stepping into them, she grabbed her cloak from a wooden peg jutting out from the bedroom wall just in case it got a bit chilly out.

It was May, that much was true, but even in May the Highlander climate never surpassed the seventies. At night it could get downright cold.

Throwing her cloak absently over one shoulder, Janet picked up her purse and headed for the door. Tonight was, after all, fish and chips night at the local pub.

As she threw open the heavy door and closed it quietly behind her, she grinned to herself that no pudgy girl worth her salt would ever let a Scottish fish and chips night go by unattended.

Being pudgy might not be in vogue, but it beat the hell out of eating salad.

"ACH EUAN, I dinna ken why we are no' wearing our own plaids. Why must we sport these . . ." Graeme swept his hand to indicate the nondescript, black garments they'd all donned and frowned. ". . . things."

Euan and Graeme's middle brother Stuart chuckled and answered the question instead. "Graeme boy, half the fun o' reivin' is leaving the mon ye reived tae guess who it was that did it. Ye dinna wear your plaid like an emblem dunderhead."

Defensively, Graeme's chin tilted upwards. "I knew that."

Euan shook his head at Stuart. He didn't think it wise to undermine the boy's pride before a dangerous activity. 'Twas mayhap only another few minutes' ride into the heart of Nairn, the village where his riders had followed the Hay entourage to.

'Twas luck, that. The Donalds wouldn't have to ride all the way into the eastern Highlands to abscond with Hay wenches after all. In another hour or two they'd have their pick of the lot.

For whatever that was worth.

Euan nodded toward Stuart, indicating 'twas time to fall behind him in the line. Stuart acquiesced, nodding toward Graeme to do the same.

The predatory thrill of the hunt flowed into the Donald's veins, fixing his features into their usual harsh relief and causing his muscles to cord and tense.

'Twas time for the Lord of the Isles to find a wife.

Chapter 2

"OH MORAG YOU'RE TERRIBLE!" JANET SHOOK HER HEAD AND grinned at her best friend's story. She had met the rascally redheaded Morag three years past when she'd first started working as the liaison between her firm and the whiskey distillery in Nairn. The duo had hit it off famously and had been inseparable ever since. "Did he really call it . . ." She waggled her eyebrows and chuckled. ". . . a love hammer?"

Morag snorted at that. "Yea he did. Can you imagine? That wee bitty thing . . . having the nerve to call it a hammer!"

Janet stretched her arms above her head as she yawned, absently thrusting her breasts outward. Many a man in the pub noticed and appreciated the view, but as usual, she was oblivious to their perusal.

Her green eyes sparkled playfully. "I've never seen it," she grinned, "but you've told me enough about it that I'd have to agree with you."

One red eyebrow shot up mockingly. "More like a love *pencil,* I'd say."

The women laughed together, then moved on to another topic.

Morag waved her fork through the air, punctuating her words as she spoke. "So are you going to take that promotion or no'?"

"I don't know." Janet sighed, her demeanor growing serious. "It would mean a great deal more money, but it would also mean that I wouldn't be traveling to Nairn every few weeks anymore. I'd be at corporate headquarters instead."

Morag's chewing ceased abruptly. Her blue eyes widened. "You wouldn't be coming to Scotland?"

Janet looked away. "No. Not very often."

"How often?"

She shrugged, though the gesture was far from casual. "Once or twice a year," she murmured.

"Once or twice a year?" Morag screeched. "Oh Janet, that's no' verra good news."

She could only sigh at that. "I know."

The women sat in silence for a few minutes, both of them lost in the implications of what it would mean to their friendship if Janet took the promotion her company was preparing to offer her. They'd hardly see each other. And they both knew it.

"Well," Morag said quietly after a few more heartbeats had ticked by, "selfish or no', I'm hoping you don't take the offer."

Janet's tawny head shot up. She searched her best friend's gaze for answers. "What will I do if they fire me?"

Morag thought that over for a minute. "We've talked about going into business together more than once," she said hopefully.

"True."

Morag grinned. "Sounds like the perfect time to do it then."

Janet's lips curled into a wry smile. "I hadn't considered that option."

"Then consider it." Morag glanced down at her watch. "But consider it as we walk back towards the inn. I'm on duty for the late shift tonight."

"Oh of course." Janet stood immediately, having momentarily forgotten that it was her best friend's job to run the small cozy inn her family owned and operated in the middle of Nairn. But then Morag didn't typically work nights. She only was this week because her brothers were off visiting friends in Inverness.

Janet didn't particularly care for either of Morag's brothers. In her opinion, they treated their twenty-five-year-old sister more like a worker bee than as a sibling and an equal partner in their deceased parents' heirloom of an inn. But Janet had never said as much to Morag. She figured if her friend wanted to talk about it, well, then she knew she was always willing and happy to listen.

The women paid their tabs and said their goodbyes to the other pub patrons, then made their way towards the door. Janet pulled on her cloak and buttoned it up after the brisk Highland winds hit her square in the face, underscoring the fact that the temperature had plummeted in the little time they'd been squirreled away inside of the tavern.

"It's foggy out there tonight," Morag commented as she donned her own cloak. "More so than what's normal."

Janet studied the tendrils of mist with a curious eye as an inexplicable chill of uneasiness coursed down her spine. Shrugging off the bizarre feeling, she closed the pub's door and followed Morag outside into the dense cloudy formation.

"Yes," she agreed as they walked down the street. "It's strange out tonight."

* * *

"Morag," Janet said as her eyes struggled to penetrate the surrounding mist, "I can't tell which way is up let alone which way heads east toward the inn."

"Neither can I." She sighed. "Good god Janet, this fog is like nothing I've ever seen before."

Janet nodded, though Morag couldn't see the affirming gesture through the swirling mist. The fog was so dense that the friends were holding hands lest they lose each other in it.

Janet looked left then right, but had no more luck seeing one way than she had seeing another. She used her free hand to burrow further into the cloak. Her heartbeat was accelerating, her skin prickling, and she wasn't altogether certain as to why. The fog was thick, yes, but that hardly accounted for the feeling of near panic that was swamping her senses. "We better be careful," she whispered. "We could run smack dab into a wall and not know it until it's too—*oomph*."

"Janet!" Morag said worriedly, unable to see exactly what had happened. She only knew for certain that she'd come to an abrupt stop. "Are you alright, lovie?" When she didn't answer right away, Morag squeezed her hand tighter, urging her to speak. "Janet!"

"I'm fine." Janet giggled. "Remember how I said we could walk smack dab into a wall and not know it?"

"Yeah."

"I did." She giggled again, her wide smile beaming. "Be careful, but come here and feel."

Morag pivoted slowly in a circle, allowing her best friend to lead her slightly to the right and place her hand on a cold stone wall. She chuckled when she realized that, indeed, Janet truly had walked into a wall. "This will make for a good story." She grinned, her eyes at last finding Janet's through the layers of mist. "I can't wait to tell everybody about—"

A shrill scream pierced their ears, abruptly bringing a halt to whatever Morag had been about to say. Their eyes widened nervously.

Janet's tongue darted out to wet her suddenly parched upper lip. "D-Did you hear that scream too?" she said in an urgent tone beneath her breath.

"Y-Yeah." Morag swallowed a bit roughly as she glanced about.

Squeezing her best friend's hand, Janet attempted to steady her breathing, but found that she couldn't. "We must leave here," she said, her heart feeling as though it might beat out of her chest. "But I can't see which way to go."

"Neither can I," Morag murmured. "Oh god Janet there's another scream!" she whispered in a panic.

"It wasn't the same as the first." Eyes rounded in fright, Janet used her free hand to clutch the wall that was now beside her rather than in front of her. She sucked in her breath when her hand didn't come in contact with a stone wall like it should have, but with a wall that felt as though it were made of . . . earth and twigs?

"What the hell?" she asked herself almost rhetorically. "Morag this wall isn't right!"

Morag didn't know what to make of such an odd declaration, so she ignored it. "Come. Behind the wall," she whispered. "The fog does no' look so thick back there."

Janet glanced toward where her friend was pointing and nodded. She said nothing as she retreated a few steps backward, stepping behind the wall she had just clutched onto, a wall that looked to belong to a home of some sort. Only that couldn't be right. Homes in the Highlands were no longer made of thatch, and they hadn't been for years and years.

Shaking her head, she thrust the odd feelings at bay and followed quietly. Only when they'd gained their position did she speak. "The fog seems to be lessening a bit," she whispered.

Wide-eyed, Morag nodded. "That could be good or bad, I'm thinking."

"I know." Janet squeezed her hand and breathed in deeply to regain her composure. She could be of no help to either Morag or herself if she wasn't thinking clearly. "If the fog lifts we'll be able to see who's causing the screams, but . . ."

Morag closed her eyes and said a quick prayer to Mother Mary. "They will also be able to see us."

"Yes."

Morag closed her eyes to finish her prayer, leaving Janet to keep vigil.

Not even a moment later, Janet watched in horror as the fog lifted a bit and the surreal scene before her revealed a large barbaric-looking man clamping his palm over a young girl's mouth and lifting her up into his overly muscled arms. He passed the girl up to another man mounted atop a horse, only then glancing over in their direction.

Janet shuddered as her large green eyes made contact with piercing black ones. She tried to clutch Morag's hand tighter, only then remembering her friend had released hers to say a prayer. "Shit," she whispered frantically, "he sees us."

"Oh my god," Morag cried out, "we've got to—"

Morag's scream caused Janet to whirl around on her heel. She watched in helpless horror as a mounted rider flew by on horseback and snatched Morag off of the ground with one sweep of a heavily muscled arm. Tears of overwhelming fright gathered up in Janet's eyes. In shock, she drew her arms around her middle and hugged herself as she listened to Morag wail for her to go get help.

Help. Yes, help.

The reality of the fact that there was aid to be found within running distance helped to snap Janet from her state of frozen shock long enough to get her to move.

She would get help for Morag. Oh god . . . Morag!

Pivoting on her sandal, she turned toward the enveloping mist, preparing to dash into it, uncaring of the fact that she would be nearly blinded, unable to see through the thick fog. Braving one last glance over her shoulder, she clamped her hand over her mouth when she heard Morag's scream and watched as her best friend's captor held her securely while riding off to only god knows where with her.

Janet's gaze was drawn toward where the lone dismounted man stood, the largest and most frightening looking of all these marauders. He was watching her, seemingly undisturbed by the fact that he knew she was about to run.

She sucked in her breath as his black gaze found hers and his lips slowly curled into a terrifyingly icy smile.

Saying a quick prayer of her own, she broke his stare and fled into the mist.

Chapter 3

JANET RAN AS FAST AS HER FEET WOULD CARRY HER. SHE SPRINTED at top speed toward . . . anywhere. She had no clue as to where she was going. She could see nothing, hear nothing, feel nothing that wasn't associated with acute fear.

The cold didn't matter. The fact that she'd tripped at least twice already and had skinned up both of her knees didn't matter. The only sight she could conjure up was the mental image of Morag screaming. The only sounds she could hear were the beating of her own heart and the gasps of air her lungs sucked in as she heaved for each breath.

She'd been running for what felt like hours but had only been minutes. She dashed through the fog, refusing to slow down no matter how weary and pummeled her body felt. She might never make it to help before she was murdered on the streets of Nairn, but she'd be damned if she wouldn't go down trying.

Pumping her arms back and forth as her body treaded through the boggy mist, she let out a small whimper of relief when she noticed a break in the fog just ahead. Dashing toward it with everything she had left in her, she came to an abrupt halt once she reached her destination.

"Oh my god," she muttered in between pants. Her eyes darted back and forth, taking in the bizarre scene around her as she doubled over to catch her breath. "Where in the hell am I?" she rasped out.

Janet's mouth dropped open in morbid fascination as her eyes flicked about the row of crude mud and thatch huts that she'd wandered into the midst of. She'd never seen anything like them. Well, she'd never seen anything like them outside of lands that had been preserved for their historic value, she mentally amended.

Snapping out of the reverie that had swamped her, she took a deep breath and reminded herself that she needed to find some sort of help. Morag was in danger. God in heaven, she thought hysterically, her best friend had literally been kidnapped off the streets! She could only hope Morag's captor didn't force himself on her before she could be rescued.

Steeling her nerves and forcing herself to behave with a calm she was far from feeling, Janet took a tentative step out of the mist and toward the row of thatched huts just ahead. She *would* get help. For Morag she would find a way.

Janet tried with every fiber of her being to make that mental vow a reality, but before she could take another step from the fog a heavily muscled arm whipped out and snatched her back into the eerie cloud formation. She opened her mouth to scream, but was forestalled from carrying it out by a large, callused hand clamping roughly over her lips and grinding into her mouth.

Frightened and quite certain he meant to kill her, she bit down as hard as she could on whatever skin she could find, bearing down until the metallic taste of blood trickled onto her tongue. It wasn't enough. The small nick she'd given him hadn't even caused him to flinch.

Flailing madly about, she gave him her full weight then, hoping it would induce him to drop her long enough to allow her precious moments to make good on another escape. Anything—even a single moment's hesitation on his part—and she'd try to flee into the mist again.

But that wasn't to be. When Janet's feet purposely shot out from beneath her and she tried to fall buttocks-first toward the ground, the same heavily muscled arms that had caught her in the first place merely swept her back up as though she were a rag doll. He whirled her around to face him, his large hand still clamped over her mouth.

"Seall dè fhuair mi," he said in a chillingly controlled tone. "Nach e tha mear."

Janet's green eyes rounded uncomprehendingly as her head shot up. She'd never heard such a language. It sounded vaguely similar to the Gaelic she'd heard some of the Highlanders in these parts speak and yet so different at the same time.

Breathing rapidly, Janet determined to look up—way up in fact—and meet her captor's eyes. He might kill her, and was no doubt preparing to do so, but she'd be damned if she'd act the coward while taking her last breath.

She was afraid to look at him, terrified in fact. She'd never encountered a man so huge, so powerfully built. The arm he had wrapped about her felt as heavy as a tree trunk, so roped with muscle it was. He was shirtless, making it easy to ascertain the fact that his equally massive torso was riddled with . . . battle scars?

Janet sucked in a deep breath from behind the giant's hand and, casting her fears behind her, shot her gaze up to meet her captor's dead-on. And then she wished she hadn't.

His black eyes drilled into her, piercing her with a possessiveness she'd never before witnessed, never experienced. The look he was bestowing upon her was so primal that it terrified her.

He didn't mean to simply kill her, she now knew. No. Escaping him would never be that easy. He meant to have her, to rape her.

Janet's last coherent thought before falling into the first faint of her life revolved around whether the barbarian would choose to kill her before, after, or . . . *during*?

And then the blackness overtook her and she thankfully knew no more.

EUAN HELD ONTO the wench's middle as her limp body sagged against him atop the destrier. 'Twas just a wee bit further they'd go before making camp for the night, getting their party as far from the scene of the reivin' they'd just done as was possible in a night's journey. The Hay would definitely retaliate. He planned to be on his own lands when they did so.

Graeme had been right after all, the Donald thought in a rare flash of humor. The reivin' had been a spot of good fun.

As he ran his hand over his future bride's plump breast and felt a nipple pop up through the fabric of her finely made outer tunic, he conceded that he'd especially enjoy reaping the benefits of tonight's coup. He could scarcely wait to rut between his wench's legs. His manhood was painfully erect just thinking about it.

Euan absently toyed with the nipple, plumping it up between

his forefinger and thumb as he considered where the closest village with a priest might be located.

He wouldn't fuck her wee body until he owned it by law, so he'd have to make certain she was his in posthaste.

The Lord of the Isles would be made to wait but so long.

Chapter 4

JANET, WAKE UP. PLEASE LOVIE PLEASE . . . *WAKE UP*."

Janet could hear Morag calling to her from somewhere in the back of her mind. But everything was so hazy, so obscured. Her best friend's voice seemed miles away. Her eyelids felt heavy, the muscles of her body were on fire, her knees felt as though someone had raked them across a serrated blade.

"Janet *please* . . . please wake up."

Black eyes. A man. Morag's screams.

The night's activities slowly began to unravel in the fogginess clouding her brain . . .

But she'd gotten away! She'd fled into the mist for help. For—Morag. Oh god . . . Morag!

But no. The man had stopped her. The battle-scarred . . . warrior? A warrior?

"Janet, for the love of Mary would you open your eyes." This in urgent tones from Morag.

Morag? Morag was here? She'd gotten away? Oh . . . Morag!

Ice-cold water pelted Janet in the face, waking her up instantly. She bolted upright, sucking in huge gasps of air, the frigid liquid shocking her into alert mode.

She blinked a few times in rapid succession as her eyes took in the strange surroundings. Animal rawhides enclosed her on three sides, the bark of a large tree on another. The tiny space she was sitting in consisted of earth and animal furs.

A tent. She was sitting in some sort of primitive tent. Her gaze clashed with Morag's. "Where are we?" she whispered.

"Oh lovie," Morag said as she ran a hand through Janet's mane of unruly tawny curls. "I didn't think you'd ever wake up."

"I'm fine." Janet sat up straighter and forcibly shook the remaining cobwebs from her brain. "I'm awake. Morag, what's going on? Who are those men? Where have they taken us?"

"I don't know." Morag worried her bottom lip as she threw a long red tress over her shoulder. "I can no' understand a bloody word of what they are saying to me, Janet. These men . . ." She lowered her voice and leaned in closer to her best friend. "These men are dangerous. We must run away!" she said urgently. "Preferably *before* they come back to interrogate us again!"

"Interrogate?" Janet's eyes widened. "They've interrogated you?"

"They've tried." Morag sighed. "Janet, they can no' understand what I am saying to them any more than I can comprehend what they are saying to me."

"How can that be?" Janet shook her head slightly, more confused than frightened, which was saying a lot. Her eyes darted back toward Morag's. "That makes no sense."

"I know." Morag was quiet for a pregnant moment as she studied her friend's features.

"What Morag? What is it?"

"It's just . . . it's . . ."

"Yes?"

She sighed. "Janet, something verra strange is happening here. Something . . . something isn't right."

Janet was surprised she was able to find a chuckle amidst the chaos, but she did. "No kidding," she said wryly.

Morag didn't return her mirth. "I'm serious Janet. I do no' just mean the fact that we were kidnapped in the heart of Nairn by a bunch of over-large, non-English speaking men. It's . . . it's . . . more than that." She took a deep breath and glanced away.

Janet clasped her hand and squeezed it. She had felt those same odd premonitions since she'd first laid eyes on the fog when they'd trekked out of the pub. "Tell me," she said under her breath. "Tell me what you think is going on."

Morag nodded, deciding to waste no more time. "Bear in mind before you dismiss my musings as nonsense that I have been awake since this entire sordid mess began. I have seen things you have no' seen, or things you have no' seen yet anyway."

Janet's heartbeat picked up. Her skin began to tingle as it had back in the mist. She didn't have any idea what Morag was about to say, but whatever it was she knew she wasn't going to like it. "Go on."

"These men . . ." Morag's eyes widened as her voice dropped. "These men are no' like any men of our acquaintance, Janet. Their bodies are covered in battle scars, they ride upon horses instead of in cars." She waved a hand through the air. "They carry swords and wear almost no clothing save scratchy blackish plaids for the love of Mary!"

Janet drew her knees up against her belly and wrapped her arms around them.

"We traveled on horseback for hour upon hour last evening and no' once, *no' even once*, did I see a home of normal appearance." Morag began to shiver. She rubbed her arms briskly, warding off the chill. "Every last home I saw with my verra own eyes—every last one, Janet!—was made of thatched twigs and clay."

"Like something out of a history book?" Janet murmured. She closed her eyes briefly, remembering only too well the row of thatched huts she'd run into before the gigantic dark-eyed man had captured her.

"Yes," Morag sobbed quietly, "just like something you'd see in a history text, or on a tour of preserved relics. Only people *live* in these relics."

Janet sucked in a deep tug of air. Her lungs burned, felt heavy. "So what you are saying," she rasped out, "is that . . ."

No! Things like that don't happen!

"What I'm saying," Morag continued for her, "is that . . ." She looked away, couldn't go on.

Janet closed her eyes. ". . . That we've traveled through time."

The words hung there between them, feeling more than a bit strange on the tongue and yet, perversely, feeling more than a bit right as well. Morag was the first to speak. "Well," she murmured, "as fantastical as it sounds, I for one do no' think we are in our own time any longer."

Janet's eyes flew open. She blew out a breath. "You sound quite calm about such a terrifying possibility."

Morag shrugged helplessly. "I've had more hours awake to deal with all of this than you."

"True," Janet murmured. She searched Morag's eyes as she considered for the first time since she'd awakened just what else her best friend might have seen, might have been made to endure. "Morag . . ." Her throat felt dry, parched.

"Yes?"

"The man who took you. Did he . . . I mean . . ." She stumbled over her words, unable to find the right ones. "Did he . . ."

"No." She shook her head. "He fondled me a wee bit, but he did no' rape me thank the lord."

Janet released a shaky breath. "Thank god for that at least."

"But he will," Morag said quietly. "They mean to do with us what they will, Janet. Make no mistake." She shivered. "The way the fairer-headed man looks at me, the way I saw that brutal-looking black-haired man staring at you . . ." She let her words trail off portentously, not finishing her sentence.

"Shit." Janet drew her knees in closer to her body. "What do we do?"

"We escape."

"But how?"

Morag found her first chuckle. "I have no' got that far in my plans."

Janet snorted at that. "And if our time travel theory is correct and we are indeed existing in some prehistoric, barbaric era . . ." She shook her head slightly as her gaze found Morag's. "Then what good is escaping? Where will we go?"

Morag nodded definitively. "Back toward Nairn."

Janet raised a brow as she considered that. "Good idea. Maybe that weird fog will still be there and we can get back home."

"Exactly."

"Or maybe this is just a dream."

"Maybe."

Janet sighed. "But you don't think so."

"No." Morag shook her head. "I do no' think so."

The women stared at each other until Janet broke the silence. "Well then, the only thing left to figure out is how we get out of this . . ." She flung a hand towards one animal pelt wall. "Thing."

Morag chuckled softly. "Unfortunately, that will be the most difficult part to figure out." She patted Janet reassuringly on the knee, causing her to wince. "But we—oh dear, what's wrong? Is it your knee, lovie?"

"Yesss," she hissed as she sucked in air between her teeth.

"Let me see." Morag undid the buttons on Janet's cloak, carefully tugged it open, and quickly ascertained how bad the situation looked. Since Janet was wearing a sundress that only came to mid-thigh while standing, it rode up even further while sitting, making it easy to see that her knees were badly skinned up. "Ouch." Morag winced sympathetically. "I take it you got scraped up whilst running?"

"Yes. I—"

One of the animal pelt walls flapped open and the figure of a brooding, dark-haired man emerged. Janet's heart rate picked up, pounding inside of her chest. The women huddled closer together, a natural reflex given the situation.

The giant's gaze sought out Janet's, but was snagged a moment later by the sight of her naked leg. She swallowed roughly in reaction as she watched the barbarian study the thigh most adjacent to him. His eyes trailed from the knee upward, slow and lingering, his possessive gaze burning into her so harshly that she hysterically wondered if a cattle brand would magically appear on her leg. Why not? Everything else about this situation was insane.

He wanted her. She'd be a fool not to see it. His burning eyes said so. His meandering gaze said so. The thick erection poking against the kilt-like blackish covering he wore said so. She averted her gaze and quickly looked away.

The heavily muscled giant stood there for another moment before making his way further into the tent. His movement caused Janet's head to snap up and her body to huddle impossibly closer to Morag's. The warrior noticed her reaction and, oddly enough, slowed his movements down, approaching her in a manner that was surprisingly non-threatening for one so large and obviously lacking in grace and finesse.

Everything about the battle-scarred man spoke of command and authority. He was a warrior accustomed to taking what he would when he would. And yet he approached Janet cautiously, the way an adult would when trying to lessen the fright of a skittish child.

His large, callused hands placed softly on her knees caused their gazes to clash. Janet's eyes widened nervously. She glanced toward Morag who was shaking like a leaf, then back to the warrior squatting before her.

One hand slid slowly down her right thigh, the leg opposite the side Morag was sitting near, so her friend didn't know what the stern-looking giant was about. His grim black eyes were glazed over with desire as he trailed his hand gently over the expanse of her warm, soft flesh. He touched her as though he couldn't seem to help himself, as though there was nothing in the world he wanted or needed more.

Such a response from a man might have been an aphrodisiac

under normal circumstances, but under the current ones it was gut-wrenchingly frightening. Janet began to swallow convulsively.

Her reaction didn't go by undetected. Again, at odds with the warrior's harsh exterior, he showed her the kindness of dropping his hand from her thigh and settling it back upon her skinned knee. His eyes sharpened almost instantly, as if he had momentarily forgotten himself but was now back in control.

And then he was preparing to leave. Just like that. He dropped his hands from her knees and stood up from his squatting position.

Janet couldn't help but to notice how heavily muscled his legs were when they flexed into standing mode. Indeed, the warrior's entire body looked almost godlike it was so formidably carved.

Janet watched him exit the tent, watched as the animal skin flapped shut behind him, then cocked her head to gawk at Morag whose own jaw had dropped open. "What was that about?" she whispered.

"I don't know." Morag swallowed a bit roughly. She squeezed Janet's hand. "I-I thought he meant t-to . . ."

Janet breathed in deeply. "So did I. I—"

The tent flapped open again and her gaze clashed with the warrior's. His mask was back on, that stony impenetrable façade that she would have thought he always wore had she not witnessed that blazing look in his eyes a minute prior herself.

Her green eyes widened noticeably as he lowered his powerful thighs before her and squatted between her legs once again. Her breathing became shallow and choppy as she prepared for the worst.

Would he rape her right here in front of her best friend? Would Morag be made to watch so she'd know what was in store for her as well? The mere thought of such humiliation caused tears to form in her eyes.

Large, callused hands thrust her legs open a bit wider. Janet looked away and bit down hard on her lip. She could feel Morag's breathing growing labored as they both prepared for Janet's assault. Morag cried out softly as the warlord settled himself intimately between Janet's thighs.

No! Janet thought hysterically. This couldn't be happening! Please god . . .

Janet closed her eyes and bit down harder on her lip. The metallic taste of blood trickled onto her tongue. Her heart was beating so rapidly she could hear nothing but the pulse of it. She squeezed Morag's hand as she felt the warrior's breath come closer.

And then she felt *it*—the hardness of his erection brushing up against her leg from beneath his coarse wool covering. Panting almost hysterically, Janet clamped down on Morag's hand as the warrior placed . . . a wet rag on her knee.

A wet rag on her knee?

Confused, Janet's eyes flew open and darted toward the giant. Her breathing slowed so rapidly it halted completely for a lingering moment. The warrior was . . . good lord he was tending to her wounded knees.

Eyes rounded, she looked quizzically at the giant who didn't seem to notice her. He was busy patting icy cold rags on her knees, tenderly wiping away the dirt that had mingled with the blood on her exposed, raw flesh.

Flicking her eyes toward Morag, Janet couldn't help but to notice the bemused expression on her best friend's face. It was that of a deer caught in headlights. Clearly, she had assumed the battle-honed giant had meant to harm her as well. Playing nurse-maid was the last thing either had expected of this formidable man.

Janet's gaze slowly raked over the giant's austere features. He wasn't a bad looking man, she admitted to herself. In fact, if she'd met him under any circumstances other than the one she currently found herself in she would have found him superior in appearance.

His features were grim, but handsome. Black as midnight hair flowed a bit past the shoulders and was swept out of his eyes by a Celtic braid plaited at either temple. His eyes were dark, so brown they almost looked black. She noticed for the first time that the iciness of his gaze was lessened somewhat by sweeping, inky black eyelashes that formed an impressive crescent when his eyes were shuttered as they were now while he studied her knees.

She shouldn't be noticing these things, she told herself stiffly. The warrior might be showing her a kindness by tending to her wounds, but they were wounds his pursuit of her had caused in the first place. She was, Janet reminded herself, no more than a prisoner to him. She asked herself not for the first time, however, just why she and Morag had been captured to begin with.

Her inward musings were brought to a halt when the warrior finished his task and began to speak. His voice was a deep bass, the richest rumble she'd ever heard. She definitely didn't understand a word of what he was saying though.

"Madainn mhath. Ciamar a tha thu?" His black gaze swept over her breasts, settled on her face.

Janet pretended not to notice his perusal of her anatomy. She shrugged and answered his question with a perplexed look.

He tried again. "Dè 'n t-ainm a th'ort, te bheag?"

Her green eyes merely grew larger. She glanced toward Morag, then back to the grim-faced warrior. She shook her head slightly, again shrugging her shoulders in a helpless gesture. "I don't understand your words," she said quietly.

Comprehension dawned in the giant's eyes. They widened almost imperceptibly before he recommended them and the façade was neatly back in place. He seemed to turn things over in his mind for a moment or two, then pointed to himself and rumbled out a word. "Yu-an."

Janet shook her head, not understanding.

He pointed toward himself again, thumping a callused hand in the vicinity of his chest. "Yu-an."

She was about to shake her head again when the significance of the giant's actions at last dawned on her. Euan. He was telling her that his name was Euan. Glancing first toward Morag whose rounded eyes indicated she still hadn't caught on, she looked back at the warrior and pointed toward herself. "Ja-net."

"Joo-nat." His deep voice repeated her pronunciation—sort of.

She didn't know why, but she felt the need to correct him. "Jaa-net," she said louder, more distinctly. She pointed at him. "Yu-an." She pointed back toward herself. "Ja-net."

He smiled, giving him a softer appearance. A dimple popped out on his left cheek, which Janet found oddly fascinating. "Jah-net."

She nodded, then smiled in spite of herself, weirdly elated by the fact that they'd managed that small communication, no matter how insignificant, and no matter that she was still his prisoner.

EUAN WALKED FROM the tent feeling more than a wee bit daft. The purpose of yestereve's reivin' had been to steal Hay women. The comely wench was clearly not Hay, mayhap not even Scottish. So why did he think to keep her regardless? He shook his head and sighed as he strutted toward the campfire where his brothers and men awaited him. Wenches did strange things to men. Especially wenches who sported creamy thighs and fleshy bosoms.

He came to a halt in front of his siblings, then nodded toward Stuart. 'Twas Stuart who had caught the red-headed wench and had a wish to keep her. "'Tis as ye suspected, brother. The wenches do no' speak our tongue."

Graeme chuckled, earning him a punch in the side of his jaw from Stuart. That didn't hold back his mirth, though. "At least my fair Elizabeth kens what I say tae her."

Stuart rolled his eyes and looked back to Euan. "Ye are certain?"

The Donald nodded briskly. He thought back to the conversation that had just taken place in the makeshift tent.

"Madainn mhath. Ciamar a tha thu?" Good morning. How are you?

Nothing.

"Dè 'n t-ainm a th'ort, te bheag?" What is your name, little one?

Again, nothing.

"Aye," he confirmed, grinning a bit at the memory of he and Janet pointing towards themselves and pronouncing their names as slowly as lackwits. He quelled the small smile, his features quickly shifting back in place. "I dinna ken from where they come, but 'tis sorely apparent they do no' comprehend a word of what I'm speaking tae them."

Stuart grunted. "I dinna care, brother. I want tae keep the fiery-haired wench." He waggled his eyebrows and grinned. "I'll teach mah wee bride Gaelic betwixt thrusts in the bedsheets."

Now it was young Graeme rolling his eyes. He decided to ignore Stuart. "What of ye, brother? Will ye keep the other one?" He nodded toward Euan as he considered her appearance. "She is comely for a certainty."

Euan grunted as he shook his head wryly. "Aye. And one hell of a good runner."

A few of the soldiers surrounding them laughed at that.

Stuart grinned. "'Twill no' be easy tae chase your wench down long enough tae thrust, brother. 'Twill mayhap be a while before that bride learns Gaelic."

The laughter evolved into guffaws. Euan acceded to it good-naturedly, uncharacteristic though it might be.

The Lord of the Isles needed an heir and therefore a wife. Janet was the comeliest lass he'd ever laid eyes upon. Big, sparkling green eyes. A lush bosom. The sort of fleshy body he could lose himself in, pumping away into oblivion. His mind was made up. Why bother looking elsewhere when perfection was already awaiting him in yon tent?

"Aye," Euan rumbled. "I will keep her."

"Then ye best get busy." This from Graeme.

Euan lifted one dark brow.

Graeme grinned, then bowed mockingly toward his elder siblings. "Your comely wenches?"

"Aye?" they asked in unison.

Graeme jerked his head toward the tent where even as he spoke two women were emerging, making efficient beelines toward the thick of the forest, dashing off into it at top speed. "I dinna think they ken the honor ye give tae them, making them Donald brides." He chuckled. "In fact, looks tae me as though they are getting away."

Chapter 5

JANET GLOWERED AT THE GIANT BRUTE STANDING BESIDE HER, his bulging and vein-roped arm plastered about her waist. So much for her ill-fated escape attempt, she thought glumly. The only thing it had garnered her was *his* undivided attention, not to mention being forcibly separated from Morag as though they were two naughty girls being grounded from playing with each other by their fathers.

So now she stood beside her captor who, much to her disgruntlement, looked extremely handsome now that he'd cleaned himself up a bit. Frightening, but handsome nevertheless.

He was wearing a clean plaid of muted blue and green with a white tunic beneath it. His plaid was draped over one arm and held together by a large emerald jewel at one shoulder. The garment fell just above his knees, showing off legs too well muscled to belong to a human.

Janet's lips pinched together. It wasn't fair that a man so dastardly should look so good.

Men who had the look of soldiers began to gather in on all

sides. At first Janet thought it was to make certain she didn't try to flee—as if she could with Euan's tree of an arm clamped around her!—but now she wasn't so sure. They didn't seem to be paying her much attention in fact. Their interest seemed to lie with the short little man standing in front of her and Euan wearing a scratchy looking robe with a hooded cowl and speaking in some other foreign tongue she couldn't make heads or tails of.

Janet sighed. It had been a long day. It felt like days ago that she and Morag had attempted to fly the coop so to speak, but in reality it had only been what was probably ten to twelve hours.

After they had been recaptured, Euan and the fair-haired man that had stolen Morag had separated the women from each other's company. They'd been within seeing distance of the other at all times, but not within a range that allowed for conversation.

Janet had managed to scrape up her knees even worse while on the run, tripping over the fallen branch that had eventually permitted the big oaf at her side to catch up with her. Damn branch.

Following her rather ignominious capture, Euan had recleaned her knees in private then shut her cloak. He had pointed and growled at her clothing, making it apparent that she wasn't allowed to remove her outerwear for any reason whatsoever.

Not that she would have. She hardly wanted to show off skin to any of the men surrounding her.

Following his grunts and stern finger pointing lecture, Euan had placed her atop a horse and jumped up to sit behind her on the mount. They had ridden that way hour after hour, stopping only briefly to eat and care for the animals.

If there had been any lingering doubts in her mind as to whether or not she and Morag had managed to do the inexplicable and travel through time, they had quickly been vanquished. There was no evidence of the modern age anywhere to be found. Nothing but horses, non-English speaking peoples, shabbily dressed villagers, the occasional man or woman hawking crudely made foods and wares, and wild animals galore.

Then they had come to this place. This hole in the wall village that boasted a few thatched huts and little else. Morag had been the first to be swept from her horse and squirreled away into the very forest clearing Janet stood in right now.

When Morag had emerged from the clearing a bit later, her face had been white as a ghost's. She had been trying to tell Janet something with her eyes . . . something, but what she hadn't any notion.

Janet's gaze had fallen to Morag's clothing. The cloak she wore hadn't looked torn or borne any evidence of a man trying to rip through it to force himself on her. That had been Janet's primary concern. When that fear had been wiped away, she'd been left in a quandary, knowing full well that her best friend had been trying to warn her of what would transpire in the forest clearing, but still unable to figure out what that something was.

So now here she stood, soldiers surrounding her on all sides, Euan stoically planted to her left, a tiny Latin-speaking man just in front of her. Latin? Yes, come to think of it, his words sounded remarkably like Latin.

The smallish man produced a bolt of cloth, placed Janet's hand atop Euan's, and wrapped them together like that. Curious, Janet's gaze shot up to meet Euan's. He didn't return it. His solemn face was intent on whatever it was the Latin speaker was saying.

What was going on! she wailed to herself. If she even knew what time she was in she might be able to sort out all of these strange happenings . . .

"Tha." Euan nudged her gently, breaking her out of her reverie. "*Tha*," he repeated commandingly, nodding down to her so she'd know she was expected to repeat what he'd just said.

Janet nibbled on her lower lip as a sense of awareness slowly stole over her. *Tha.* She'd heard that word before in the Highlands. It meant *yes.* If she repeated it, what exactly would she be agreeing to?

She moistened her lip nervously with her tongue, in the end deciding that there was no point in arguing with the man. If he wanted a yes she'd give him a yes. Begrudgingly, she narrowed her eyes at Euan and phonetically repeated the word she'd been prompted to say. "Ha."

Almost immediately the Latin speaker followed up with a few more words of his own. He said . . . something. Something that made Euan smile for a fraction of a second before he lowered his face to hers and kissed her chastely on the cheek.

Congratulatory shouts rose up from the surrounding soldiers, many of them thumping the giant beside her on the shoulder, almost as if they were saying to him "job well done."

Janet chewed that over for a moment. She stilled. Her back stiffened.

Her eyes shot up to meet Euan's as she gaped open-mouthed at him. His answering arrogant smirk was all the confirmation she needed.

Good lord in heaven, the man had just married her. And worse yet, she'd agreed to it.

Chapter 6

Janet stood inside of the crude hut Euan had cloistered her inside of an hour past, wondering morosely if this pathetic place was to be her new and permanent home. The hut boasted but one room . . . one single, solitary room. A hay-strewn bed lay at one side of it, a kitchen-like area with a few clay bowls on the other, and a solitary chair in the middle. That was it. No tables. No more chairs. No anything. She hated it immensely.

Naked, Janet covered her breasts with her hands as best she could while she watched two village women remove the crudely made tub she'd just bathed in from the one-room hut. She nibbled on her bottom lip, hoping that the women would hurry up and come back with her clothes. She didn't want to be caught unawares when her husband returned.

Her husband. Janet groaned. Good lord! How would she ever get out of this mess, find Morag, return to Nairn, *and* get back to the future? The task set before her was simply overwhelming.

The wooden door opened a moment later causing Janet's head to shoot up. Her breath caught in the back of her throat and her eyes widened skittishly when she realized that the new occupant was not one of the village women that had helped to bathe her, but instead the very man she least wanted to see while naked.

Dusk was just beginning to settle over the Highlands, so there was still enough light to see the heat in Euan's eyes as his black gaze raked insolently over her body. He was erect, very erect she could easily surmise, his penis bulging against the plaid he still wore.

He closed the door quietly behind him and made his way slowly towards her. Janet sucked in her breath and took a reflexive step backwards.

Euan stopped in his tracks, approaching her cautiously again, just as he had in the tent before tending to her knees. It was then that she noticed he carried a platter of some sort. Food. Against her will, her stomach growled hungrily in reaction to it.

"Hai." He dipped his head. His blazing eyes raked over her flesh once more, lingering over long at the clipped tawny curls between her thighs, but he made no movement to touch her.

"Hi," she whispered back. She gnawed on her lower lip and looked away.

It occurred to her that it was stupid to stand there shielding her breasts from his view when her mons was completely bared to him. But nonsensical or not, she continued to cup them.

Part of it was born of fear, knowing what he meant to do to her and knowing equally well she wouldn't have enough physical power to stop him when he did. But she had spent all day long with him, first while he tended to her knees and then again for the long trek on horseback to the rugged area of the Highlands they were now in. She was afraid of him yes, but not as acutely as she'd once been. He treated her too tenderly to fear him too much.

No, it was definitely more than fear that kept her hands cupping her breasts. It was also reflex, Janet's naturally shy reaction to standing totally divested of clothing in front of a male.

Back home in the States she had endured all manner of teasing as a child and then again as an adolescent. Pudgy. Plump. Fat. Fluffy. Big-boned. Piggy. She'd heard every derogatory term imaginable coupled with her name, every euphemism there was to express the fact that she wasn't a rail and would therefore never be as desirable as every woman wanted to be to the opposite sex.

But this man, she told herself staunchly, this man had captured her, made her his prisoner, taken her against her will, even married her for the love of god! If he wasn't happy with the end result that was his own doing. Perhaps he'd even let her go once he realized his mistake.

Firmly resolved to get it over with while she was still angry enough to do it, she dropped her hands from her breasts and thrust her chin defiantly up. Her nostrils flaring, she stood there and waited for him to reject her.

His reaction wasn't quite what she had been expecting.

Euan groaned, the fire in his eyes raging brightly, licking over every lushly rounded curve, every nuance of her fertile figure. He didn't seem at all put off by her body. In fact, he gazed at her with such obvious desire that Janet's nipples involuntarily puckered up for him and her breath caught for the briefest of moments.

Biting her lip, she glanced away, shaken by both of their reactions. Now what did she do? She'd feel like an idiot re-covering her breasts at this point.

And then the decision was taken away from her as she heard him put down the platter of food and come to her. Two large, callused hands cupped her breasts and gently kneaded them like soft dough. He plumped them up with his hands, taking the nipples in between his thumbs and forefingers, and massaged them from roots to tips.

Janet closed her eyes and gasped. "No. Please. No."

From somewhere in the back of her mind it occurred to her that her voice sounded smoky with passion, not defiant with anger and fear. Euan didn't speak her language, she reminded herself, as he began to massage her breasts and nipples into a deeper state of arousal. If she wanted him to understand that his touch wasn't welcome, she'd better sound more forceful.

Janet's green eyes flew open and locked with Euan's black ones. He continued to stroke her, tug just the right amount on her nipples, just enough to where it didn't hurt but sent tremors of desire coursing through her blood instead. She opened her mouth to say no, but found herself sighing and her eyes glazing over instead.

He was handsome. Incredibly, impossibly, muscular and virile. The sort of man that would never look twice at her in her own time, but for some reason or another was fascinated by her in this one.

This was—madness. She couldn't even speak with him, couldn't converse with him, knew nothing about him beyond the fact that his name was Euan and he was well-versed in tending to wounded knees . . . among other things.

And then one of his hands dropped a heavy breast and a callused finger found the sensitive piece of flesh between her thighs and stroked it. "Oh god," she breathed out. Janet's head dipped back, her neck bared to him, all rational thought out the proverbial window. "Oh god."

Where a minute ago she would have tried to say no, she found in this moment that her feet were moving apart to give his hand better access to her clit. She closed her eyes against her worries and fears, accepting the pleasure, and moaned softly.

It was all the impetus Euan needed to further his ministrations. "Mmm, tha," he rumbled as his eyes watched her face, as his hand cupped her wet flesh and felt her liquid dewing up for him.

And then he was lifting her into his arms and carrying her to the bed. He sat her down on the edge of it and splayed her legs wide.

Janet offered him no resistance, opening them impossibly wider for him instead so that her labia was on prominent display. The entire scene felt surreal, like it had to be happening to any woman but her. A more brazen woman. A more wicked woman. Not the reserved and mousy Janet Duval.

He traced the slick folds of her flesh with one callused finger, the look on his face reminding her of someone who'd found the most glorious treasure on earth and wanted to explore every facet of it. His reaction to her body was heady enough to induce her nipples to pop out further as desire shot through her at lightning speed.

"Oh lord." He was rubbing her flesh again, stroking her clit, exploring every wet nook and cranny. Her head dangled backwards like a puppet. She leaned back on her elbows and splayed her legs as wide as they would go. He began to rub her more briskly, faster and faster. "*Euan.*"

"Mmm, te brèagha," he rasped out.

Beautiful one. He'd called her *beautiful one.* She'd understood that, knew that expression from her friends in Nairn. Her breathing grew more labored with each touch.

Faster. Faster.

Oh god the stroking was faster, brisker . . . faster still. *"Oh god."*

She was soaking his hand, saturating his fingers. And still impossibly faster. *"I'm coming Euan."*

"Tha, te brèagha," he urged her on. *Yes, beautiful one.*

He didn't need to understand her language to comprehend what words she was groaning out. Her body was telling him.

"Euan," she moaned. *"Faster. Yes . . . god—faster."* On a final groan, her head snapped back, her nipples shot out, and her labia turned a juicy red as her orgasm blew. Blood coursed into her vagina and nipples, heating her body, burning even her face.

And then he was coming down on top of her . . . already naked? She didn't know when or how he'd discarded his plaid but didn't care either. She made him do a little groaning of his own when she pulled him roughly down on top of her and wantonly wrapped her legs around his waist. She wanted him to fill her—needed him to fill her.

Euan clenched his jaw as he poised his thick cock at her entrance. If she didn't slow down a wee bit he was liable to do her a damage. "Gabh do thìde," he gritted out. *Take your time.*

But she was wild for him, his beautiful wee wife. Hot and wild. He'd never experienced such a primal reaction from a wench, had never seen a woman filled with such passion as his Janet. He was more glad than ever that he'd snatched the wrong wench for a wife.

Instead of slowing down, she gyrated her hips, thrusting them upward towards his jutting cock. It was his undoing. There was only so much a man could take, the Donald or no.

Grabbing her by the hips, he thrust deeply inside of her tight, wet flesh, groaning like a man possessed as he did so. Christ but he'd never felt anything so tight and welcoming.

"Oh Euan."

She was breathing out his name in her passion already, he thought with more than a little arrogance. Grabbing his wife's large, elongated nipples, he settled his body atop hers and began thrusting into her in long, deep strokes. He rolled the nipples around with his fingers, tugging at them in the way he'd discovered she liked.

"Faster."

She groaned out that foreign word over and over again. As much as he wished it otherwise, Euan knew not her meaning. He continued burrowing into her in long, agonizingly languid strokes.

"*Faster,*" she all but shouted, this time arching her hips to pummel at his cock in quick strokes.

Ahh. Now *that* he understood.

Euan released his hold on Janet's breasts and came down fully on top of her. Twining a handful of her long, sweetly scented hair around his fist, he locked gazes with her just before he rammed himself home.

She groaned, her head falling back upon the bed as he rode her body hard, fucking her sweet cunt in fast thrusts. "Tha domh phuiseag fearachdainn math," he said hoarsely. *Your pussy feels good.*

Sweat-soaked skin slapped against sweat-soaked skin. The sound of Janet's sweet cunt sucking up his manhood reverberated throughout the shepherd's hut. Euan growled as he went primal on her, fucking her harder and faster, riding the body he now owned by law into ecstasy and oblivion.

"Euan."

His name on Janet's lips as her back arched and her body climaxed for him was powerfully arousing. She shivered and convulsed, moaning wantonly as she burst all around him.

In one fluid movement, he grabbed her hips and rammed himself inside of her body, over and over, again and again. Quick strokes. Deep thrusts. Flesh slapping flesh.

His muscles corded and bunched. His jaw clenched. He rode her fast, hard, like an animal. "*Leamsa.*" *Mine.*

And then he burst.

Nostrils flaring, Euan's black gaze collided with Janet's as he thrust home once more, then on a groan of completion, spurted himself deep inside of her.

They held each other like that, both of them spent and breathing deeply, both of them too exhausted and replete to speak.

Euan bent his neck to sip gently from her lips. Janet accepted him without hesitation, sweeping her tongue out to meet with his. They kissed slowly for a minute or two, sweet and languid brush strokes until their mingling stopped completely.

Entwined with each other in every way possible, they fell fast asleep.

Chapter 7

SHE WOKE UP TO THE FEEL OF A TONGUE SLIDING ALONG THE folds of her swollen flesh. The tongue was tantalizingly rough and slick, rimming her labial folds with precision, flicking across her clit, rimming, flicking, rimming, flicking . . . *god*.

She moaned in reaction, her eyes not yet opened, her brain still drunk on pleasure and sleep.

The tongue was joined by firm lips, lips that closed over her swollen clit and helped the tongue to suckle her. Flick, suck, flick, suck, flick, suck . . . *oh yes*.

She ground her hips to meet the tongue and lips as her nipples stabbed up high into the air.

Flick, suck, flick, suck.

Suck, suck, suck, suck . . . *Euan*.

Janet's eyes flew open and her hips flared upward on a groan as she climaxed into his mouth. *"Oh god."* Instinctually she wrapped her legs around his neck and buried his face further into her flesh, wanting him deeper, needing him to suck her dry, wanting the pleasure-pain to never relent.

"Mmmm." He lapped at her like a dog, slurping up the juices that trickled out of her engorged flesh, then sucking again—harder, torturously harder until—

"Oh my god." Janet reared up off the bed, screaming because the pleasure was so acute. *"Yes Euan."*

Reflexively her body tried to disjoin from his mouth, uncertain it could handle falling over such an all-consuming precipice of pleasure. Euan grabbed her hips in reaction, simultaneously shoving his mouth deeper into her cunt and suckling from her clit harder.

"Oh Jesus god. Oh my . . . god!"

Janet's hips tried to thrash about, but he held her steady, not letting go, never relenting. "Mmmm," he growled, vibrating her clit all the more. His sucking became merciless, faster—harder.

Her head flew back, her nipples hardened and elongated impossibly further, blood rushed to her face. *"Yes . . . oh yes!"*

And then she was there, falling over the precipice, screaming from the ecstasy, wanting more, needing to be filled and fucked.

Euan flipped her over with a growl as he came to his knees, wanting to take her from behind on all fours. "Dinn," he gritted out, nudging the back of her head gently.

Lying on her elbows, Janet looked over her shoulder and made a face, not understanding. She arched an inquisitive brow at him.

"Dinn," he stated with more force, again nudging her head. His eyes were blazing, his muscles corded, his thick cock jutting and swollen. "Dinn."

Janet's lips formed an O. He wanted her upper body pressed down further. She complied readily, spreading her legs far apart, sliding off of her elbows and pressing her head and torso further towards the bed, her buttocks and labia dipping upward for his use.

He grunted arrogantly then cupped her labia from behind and pressed his palm and fingers upwards. "Suas."

That must mean "up," she told herself wryly. Her face heating up despite the night they'd already shared together, Janet submitted, keeping her head and torso down while simultaneously thrusting her labia and buttocks up into the air as high as they would go.

It was a wicked feeling, she thought, being on display like a man's personal whore. But when Euan expelled his breath on a groan while running his hand over her exposed flesh, she decided that wicked could be a good thing.

"Leamsa."

He growled out that word again, the word he had used the last time he'd fucked her, the word he was even now repeating over and over again as he rubbed her wet flesh.

Mine. Janet somehow understood that *leamsa* meant *mine.* Her body reacted to his possessiveness, her nipples hardening and her breath quickening.

"Leamsa."

She gasped as he impaled her, her flesh slurping up the impressive length of his cock, her labia reflexively arching skyward for more. He gave it to her.

Euan gritted his teeth as he slid in and out of her, thrusting into her depths in long, penetrating thrusts. "Leamsa."

"Oh god."

He pummeled faster, pounded harder, thrust into her to the hilt. Over and over. Again and again. "Leamsa."

The slapping sound of her soaked flesh sucking up his cock

reverberated, grew louder and lustier as she grew wetter and wetter. "Leamsa."

Janet thrust her buttocks back towards him, meeting each of his thrusts as he gave them to her. The harsh jiggling of her breasts caused her already sensitized nipples to grow that much harder. "*Euan*," she moaned out. "*Oh god . . . Euan.*"

She buried her face in the bed furs as her body began to convulse, her labia contracting around his steely flesh. She half screamed and half sobbed from the pleasure, so powerful was her orgasm.

"*Leamsa,*" he roared possessively, his jaw clenching. His callused fingers dug into the flesh of her hips as he thrust faster and faster, harder and harder. His muscles were tensed, the veins in his neck and arms bulging, his balls impossibly tight from the need to burst.

Janet moaned, continuing to meet his thrusts with thrusts of her own. "*Yes Euan,*" she groaned, "*god yes.*"

And then she was coming again, pulsing around him again, contracting again, moaning like a mortally wounded animal because the pleasure was so acute as to border on the painful.

"Tha, te bheag," he gritted out, "taom a-mach e." *Yes, little one. Pour it out.*

"*Oh god.*" Waves and waves and waves of pleasure shot through her, jutting out her nipples like hard gems, heating her face like a furnace, sending her over a cliff of sensation.

"*Leamsa,*" he growled definitively, slapping into her deeply for a final thrust. Gritting his teeth and closing his eyes, he groaned as he erupted, spurting his orgasm deep inside of her.

A suspended moment later, when the intensity had died down

a bit and some sense of rational normalcy settled in, Janet began to wonder why Euan was still holding onto her hips, thereby forcing her buttocks and labia to remain skyward. Confused, she drew herself up as far on her elbows as he would allow, then glanced over her shoulder to study his face.

The mask was back, that stone cold façade that broached no argument and allowed no leniency. And yet, conversely, his black eyes blazed more possessively than she'd ever seen them before.

A chill of foreboding swept through her, causing her eyes to widen and her throat to parch. He was about to do something—or say something—and she had no idea what. All she could do was wait. Sit there on all fours, her labia on display for him, and wait for whatever it was that he was about to command.

And then his large, callused hands were reaching under her and grabbing her breasts. He found the nipples, pinched them between his thumbs and forefingers, and locked gazes with her. "Leamsa," he said softly. Too softly. He tugged at them a bit so there would be no mistaking his meaning. "Tha?" *Yes?*

Janet's eyes widened further.

"*Tha?*" he asked more sharply, pinching her nipples again.

He wanted her to say it. He wanted her to acknowledge an ownership of sorts over her. She hesitated for a moment, uncertain as to what she should do. She didn't want to stay in the past, no matter how enjoyable these past few hours had been.

Eventually, however, the look in his eyes scared her into nodding. She would not say the word, but she would nod.

When she submitted Euan released one nipple, then used his free hand to trail down to the soaked and swollen flesh between her thighs. He slid two large fingers in her to the hilt, then met her gaze once more. "Leamsa," he murmured, his deep voice a rumble of authority and power. "Tha?"

She nodded briskly.

"Tha?" he asked again, louder, angry now.

She nodded again, assuming he hadn't seen the small gesture.

"*Tha?*" he bellowed, thrusting his fingers in again and pinching one of her nipples.

Janet's eyes widened nervously. He wanted her to say it—aloud. He wouldn't settle for anything less.

She swallowed harshly as her gaze clashed with his for a final time. Clearing her throat nervously, she nodded once more. "Tha," she agreed quietly.

With an arrogant grunt, he began to massage her clit with one hand and the nipple he was still latched onto with the other. She groaned, her head falling limp as he rewarded her for her compliant answer.

And then he was impaling her all over again and Janet thankfully had to concern herself with rational thought and worries of ownership no more.

Chapter 8

Janet had been surprised when Euan had awoken her a few hours later indicating that they were going to depart this place where they had shared so much passion together. He had taken her again, thrust himself into her with a groan as though he couldn't seem to help himself, as though her body was the most soothing place in the world for him to be. He had brought her to orgasm at least twice, maybe three times. She had been so groggy with pleasure and peaking she could no longer remember.

Euan had given her a new dress then, a floor length green number that was not only quite beautiful, but also more appropriate for his world. She could only assume that he'd somehow acquired it during the bath she'd taken after he'd married her.

And then he had taught her several new words by leading her outside and pointing to various things. He had been patient in his instruction, which had surprised her. She didn't know why she was surprised really, for he'd been extremely gentle with her ever since he'd captured her.

Perhaps she'd been taken aback because of the way Euan

bellowed orders at his men. She'd quickly surmised that he was the leader amongst the group for everyone catered to him efficiently and unquestioningly. If he barked out a command, it was obeyed and answered instantly. It was through these exchanges that by the second day of their journey from the village Janet found herself picking up more and more words from Euan's tongue.

Janet was pleased that she seemed to be learning key words and phrases from his language rather rapidly. Not enough to where she could yet carry on meaningful conversation—they'd been together but three days after all—but enough to where she was slowly beginning to comprehend what he meant without his having to point at whatever thing or action he was trying to describe.

The past three days had felt much like a dream to Janet. Riding through the Highlands on horseback, the brisk winds hitting her in the face, stopping to look at the wares of the occasional nomadic craftsman, making camp—and making love—with her husband at night.

Her husband.

The knowledge that she even had a husband, let alone one that had died hundreds of years before she'd been born, was what felt more surreal than anything else. And weirder still, she wasn't altogether certain how she felt about it.

Three days ago Janet would have escaped Euan at first opportunity. Today, if given the choice, she wasn't certain what she'd do. Such an admission was not only startling to her, but terrifying as well.

And Morag—oh how she missed Morag. Janet had no idea at all as to how her best friend was faring. Morag and her captor, a man Janet could safely assume was now Morag's husband, had ridden out ahead of she and Euan the morning following the weddings.

Where Morag had been taken Janet couldn't even begin to speculate. Worse yet, she wasn't well-versed enough in Euan's tongue to put such a higher level question to him. It was one thing to be able to ask for food and drink, quite another altogether to express feelings and concerns. She felt as though she were floating along like a piece of driftwood, unable to control her own destiny and uncertain as to where the waters would lead.

On the fourth day of their journey their entourage had been attacked by a group of bandits that outnumbered their party three to one. One minute Janet had been eating an apple as she rode in front of her husband on his mount and the next she was startled into dropping the piece of fruit by the sound of ear-piercing war cries followed by the thunder of hooves as a group of sword-wielding men assaulted them from the south.

Wide-eyed, her gaze had shot up to Euan's. He had paid her no attention, dashing off toward a tree with thick, high branches instead, and placed her into it for safe-keeping while he'd galloped back to charge directly into the fray.

Janet had been frightened. Not only for herself, but for Euan as well. Tears of frustration and terror had welled up in her eyes as she'd watched him ride off, watched him engage in a fight in which the numbers greatly out stacked any hope of a Donald victory.

A Donald. Janet now understood that her last name was Donald, or MacDonald. Apparently the two names were interchangeable, but since she knew from her own time that "Mac" meant "son of," she could assume that in these times the "Mac" was dropped as redundant, leaving whatever name was behind it to stand solo.

Not that she'd thought about something as inane as name trivia as she'd watched the skirmish unfold. She had considered the naming business later on, after the Donalds had surprised her by quickly vanquishing the threat to them.

It had been chilling, watching her husband kill men before her very eyes, watching as his heavily muscled and vein-roped arm had bore down on men with such force that his sword had neatly sliced through their now dead carcasses like butter.

He had worn that mask again, that stony façade that was so much a part of him . . . a part of him that was always in place save for the moments of passion they claimed together at night. But she supposed such a mask was necessary in this world, a needed way of severing all emotion from whatever job had to be done in order to keep your wits—and life—intact.

And so now here she stood on the fifth day of her journey, gazing out into the frigid Highland waters from shore as she watched a large boat being made ready for them to take to . . . well she didn't know where precisely, could only conjecture from the bits and pieces of Scottish history she'd gleaned while working in Nairn.

Janet knew that the clan MacDonald heralded from the Isle of Skye, that tiny dot of an island in the Hebrides where a man known as the Lord of the Isles had ruled as a king of sorts over the Highland clans in medieval times. She could only surmise, therefore, that since her husband's last name was Donald, or MacDonald, Euan must be of this lord's direct clan.

Janet felt weary, tired and bone-weary from their long journey. And she was confused, still overwhelmed by everything that had taken place this past week. And what's worse, at least to her way of thinking, was that she deeply suspected that she was beginning to grow feelings toward her husband that she wasn't particularly interested in having. Attached feelings. Caring feelings. Feelings of . . . love.

It was just that he was so . . . good to her. Euan made her feel special and loved and desired—three things she had never felt for a man back in her own world, most likely because no man had ever felt them for her either. The way he looked at her, the way he held her as though he'd never let her go or let anyone take her from him . . . it was heady stuff. Heady stuff that had little by little evolved into a deeper affection for him.

But how did he feel for her? she wondered. It was hard to speculate when she wasn't versed enough in his language to speak with him! But, Janet thought somewhat nostalgically, it was only when looking at her—just her—that his mask slipped from place, and bits and pieces of what in any other man would have been termed vulnerability could be seen.

Leaning against the bark of a tree, Janet had closed her eyes for barely a moment when the feel of soft lips placing kisses on her mouth startled her into opening her eyes. She kissed him back without qualm, then smiled up at the gentle giant towering over her. Well, gentle might not be the best term used to describe him, but he was gentle towards her at any rate.

Euan didn't smile at her, but then he never did. She could see the affection for her in his eyes though, the way they seemed to sparkle whenever he looked at her—and only when he looked at her. "Ciamar a tha sibh?" he asked somewhat briskly.

Janet cleared her throat a bit, answering him in broken Old Gaelic. "I am well. How are you?"

"Good. We will travel tae my lands today."

She looked at him quizzically.

"Land," he repeated quite patiently. He stomped his foot on the earth below him and repeated the word. "Land." When her eyes lit up with comprehension, he grunted, his usual response when pleased with her ability to learn quickly.

"We will go on the boat?" she asked him, pointing toward the large wooden vessel in case she was using the wrong word.

Apparently she hadn't. Euan nodded, speaking slowly so she'd understand him. "Aye, we will. 'Twill take most of the day."

Janet noticed that he didn't seem terribly put off by such a notion. And then she understood why when he backed her up against the tree bark and pressed his erection into her belly. The glazed over look in his eyes coupled with his thick erection let her know in no uncertain terms just what he planned to do with her to while the hours away on the boat.

"Mmm Janet," he murmured against her ear, "I need tae love ye."

Janet's body responded immediately, her nipples hardening and her breath catching. She knew her own eyes were glazed over, could feel them narrowing. "Yes," she whispered.

And then Janet did something she never would have been bold enough to do to a man in her own time. Reaching up under his plaid, she wrapped her palm and fingers around his thick cock and began to masturbate him.

Startled, though not unpleasantly so, Euan sucked in his breath. "Ah Janet." He closed his eyes, clearly trying to steady himself, and pushed at her hand. "Stop," he said gruffly. "Later, wife."

But Janet wasn't listening. She felt empowered by the response he always gave her, brazen and daring.

Euan was given only a moment to wonder at the mischievous look suddenly in his wee wife's eyes, his own nearly bulging from their sockets when she dropped to her knees and her head disappeared beneath his plaid. Right here under a tree. Where anyone could walk upon them. She was massaging his balls underneath his plaid.

"*Chan eil*," he hissed under his breath. *No.*

But again, Janet wasn't listening. She'd never done this for him before and suddenly she wanted to do it more than anything on earth. She took him into her mouth, sucking from tip to base, deep-throating him in one suck. She was elated when he gasped in astonishment, then acquiesced to her on a low moan.

Obviously this wasn't an activity women of his time knew much about. Good, she thought wantonly. The realization that for once he was more of a virgin in this arena than her made her all the more determined to bring him to orgasm.

"*Janet*," he said harshly, a disembodied voice from where she couldn't see him on the other side of the plaid.

And then she was pumping him in and out of her mouth in quick sucking strokes, letting his cock go almost the entire way out of her mouth before suctioning him back in with her lips and tongue. She knew the smacking sounds of her suckling were as much a turn-on to him as they were to her.

Janet realized the exact moment when Euan mentally capitulated. His breathing ragged and choppy, he thrust the plaid from around her so he could watch his cock disappear into the depths of her mouth and throat. He groaned at the wicked sight, his muscles cording and tensing. "Aye, Janet," he said hoarsely. "Dinna stop kissing me."

Grabbing her by the back of the head with both large hands, he helped to ease himself in and out of her mouth, riding her faster and faster, much as he did to her pussy while mating.

Janet gave him everything, holding back nothing. She sucked him hard, faster and harder, in and almost out, over and over, faster and faster. Kneading his tightly drawn scrotum with both hands, she suckled on him relentlessly, knowing from his now incessant moaning that he was about to burst.

"Tha, Janet," he gritted out between pants, his jaw clenching as he continued to ride her mouth, "doit mo bhod." *Suck on my cock.*

And then he was coming, riding her hard as he spurt into her mouth, moaning louder than she'd ever heard him moan before, uncaring if anyone heard what they were about.

Janet drank of him, sucked every drop of him dry, until his cock once again lay flaccid and sated in the nest of dark curls at his groin.

Euan drew her up to her feet, hugging her tightly against him, as if thanking her.

FIVE HOURS AND three blow jobs later, Janet decided that she had created a monster. Her jaw was sore, she was slightly seasick from the rough movement of the waters in a postage-stamp-sized cabin that boasted one tiny bed of animal furs and a few small slits for breathing in oxygen, yet she couldn't seem to stop herself from obliging his carnal longings.

Clearly, Euan was enthralled with the new form of pleasure she'd introduced to him. He hadn't left her side once. Not even to go check on the voyage's progress.

Three times now Janet had fallen asleep with a sated cock in her mouth and three times she had been woken up to a stiff, thick erection poking at her lips, wanting entry. She always gave it to him, of course, then secreted away a smile when she'd hear her husband moan as he closed his eyes and laid back to enjoy a special treat.

Janet honestly didn't know how her jaw was withstanding so much sucking, but it was. Every time she got sore to the point where she didn't think she could carry on, it took but one glance toward Euan's face to change her mind.

His expression while she sucked on his cock reminded her of what she assumed a little boy who'd discovered masturbating for the first time would look like—gloriously enraptured. A man who had found and captured Nirvana.

EUAN SIMPLY COULD not get enough of his wife's suckling. He knew he was being hard on her poor mouth, but he kept awakening from his slumber with a rock-hard erection and a new load of juice that needed to be relieved. And by the saints, 'twas bliss the way Janet relieved him. He'd never before experienced such a sinful delight.

"Ah Janet," he murmured, as he watched her beautiful mouth slurp up his cock, "keep kissing him," he groaned. "Dinna stop, love."

Love. Not a word he'd expected to feel for his wife. Not a word he'd felt for any female save his daughter Glynna.

Nay. With Janet he had felt lust upon seeing her, more lust than he'd ever entertained in his life. Lust that had driven him to capture her twice, lust that had speeded him towards the first village with a priest just so he could rut inside of her, lust that had kept his cock hard and pumping his cream into her more often than he'd believed to be possible.

But somehow over the course of the journey back home, over the course of fucking her mindless and spewing inside of her several times a night, the Lord of the Isles had fallen in love with his captured bride.

He would never let her leave him. Never.

Euan sucked in his breath and groaned as Janet released his cock from her mouth and bent lower to suckle of his man's sac. Running his fingers through her long curly hair, he closed his eyes and enjoyed the bliss.

Nay. He would never let her go.

Chapter 9

THE CASTLE WAS BEAUTIFUL. JANET SIMPLY COULDN'T GET OVER how gorgeous it was, a mythical looking place that was probably no more than a shell of a relic in her time if indeed it still stood at all. Honestly, she didn't know. Although she'd heard a great deal about the Isle of Skye, she'd never actually visited it. But she was here now. And wow was it awesome.

The entire island was the most lush, picturesque place she'd ever laid eyes on. Emerald green grass, true blue skies, fragrant bluebells that stood at attention in the wind. It was breathtaking.

And the castle—simply indescribable in its wonder. She gawked at the fireplace in the great hall where she was currently standing, taken aback by how large it was. She would easily be able to stand upright in it and still have a bit of head room. It was that tall. And the width—twenty replicas of her could stand side by side in it. She imagined it took a great deal of kindling to light so massive a structure every day.

And then there was the little girl. Glynna if she'd understood Euan correctly. She was roughly six years in age and about the prettiest little thing Janet had ever laid eyes on. There was no doubt as to who had fathered this child. If the jet black curls and stubborn jaw hadn't given away her parentage upon first glance, then the way she'd flung herself into Euan's arms upon seeing him certainly would have.

What's more, it was obvious that the father was deeply in love with the daughter. Euan had actually broken into a full smile upon seeing Glynna, bending down, scooping her up off the floor, and affectionately rumpling her fine coif of a hair-do.

Janet had smiled while watching, mesmerized by the sight of it. She'd always wanted children, but she had never thought she'd have one. She didn't know how she felt about having one now. Latching on to Glynna, a motherless little girl who even now was holding her hand as she stood next to Janet and watched her father order this man and that man about, was paramount to all but giving up any hope of returning to the life she'd known but a week ago.

But did she want to return? Janet wondered silently for at least the fiftieth time. What was there for her really, especially with Morag here in the past? A job she was probably going to get fired from? An empty apartment in Cleveland she rarely saw?

There was no man in her former world who was special to her. No family either for that matter. Her parents had been dead for over five years, killed in a diving accident three days before Janet's twenty-second birthday.

Neither did she boast any real friends in the future save Morag—Morag whom she was still yet to see. She was beginning to worry that she'd never see her a—

"Janet!"

Wide-eyed, Janet whirled on her heel at the sound of that very welcome voice. Smiling brightly, she continued to clutch Glynna's pudgy little hand as she opened her arms and giggled when her best friend came bounding into them. "Morag!" she laughed.

"Oh Janet!" Morag hugged her tightly. "I was so verra worried for you!"

"I'm fine," she promised, hugging her back. "But what about you? How are you?"

Morag released Janet and stepped back a bit. It was then that she noticed Glynna for the first time. She smiled down to the little girl. "And who is this?"

"Glynna," Janet answered.

"Euan's daughter?"

"Yes."

Glynna smiled, displaying neat white teeth. "Hallo, milady," she whispered very sweetly in Old Gaelic.

"Hallo," Morag answered back with a grin, apparently having learned about as much of the tongue as Janet had. "You are verra pretty, Glynna."

"Thank-ye."

Janet's brow furrowed. Obviously Morag had learned a bit more of the tongue than she had. She reverted back to English. "How did you know those words? And how did you know Euan's name?"

"Stuart."

"Stuart?"

"Yes Stuart," Morag responded. Her cheeks pinkened a bit as she cleared her throat. "My, uh . . ."

"Husband?"

She nodded. "I tried to tell you that day in the forest but—"

"It's okay," Janet said wryly, "I pretty much figured it out for myself."

"Among other things, I'd wager."

Janet shook her head. "What's that supposed to mean?"

Morag chuckled. "We were in the same boat as you and your husband, you know, even if the men would no' let us see each other until we docked."

"And?"

She grinned. "Your man was doing more than a wee bit of moaning from what I could hear all voyage long."

Janet's face flushed with heat. She couldn't hold back the small smile that tugged at the corners of her lips though. "So glad I was able to unknowingly provide entertainment," she murmured.

Morag smiled, chucking her playfully under the chin. "Quit blushing. You have the look of a turnip."

Janet happened to glance down just then and noticed that Glynna was watching a little girl across the room play with a doll. The look in her eyes was one of unadulterated longing, a child desperately wanting to play, yet she made no move to dislodge herself from Janet's side even though it was obvious she'd rather be doing little girl things.

Good lord, Janet thought, she'd never met a child so in control of her naturally playful and exploratory nature. Not a good thing at the age of six, to stand off to the side rather than indulge. She turned to Morag. "Do you know the word for 'play'?"

"Hmm." She thought that over a minute, then threw a word at Janet.

Janet nodded her thanks then turned back to Glynna. "You may play now if you would like." She smiled down to her.

Glynna's return smile was so big as to border on bursting. Janet now understood that when Euan had first brought the little girl to her side, he must have instructed her to remain with Janet unless told otherwise. Good grief how boring for a six year old!

"Thank-ye, mum."

Janet's back stiffened. She hadn't been expecting such an endearment so soon, if at all, and she was confused as to how she should feel about it. It was frightening. And yet heartwarming at the same time. Realistically she knew the little girl was probably only calling her by the name she'd been told to use, but it didn't keep her heart from swelling up just a bit. "You're welcome," she said softly, scooting her gently away from her skirt. "Go play now."

Morag chuckled as the little girl bounded away. "She is a verra pretty wee thing."

"Mmm yes. She is."

The conversation turned then as they caught each other up on all that had transpired since they'd been separated. "I love it here." Morag waxed nostalgic as she spun around in a circle and took in the massive great hall and its bustling activity. "Stuart might be a bit high-handed at times, but he's good to me, gentle with me. No' at all a tyrant as my damned brothers were."

Janet didn't know the first thing about Stuart, but she could agree with that bit about Morag's brothers. She shook her head, bemused. "Are you telling me you don't want to go back to the future?"

Morag sighed, then shrugged. "I really don't know, Janet. I was no' thrilled with my life back in Nairn, hated it in fact. I would have gone crazy had I no' had you for a friend."

"I know what you mean," Janet murmured, her catlike green

eyes straying to absently watch Glynna play dolls with her friend. "But I can't imagine life here will be easy either." Her brow wrinkled as she considered something. She glanced back toward Morag. "Do you even know where we will be living once we leave the castle? Are Euan and Stuart sort of like, I don't know, soldiers to the big guy here or something?"

Morag's mouth dropped open. "You mean you do no' know?"

"Know what?"

Morag chuckled. "Janet lovie, Stuart is a soldier to the big guy as you so aptly named him, but Euan *is* the big guy."

Janet's eyes blinked a few times in rapid succession. She wasn't exactly sure what Morag . . . oh my.

Janet's eyes strayed across the hall to where her husband was instructing a man to send a message from him to another laird. She couldn't eavesdrop on much of the conversation—they were standing too far apart—but she did manage to make out the last sentence he'd uttered. *Tell him Mac Dhonuill nan Eilean sent ye.*

Mac Dhonuill nan Eilean?

Janet's breath caught in the back of her throat. She swallowed roughly as her eyes darted back toward a grinning Morag.

"That's right," Morag nodded. "You married the MacDonald of the Isles."

Chapter 10

EUAN GAZED DOWN AT THE SLUMBERING FORM OF THE WOMAN sound asleep beside him. He'd loved her hard this eve, ridden her sweet cunt twice and her wanton mouth once before he'd felt sated enough to leave her be.

'Twas little wonder, he thought with more than a wee bit male pride, that his lady wife was snoring louder than Auld Sheumais did when he'd been hitting the ale overlong. Of course, he conceded in a rare flash of amusement, her snoring was also making it difficult to fall asleep.

Reclining on his elbow, Euan ran his fingers through Janet's shiny mane of curls, brushing a few stray ones back from her hairline. 'Twas hard to believe that a woman so finely made was his. 'Twas not just her plump breasts and woman's hips that tempted him so, nor even the way she gave herself over to him so willingly.

'Twas her heart as well. The way she was with wee Glynna, taking to her these past few weeks as if she'd birthed her herself, spending time with her and making her feel important.

'Twas also the way Janet made him feel. When he held his

wife in his arms and made love to her, or simply when his eyes clashed with hers from across a chamber, he felt . . . alive. Whole and content. 'Twas the first he'd felt this way in—well mayhap in forever.

Euan bent his neck to kiss Janet softly on the lips. He hadn't been expecting it, but was pleased when she woke up, blinked a couple of times as if coming out of a daze, then smiled slowly before pulling his face down atop hers to kiss him more thoroughly.

They kissed for a few minutes, softly moaning into each other's mouths as their tongues swept back and forth over the other's. After a bit more of this languid loving, Euan raised his dark head and gazed down into Janet's eyes. "Ye're awake," he murmured.

"Yes." She nibbled on her lip for a moment. "Plan to do anything about it?" she whispered, her cheeks tinting scarlet as the words tumbled out.

Euan couldn't help but to grin, something he found himself doing quite a bit of lately. And now that his wife understood his tongue almost as well as he did, he'd discovered much to his delight that she had a wondrous sense of humor. She never bored him. Never a dull moment at the keep with Janet about.

'Twas not her words that caused his grin this time, though, but the fact that her cheeks were pinkened. As many times and in as many ways as they'd loved each other, it never failed to amuse him when Janet would suddenly turn shy on him. "And what," he murmured, "would ye have me tae do aboot it, vixen?"

She grinned at his endearment, having never thought of herself in such outrageous terms before. Or at least not before meeting Euan. She'd been telling herself for weeks not to form a deeper attachment to him, not to let herself fall any more in love with him, until she knew with stark clarity just what it was that she wanted. Did she want to remain in the past or try to find her way back to the future?

But as usual where Euan was concerned, the moment he gazed into her eyes with longing she brushed her concerns aside and refused to deal with them. It was wrong, she knew, but she couldn't seem to help herself.

"Hmm," she teased, pretending to think his question over. "Perhaps you could read to me by the fire or—"

Euan half growled and half grinned as he came down on top of Janet and settled himself between her thighs. She giggled, running her hand along the strong line of his jaw. It was always good to see the proof of him feeling carefree and lighthearted. Since arriving, she'd quickly discovered that such common things were contrary to his nature, most likely born of his position in life. From a young age, he had ruled many. Not only that but he'd been responsible for the rearing of his brothers as well.

He entered her welcoming flesh in one long thrust, gritting his teeth as he did so. 'Twas like a bit of heaven on earth, being deep inside of her. "I've got a treatise ye can ponder o'er, lass."

Janet's eyes widened on a laugh. She'd never heard him crack a joke before. He'd done it fairly well for a novice. "Oh do you now?" She grinned, wrapping her legs around his waist. "Anywhere near as good as *The Odyssey?*"

"Much better, I'm thinkin'." He rotated his hips and thrust deeply to underscore his words.

"I see," Janet gasped. "And what is the name of this treatise?"

Euan slid into her flesh again, causing his wife to suck in her breath. He ground his teeth, beads of perspiration forming on his brow. "I call it *Mac Dhonuill nan Eilean Falls in Love*."

Janet stilled. MacDonald of the Isles falls in . . . love? She had been expecting a witty return, not a declaration of his feelings. Her eyes darted up to meet his, rounding when she saw the affection in his gaze. She realized at once that her husband was deadly serious. *He loved her.*

"Oh Euan," she whispered, "thank-you so much for telling me that." *It made her decision so much easier.*

He grunted a bit, hopelessly attempting to conceal the rising color in his cheeks. "Have ye nothing tae say back tae me, wife?" He glanced away, wishing he hadn't asked as much.

It dawned on Euan that for the first time in his life he was feeling quite vulnerable. He quickly decided he didn't care much for the feeling, but also realized there was naught to be done about it. "Forgive my tongue," he said gruffly, "I should no' have—"

"Euan," Janet murmured, clutching his face between her hands as she searched his eyes.

"Aye?"

She smiled. "I love you too."

The heat in his face went from pink to crimson, endearing him to his wife all the more. "Of course ye do," he grumbled under his breath. "Let us speak of these silly things no more, ye ken?"

She grinned. "But I really love those silly things."

He sighed like a martyr. "Did I know ye were tae be so bluidy demanding, I mayhap would no' have stolen ye, Janet mine."

She slapped him playfully on the rump for that. "Oh really?"

Euan grinned, then shook his head slightly as he studied her features with a serious expression. "That's no' the truth," he murmured. "I would have stolen ye no matter the circumstance."

"Why?" she whispered.

He kissed her softly on the lips. "Because I love ye." The dimple on his cheek popped out as he added teasingly, "Daft wench."

Chapter 11

Lack of TV—not a problem. No electricity—who cares? Non-flushing latrines made of stone—kids' stuff.

Janet breezed around the keep for the next couple of days feeling drunk on giddiness. He loved her. Handsome, virile, sexy Euan was in love with mousy Janet Donald nee Duval.

So it was much to her chagrin when Morag squirreled her away in an alcove on the second day following Euan's pronouncement of love, wanting to escape.

"I can no' stand to be with Stuart, Janet." Morag threw a lock of red hair over her shoulder. "Did I say he's no' as bad as my brothers? Ha! He is a thousand times worse!"

Janet cleared her throat. "What did he do?"

"What didn't he do is more the question needing to be asked," Morag huffed. "He tells me what to do, orders me around like a bloody personal servant, he . . ."

Janet listened with half an ear as Morag detailed the longish litany of her husband's sins. She knew Morag—and her temper—well. Even though her best friend didn't realize how she got when she was in a pique, Janet understood implicitly that she'd change her mind about wanting to leave Stuart once she cooled down a bit. She knew Morag loved him. It's just that Morag always became agitated whenever a man displayed even a hint of behavior that smacked of her brothers'. A fact Janet could hardly blame her for.

"So are you with me or no'?" Morag finished her tirade with a definitive nod of the head. "Or do you plan to make me find passage back to Nairn myself?"

Three years of experience enabled Janet to deal with the potentially explosive situation pragmatically. She knew Morag would change her mind once she let off a bit more steam. It was just a matter of distracting her until then.

Janet pretended to turn the matter over a bit. She narrowed her eyes and gazed thoughtfully toward the ceiling. "I don't think we should discuss this here. Let's go take a walk outside," she whispered.

Morag's blue gaze rounded as if she hadn't expected Janet to capitulate in the slightest and, in fact, had been hoping she wouldn't. That only confirmed Janet's initial suspicion—Morag just wanted to vent. "Y-You want to discuss it outside?"

"Of course." Janet shrugged. "This is hardly the sort of thing we can talk about in here."

Morag was so taken aback it didn't occur to her that there was no reason they couldn't talk within the castle walls because nobody would understand them anyway. "Well . . ." She scrunched up her face and cocked her head. "You want to leave Euan?" she squeaked out.

Janet decided not to bother playing games. Clearly, Morag had no desire to leave. Not deep down inside at any rate. "Not any more than you want to leave Stuart." She held out her hand and smiled. "Come on. Why don't we go outside and take a nice brisk walk and you can tell me all about what a jerk he is and then you'll feel tons better and more ready to confront him."

Morag chuckled. "You know me too damn well, lovie."

"Lucky for you." Janet grinned. "If I was any other woman we would have been halfway to Nairn by now."

"I DINNA KEN her problem," Stuart growled, his sword clashing against Euan's. They were sparring in the lower bailey, honing their skills.

Euan disarmed him almost immediately, then pointed the tip of his sword just under his brother's chin. "Ye best figure it out, mon. 'Tis affecting your concentration." He released him and resheathed his weapon.

Graeme, who had been watching from the sidelines, chose that moment to amble over and do a little grumbling of his own. "At least ye have a wench tae moan o'er, Stuart. I still can no' believe Auld Sheumais let wee Elizabeth get away from him." He threw his hands in the air dramatically. "All the mon had tae do was watch her whilst I took a piss!"

Stuart found a grin at that. "He'd been hitting the cups again, no doubt."

Euan snorted. "As always." He shook his head, then rumpled Graeme's hair affectionately. "'Tis tae young ye are tae worry o'er a wench, boy. Ye'll get another. I'll find ye a betrothed myself come Michaelmas when a few of the clan leaders come tae sup."

Graeme shivered at the notion. "I can scarcely contain my excitement, brother. Will ye betroth me tae that MacPherson wench who possesses a face with a frighteningly close resemblance tae that of a pig, or will it be the dowered daughter of the MacInnis with the over-large teeth?"

Euan and Stuart couldn't help but to chuckle. "Well," Stuart teased, "what is your preference? A pig face or over-large teeth?"

Graeme didn't see the humor in the situation. He sniffed at such a choice. "Ye best save your ill-wit for one who can appreciate it. Since I dinna care for it and since your lady wife is planning tae run away from ye, one must wonder—"

"Back up, whelp," Stuart interrupted. His smile faded abruptly. "What do ye mean Morag plans tae run away?"

Graeme's eyes widened. "Well," he stammered out, "she was mayhap no' serious. Mayhap she was just grumblin' aboot because she was mad at—"

"Graeme," Stuart ground out, "tell me what ye heard."

"Aye," Euan rumbled, his thoughts turning to Janet and her close friendship with Stuart's wife. "Tell us."

Graeme sighed, thinking the scene he'd witnessed this morn not worth the telling of it, but eventually he gave in with a shrug. Why not? "I dinna ken most of what she said for she was mutterin' tae herself in that foreign tongue of hers, but after ye stomped off from the great hall this morn she grumbled under her breath in Gaelic that she was off tae find Janet and leave this place forever."

A chill of foreboding coursed down Euan's spine. Janet had never even confessed to him from whence she'd come. If she got away, he wouldn't have the foggiest notion where to hunt her down to.

"Damme!" Angered, Stuart cursed up a mild storm before turning back to his brothers. "I best go see what the wench is aboot."

"I'll come with ye," Euan murmured.

Stuart's eyes rounded comprehendingly. He nodded. "Let us go."

Chapter 12

MORAG TWIRLED A FRESHLY PICKED BLUEBELL BETWEEN HER fingers and smiled as they walked alongside the perimeter of the wall that led toward the waters surrounding Skye. "You were right," she admitted with a grin, "I feel a lot better now. Sunshine and sea breeze was just the thing."

Janet tossed a tawny ringlet over her shoulder and smiled. "It is quite beautiful here, isn't it?"

"Mmm. Like a dream."

Janet stopped when they came toward an area of the wall with a hole in it. Gliding up to it, she put her eye against it and looked to what was beyond the stone structure. "Wow. Morag come look at this. The beach out there is about the prettiest thing I've ever seen."

Morag tried to oblige her, but wasn't able to see anything. "I'm shorter than you by a good three inches and you are standing on tiptoe. I canna see a blessed thing."

Janet chuckled. "Too bad. It's so pretty."

Morag thought that over for a second as she surveyed the wall. "We could try to climb to the top using these holes as footfalls."

Janet wrinkled her nose at that. "What if we fall? No thanks!"

Morag sighed. "Janet, we may love our husbands but let's face it, there is no' a damn thing to do in this time. If we fall, so what. At least trying to climb the wall gives us something to do for the next fifteen minutes!"

Janet half laughed and half snorted. "True."

Five minutes later the women had gotten no more than halfway up the wall when the thundering sound of horses' hooves came rumbling from the castle bailey charging toward them at top speed.

Morag crinkled up her face, glancing over her shoulder without letting go of her hold on the wall. "Is that my Stuart?"

Janet used one hand to shield her eyes from the sun's glare. "Yep. And that looks like Euan with him too." She winced when she heard Stuart's cursing. "Wonder what's got him so upset?"

Morag's eyes widened. "You do no' suppose we are under attack?"

Janet wasn't given the opportunity to answer. Twenty mounted men came to an abrupt halt at the wall just then, all of them staring straight up at the women from below ground. They looked distinctly uncomfortable, Janet thought, which seemed a bit odd. But then again, Stuart was cursing loud enough to wake the dead. That would make anybody uncomfortable.

"What are you bellowing over now?" Morag screeched, her nostrils flaring as she glanced defiantly down toward her husband.

Stuart didn't answer that. He didn't bother. Janet thought his face looked red enough to start a campfire off of. "Get," he said distinctly, spacing out his words evenly, "down from there now."

Morag chose that moment to contradict him. "No," she sniffed. "I will no'."

A tic began to work in Stuart's jaw which Janet found curious. He really seemed to be overreacting to the situation if indeed she and Morag's excursion up the wall was what had set him off.

"Morag!" he bellowed. "Running away will do ye no' a bit of good. I will find ye every time. And punish ye just as I will when I get my hands on ye!"

Morag rolled her eyes. "Oh sure, like I'll come down now," she said dryly, "knowin' you plan to punish me and all." She sighed. "I mean really Stuart, you—" She broke off as she glanced toward Janet. Confused, she threw her a baffled look before doing the same to her husband. "Wait one moment. What do you mean aboot running away, Stuart? I was no' running away. We were but climbing the wall to get a look at the beach on the other side."

A few muffled laughs rose up from the soldiers on horseback, inducing Janet to wince. Geez but she couldn't blame them. She knew for a fact Morag was telling the truth, but climbing a wall to look at the beach? It truly did sound like a lie, and a weak one at that.

"Climbing a wall tae look at the bluidy beach?" Stuart laughed mirthlessly. "How lackwitted do ye think I am, woman?"

When Morag opened her mouth to speak, Janet forestalled her by coming to her defense. She was afraid that, as angry as her best friend was, she might have chosen to actually answer Stuart's question thereby getting herself into hotter waters with him. "It's the truth," she said with a nod, gazing down at her brother-in-law. "She wasn't running away. We were just bored and we wanted to—"

"Enough."

That one word, uttered quietly yet icily from Euan, was enough to send a shiver up Janet's spine. She flicked her gaze down toward her husband, swallowing roughly when she realized how angry he was. But there was more than anger in his expression. There was something else. Something that looked remarkably like . . . pain.

Oh no! she thought in a flash of realization, Euan actually believed that Morag had been trying to run away. And worse yet, Janet now understood that he believed her to be guilty of the same crime. Her eyes rounding, she implored her husband to listen. "You don't really think I was trying to run from you do you?"

He said nothing. Merely stared at her.

"Do you?" she asked shrilly.

Euan was wearing his mask again, Janet noted with more than a little trepidation. His black gaze was boring holes into her, the line of his jaw stubborn and unbending. Her eyes widened nervously.

After what felt like an eternity, Euan broke his harsh gaze from hers and threw a command at one of his men. "Get her down from there," he said with seeming indifference. "And lock her in my bedchamber."

Chapter 13

JANET'S CHEEKS PINKENED WITH MINGLED ANGER AND embarrassment as Euan's man Niall escorted her back to her sleeping chamber. Her only consolation was that the gruff warrior looked as though he felt sorry for her. In fact, just before he locked her inside he turned to her and mumbled sheepishly, "For the record, milady, I do no' think ye were tryin' tae escape."

And then he was gone, leaving Janet alone to stew. She was angry. Very angry. But also quite frightened. The final look Euan had thrown her way before galloping off had been laced with promises of retribution. She could only wonder at his punishment.

One side of her, the indignant half, wanted to stay right where she was and await his arrival so she could rage at him for treating her like this, for not believing her when she'd told him the truth. But the other side of her, the pragmatic half, wanted to bolt. Janet had no clue as to how her husband planned to punish her for her alleged sin, but she conceded rather gloomily that none of the scenarios she was coming up with in her mind boded well.

Janet paced back and forth in the bedchamber, uncertain as to what she should do, what she should say, when Euan finally saw fit to make an appearance. Just then the door came crashing open, causing Janet to whirl around on her heel and dart her eyes nervously toward her husband.

He looked angry. Very, very angry. For some reason or another she wasn't afraid of him any longer though. For some reason or another rather than cowering as most would have and she probably should have, she found her eyes narrowing acidly and her lips pinching together. "Go away," she seethed, turning around, giving him her back. "I have nothing to say to you."

It took Euan five long strides to reach her. When he did, he whirled her around to face him. "I'm certain ye are verra angry with me," he gritted out, his nostrils flaring, "for putting a stop tae your grand plan. But ye will do as I bid ye regardless."

That was too much. She thumped him on a steely arm, not that the big ogre so much as flinched from it. "This is ridiculous!" she screeched, raising her voice to him for the first time since they'd met. "I wasn't trying to run," she fumed out, "and I resent the fact that you don't believe me!"

His nostrils were still flaring as he searched her gaze. He looked like he wanted to believe her but was afraid to hope. And then the vulnerability in his eyes was quickly masked and the steel replaced it. "Take your clothes off," he ordered her.

Janet's eyes widened. Her chin went up a notch. "No."

"I said," Euan repeated icily, "take your clothes off." A tic was working in his cheek now.

"I heard you and I said no." She crossed her arms defiantly over her breasts.

Apparently he didn't care for that answer for the next thing Janet knew he was lifting up her skirt and removing her dress himself. She struggled, indignant now. "How dare you!" she sputtered as the dress went over her head and sailed towards the other side of the room.

"I am Euan Donald, Mac Dhonuill nan Eilean," he said arrogantly. "I dare what I will." His black gaze raked her body insolently. "Go lie on the bed."

"Are you deaf?" she screeched. "I don't wish to speak to you let alone have sex with you! You didn't believe me when I told you the truth and I have nothing more to say to you!"

A vein in his neck began to pulse as his face stained red with anger. "Ye expect me tae believe ye were climbing up the wall tae see the beach!" he roared.

"Yes! I expect you to believe it!"

Euan growled like a trapped animal, the need to believe his wife warring with rational thought. He didn't know what to think in that moment, just knew that he needed to be inside of her. *"Get on the bed,"* he bellowed.

Her chin lifted impossibly higher. "No!"

He slashed his hand through the air. *"Now."*

Janet's eyes widened at the unadulterated pain laced in that one word. It was that knowledge, and not the order itself, that sent her legs gliding toward the bed. Climbing up on top of it, she sat there on her knees and waited, uncertain as to how she could convince him she had been telling the truth out there on the wall. It was paramount that she convince him. She didn't want him hurting inside.

"Why did ye run?" he asked as he took off his clothing and joined her on the raised bed. "Did ye really think I'd let ye go?" He ground that question out through a clenched jaw as he came down on his knees in front of her and took her breasts in his palms. "Ye should have known better, *Seonaidh, leamsa.*" *Janet, mine.*

She met his tortured look unflinchingly. "I did not run from you."

His black gaze softened somewhat, but Janet could tell he wasn't yet totally convinced. He was beginning to believe her, though, which gave her new hope.

And then Euan was massaging her nipples, rubbing them between his thumbs and forefingers and Janet found her lips parting on a breathy sigh under the sensate assault. "Ye have beautiful thick nipples," he said gruffly as he plumped them. "I want them pokin' straight up in the sky for me tae suckle of."

Janet gasped as his lips closed around one diamond-hard nipple. He slurped it into his mouth, closing his eyes as if to savor it, rolling it around between his tongue and teeth. Liquid desire shot through her, dampening the flesh between her legs and elongating her nipples further. She ran her fingers through his hair and mashed his face into her chest. "Yes, Euan," she breathed out. "Oh yes."

He drew from her hard then, sucking on her nipples incessantly until she was panting for air and he was primal with the need to fill her up with his cock and his cum.

"Whether ye want me or no'," Euan rasped out in a moment of unveiled vulnerability, as he pushed her down onto her back and settled himself between her thighs, "I will always want ye. I will always need ye."

Janet's eyes closed briefly, saddened as she was by the pain in his voice. Her eyes opened and clashed with his. "I love you, Euan. I swear to you," she promised softly, "that as ludicrous as my explanation might have sounded back there at the wall, it was the complete and total truth." She wrapped her legs around his waist. "I will never run from you. I love you."

He lay poised above her, his eyes searching hers frantically for the truth, hoping against hope that he could believe what he'd been told.

"Tha gaol agam ort, a Euan." *I love you, Euan.*

He impaled her in one long stroke, inducing Janet to gasp as he filled her. "I love ye tae," he rasped out, his teeth gritting at the exquisite feel of her tight flesh enveloping him, sucking him in.

Janet clutched his buttocks in her hands and stroked them soothingly. "Do you believe me then?" she whispered. "Please tell me you do. Even if it's a lie. I couldn't bear it if I thought you believed Stuart."

Euan kissed her lips gently, sipping at them. "I believe ye, my love. And that's no' a lie."

Janet had no time to respond to that pronouncement, for within the next breath her legs had been thrown over his shoulders and Euan was drawing himself up to his knees. His callused fingers digging into the flesh of her hips, he held her steady and impaled her to the hilt.

"Oh yes."

"Mmm," he said thickly as he began to rock in and out of her cunt in long, deep strokes, "ye feel so good tae me." He thrust harder and deeper, his strokes becoming faster and more penetrating.

"Oh god."

The sound of her vagina sucking up Euan's steely flesh was as much of a turn-on to Janet as her husband's primal pumping. She bore down on his cock, meeting his thrusts, loving the deep mounting he gave to her when her legs were splayed wide over his shoulders. *"Faster."*

Euan's jaw clenched tightly, his muscles cording and tensing, the veins on his neck and arms bulging. Grabbing her thighs, he pounded into her slick flesh.

Faster. Harder. Faster still.

"Oh yes."

And then Janet was coming, her back arching and her head falling back in ecstasy as she moaned wantonly for him, her nipples stabbing upwards as her sopping flesh contracted around the length and breadth of him. *"Yeeeeesssss,"* she groaned, gyrating her hips at him as her cunt sucked every bit of pleasure from him that she could.

"Janet." Euan used his fingers to clamp down on her jutting nipples as he thrust into her once, twice, three times more. Throwing his head back, he made a guttural sound as his orgasm ripped through him, spewing into her flesh.

Both of them dripping in perspiration, Euan held his body over Janet's while they both steadied their breathing. He kissed her softly on the lips, then eased her splayed legs from off of his shoulders. Coming down on the bed beside her, he drew her into his arms. "I love ye," he murmured, kissing her temple.

She smiled contentedly. "I love you too."

They were silent for a long while, enjoying the simple pleasure of basking in each other's embrace. Eventually it was Euan who broke the languid quiet. "I was wondering aboot something," he said, stroking her thigh as he spoke.

"Mmm. What about?"

"Ye are no' of the clan Hay."

Janet grinned, sensing the question that was coming. "No I'm not."

"Where did ye come from then?"

"It's a long story."

"We've plenty of time."

She smiled up at him, running her hand across the impressive width of his chest. "True. But before I tell you that story, I have something else I'd like to tell you first."

Euan cocked a black eyebrow. "Sounds intriguing. And ye sound mischievous. Should I round up a tankard of ale before we talk?"

She grinned. "You might need two."

Epilogue

EUAN DONALD, LORD OF THE ISLES, MASTER OF ALL HE SURVEYED, swiped an unmanly tear from his eye as he watched his beautiful wee Janet suckle their hour-old son, Alistair. Bonny Glynna was sitting next to them on the bed, grinning down at her new baby brother as she held onto one of his tiny hands.

He thought back on that eve several months past when first his wife had told him she was carrying his bairn. She had been right, he thought with a grin, he had needed more than one tankard of ale. Though not from the announcement of his son's conception but from the tale of how Janet had come to be with him in the first place.

Odd, but Euan had believed every word, having decided after that day at the wall to never doubt his wife again. He wasn't a man given to trusting others, yet Janet he trusted both implicitly and explicitly. 'Twas a good feeling, having another in the world he knew he could always rely upon.

"Look da'," Glynna giggled, "he's all red and wrinkly."

Janet laughed. "I'm sure he'll grow out of it, sweetheart."

Euan grinned at his wife and daughter as he strode toward the bed to join his family. "Let's hope so. Otherwise he might no' be verra popular with the ladies."

Janet and Glynna giggled at that, warming his heart.

It occurred to Euan as he sat down and gathered his wife and children closer to him that a year ago when he'd first set out to steal a bride, he had never anticipated finding such bliss. Fate was a funny thing.

Thank the saints.

DRAGONS and DUNGEONS

Tawny Taylor

ACKNOWLEDGMENTS

Thank you to my editor, Sue Ellen Gower, who has the patience of a saint and an eye sharper than a surgeon's scalpel.

And my husband, David, who may not have eighteen-inch biceps, but he has a heart ten times bigger than your average romance hero.

Chapter 1

KAYA CORDOVA HAD READ SOMEWHERE A LONG TIME AGO THAT the devil was the most beautiful angel in heaven. That was, before he was booted out of paradise, of course. At the time—she was probably in grade school then—the significance of that statement had been lost to her. But now that she was staring straight into the eyes of what had to be Lucifer incarnate, she had no doubt of its validity.

Today the devil had taken the form of a six-foot something, sun-kissed blond, suntanned, muscular god in crisp, finely tailored clothes that fit him like a second skin. And unfortunately for Kaya, he had just entered the winning bid on the one item that she had desperately wanted. Damn. And damn.

The second the auctioneer acknowledged his victory, bidder number nine, as he was officially known at the private auction, gave Kaya a slightly gloating but wickedly sexy smile.

In contrast, she maintained her dignity, although she wasn't above sticking her tongue out at someone who had completely ruined her day, week, month. Naturally, as was her luck, the item she'd just lost to the incredibly yummy Mr. Nine, was the last item left to be auctioned. She'd held out, bidding conservatively on the earlier artifacts, accurately anticipating she'd need every penny of her budget to buy the last item, a piece of a large collection reportedly smuggled into the United States by an ex–United States Marine turned treasure hunter.

Everything she'd seen today was valuable, would potentially bring a small fortune for Kaya's boss, a woman who owned a shop that specialized in rare Asian antiquities. But that last piece, a copperplate imprinted with some form of ancient writing, Kaya had a feeling that was priceless.

Being half-Filipino on her mother's side, the fact that it had been found near the mouth of the Lumbang River in the Philippines by a man dredging for sand, and sold for pennies to the Marine back in the 1980s, made it even more intriguing. How old was the copperplate? What did the inscriptions mean? Was it real, or one of the many fakes that had been offered to Americans with deep pockets and the hunger to own a piece of international history?

Kaya grumbled at her loss as she reluctantly shuffled toward the exit, mindful of the winning bidder's unhurried gait. He strode like a proud peacock toward the cashier to pay for the artifact she wanted so badly her belly ached. If only she'd had another few thousand dollars to work with! Then again, that was probably for the better. Although no longer a novice buyer, she would've been tempted to keep bidding, forgetting what she'd learned ages ago—not to fall in love with something and bid beyond her budget. In this case it had been so tempting.

And speaking of tempting . . .

Her head turned and her gaze glued itself like a fly on flypaper to the man responsible for her temporary discouragement. Never mind what he'd purchased, the man himself was walking, talking temptation right down to his well-shod toes. If not for her strong sense of self-control, she would have done just about anything to run her fingers through those flirty blond curls, trace the line of his jaw with her tongue, maybe even nibble on one of those adorable earlobes. And don't get her started on the dimples! Dimples were her weakness.

"That man is trouble with a capital T." She sighed and forced herself to keep walking, even though she wasn't watching where she was going. After taking only a few steps, however, a high-pitched yelp made her stop.

"Sorry!" She apologized before she turned to look forward. She realized the instant she did that she'd slammed into the petite but friendly looking young woman who'd formerly occupied the seat next to her during the auction. "Oh! I'm so sorry," Kaya repeated, still slightly distracted. For some illogical but frustrating reason, even now her gaze seemed to want to stray to the left where it would find Mr. Nine's slightly mocking smile and blue, blue eyes.

They were bluer than any eyes she'd ever seen. Very striking.

"It's all right. I've taken worse," the woman said, giving Kaya a friendly, not at all mocking smile. So unlike Mr. Nine's. "I took ballroom dance lessons with my cousin once. At thirteen, he was six-five and a hair shy of two-fifty. He broke two of my toes the first night." She tipped her head and glanced beyond Kaya. "That copperplate was something, wasn't it?"

"Yes it was, assuming it isn't a forgery," Kaya said, trying to hide her disappointment. "Since it hasn't been authenticated yet,

I wasn't at liberty to bid any higher. There've been too many fakes coming out of the Philippines lately to risk it."

"I'm new to this sort of thing, so I'm hardly an expert, but that makes sense to me." The young woman offered her hand. "I'm Mary, by the way. Mary Stratford."

"Kaya Cordova." Kaya gave Mary's tiny hand a firm but relatively gentle shake. Standing as close as she was to the pretty, petite woman, she felt like a horse, all big and clumsy. It seemed like all it would take was a wrong move—or even a light breeze—and the little woman might shatter like glass into a gazillion pieces. "I'm not two-fifty, thank God, but I'm no lightweight either. I didn't break any bones, did I?" She motioned toward the foot she assumed she'd stomped on.

"Not a one." Mary followed the line of Kaya's fleeting gaze, from her foot to the cashier. "I'd pay good money to see the smug smile knocked off that man's face if he learned he just spent over twenty thousand on a worthless piece of industrial waste turned priceless artifact."

"For some reason, I don't believe we'll get the satisfaction. Besides, looking at his clothes, I have a feeling twenty thousand is nothing to him."

"Oh well," Mary said on a sigh. "As they say—the rich get richer. Speaking of rich, I've got to get to the airport. I'm off to Chicago to catch another auction. Sorry you didn't get this one, but you'll get the next."

"I hope you're right. Good luck in Chicago." Kaya pushed open the door and held it for Mary.

Mary gave her an over-the-shoulder thanks as she hurried out the door and into the soggy, cold late morning. She shuffled down the two front stairs to the ground level. Kaya followed Mary outside but stopped under the wooden overhang, not exactly eager to dash through the monsoon dumping water from the sky by the bucketful.

Thanks to the downpour, the air had chilled nearly twenty degrees to a crisp fifty-something. Because it had been a lot warmer earlier, Kaya was wearing only a light sweater over her lightweight, short-sleeved dress. That loosely crocheted garment wasn't going to offer even meager protection against the gale-force winds, any more than it was going to keep her dry. "Stupid Michigan weather. I wish it'd make up its mind and decide whether it's winter or summer," she muttered to herself, hugging her sweater around her body. "What's wrong with some transitional weather? Say a nice, comfortable sixty degrees?"

A particularly strong blast of wind that made her shiver and coated her face with a cold mist was the only response she received.

It was then that she decided she had two choices . . . either A—go back inside and wait out the storm, or B—make a run for it. Since she was expected back at the store in less than an hour, and the all-encompassing gloom didn't look like it was going to break before next week, she figured she had no choice but option B.

She just hoped the Dry Clean Only tag on her dress didn't mean the garment would shrink to toddler-size when exposed to water. She'd had that happen once. And once should have been enough to keep her from buying Dry Clean Only clothes altogether. A grown woman with fairly ample curves wearing a dress that would fit your average four year old was not a pretty sight. Today, she'd have to take her chances.

Preparing to run into an icy-cold downpour was a lot like

TAWNY TAYLOR

getting ready to dive into the Detroit River in the middle of January. It required a bit of time, some deep breaths, and a little bit of jogging in place to get the blood pumping, which were all good reasons why she didn't make a habit of swimming in January or making mad dashes through thunderstorms to her car. For one thing, time was something she rarely possessed an excess of. Second, deep breathing made her dizzy and her hands numb. And third, running in three-inch heels was dangerous, especially in slick-soled three-inch heels that tended to slip on wet asphalt.

Thanks to the difficulty in running and a bit of reluctance—Kaya had never been the kind to dive into water, frigid or otherwise. She'd always been more the toe-in-the-water kind of girl—she hadn't made it more than a step or two away from the front door before a big, black limousine swooped around the corner and came to a skidding stop in front of her. Muddy water coated the lower half of her body and she prepared to give the passenger inside a good, nasty glare when the passenger door opened. Instead of some rich snob stepping out of the car like he was preparing to walk the red carpet, only an arm jutted out. A hand caught her dress at about hip level and yanked.

Out of instinct, she jumped backward and tipped her head to look down in the car, spying none other than sexy Mr. Nine grinning at her from the backseat.

"Hi there," he said, looking absolutely amazing in the dimly lit interior of the car. His dimples were on high beam, his smile too. "I'd like to give you a ride to your car."

She was grateful for the shelter of the overhang as she stood by the side of the car trying to pry her tongue loose from her throat. If she was going to stand there for a while, her jaws snapping open and closed like a possessed mousetrap, at least she wouldn't get drenched. Then again, the look Mr. Nine gave her, one of the flirty, render-a-girl-brainless varieties, made her so hot she was tempted to throw herself into the biggest puddle she could find for some relief.

After indulging in a sigh that finally knocked her tongue free, she shook her head. "Thanks, but no. I'm just parked over there, not more than twenty yards away."

"Are you sure I can't change your mind?"

I could think of one or two ways you could. "No, thanks. Although this storm is getting bad, I don't think I need an ark to get there yet. Appreciate the thought, though." She tried to step farther back from the car, fearful of getting her toes run over when it pulled away, but his firm grip on her dress kept her from backing too far. Puzzled, she gave him her best, practiced "what's up?" look.

"Please," he answered. "I'd like to speak to you."

"About what? What could you, the person who obviously got what he wanted, want to talk to me—the one who didn't—about? I don't have anything you want."

Silent laughter making his eyes glittery, he mumbled something incoherent that made her blush then added, "About this." Those two sweet dimples poked into his cheeks as his mouth curled into a naughty smile that made her knees all weak and trembly. He lifted a black case which she assumed held the copperplate.

"Yes, I know you have it. You bought it. What do you need me for?"

"Please. I have a few questions. And I promise, if you're worried about getting into a car with a strange man, I'm not suggesting anything sinister and I've never been convicted of a crime."

"Thanks for clarifying. Yes, I was worried you might be a crazed monster who entices women into your lair during our infamous Michigan downpours and then does unmentionable things to them."

"Wow, you have me pegged already. Want to risk it anyway?" he joked. Those dimples became even deeper.

She chuckled to hide a near-swoon. Charmed almost out of her mind and curious about what he wanted, she looked into those big blues for some sign of subterfuge. What she saw was confusing but not threatening. But before she made her decision, he made it for her. When she reached down to smooth her windblown dress against her legs, he caught her by the wrist and yanked her inside. The door slammed the second she was in the car.

Alarmed, and feeling off balance, her body basically sprawled over his, her chest on his belly, her groin on his thigh, she glared up at him and shook a scolding finger. Funny little tingles and zaps buzzed through her body, like little bolts of static electricity as she warned, "If you try anything funny, I'm outta here." Still not comfortable with the situation, although the position was growing on her, she gathered herself together, settled into the black leather seat, smoothed out her wrinkled dress and tried to fake a casual, confident air. "Hmm. This is cozy. I could get used to this."

"So could I."

So much for her confidence. It crumbled at the sound of those three little words. Then things went from bad to worse. When he winked then glanced meaningfully at her crossed legs, she just about died. Sure her face was as red as a stop sign, she tugged at her skirt, which was slowly inching up her thighs, no doubt the result of the drenching she'd received when the car pulled up. To keep him in his place—or at least attempt to—she gave him her best mean eyes, the ones she used regularly to intimidate any door-to-door salespeople who chose to ignore the "No Soliciting" sign plastered to her front door. "You, behave yourself."

"I'm doing my best to tame the beast, I swear. Here, I'll play polite host. Can I offer you something to drink?" he asked, motioning toward the minifridge.

"No, thanks. Call me silly, but I have this rule. No alcohol before noon." *And no alcohol while locked in a moving vehicle with a man who makes my head swim.*

He glanced at his watch then blinked wide-eyed at her, clearly trying to look innocent. It wasn't working. No sirree.

But it did make him look cute.

"Well, then, we'll just have to wait ten minutes." He pushed the intercom and asked the answering female voice to carry on.

"Carry on? What's that mean?" Kaya watched as the stretch limo did indeed carry on, gliding across the parking lot like it was floating rather than rolling on the road, past her car and onto the street. "Um, where are you taking me? I agreed to a ride to my car, not a tour of the city."

"We're . . . um, taking the scenic route." His crooked smile still firmly in place, he leaned forward and offered his hand. "Name's Jestin Draig."

Whew, being up close and personal to the body that possessed that wicked grin was doing some very interesting things to her, especially the parts south of her waistline. Shockwaves of awareness paraded up and down her spine like a marching band playing a Sousa march, which in turn made her inner girly parts start strutting to the beat, waving flags and tossing batons. "Jestin? Not Justin?"

Despite the parade going on in her body, she hesitated before taking his hand. Surely there was extreme danger in shaking hands with the devil. She'd never been the kind to embrace extreme danger, in any form, male included. Heck, just being in the car with him—a complete stranger—was a first for her. She stared at his hand, trying to decide what to do.

He cleared his throat, an action that naturally lured her gaze to his face. "And you are?"

That had been a good move on his part—making her look at his adorable face. Now, she was practically dumbstruck, again staring into impossibly blue eyes. It only took a few seconds for the playful twinkle in those eyes to melt her reservations almost completely. Her girly parts broke into a chant, *Go, team, go!* and she reached for his hand. "Kaya Cordova."

The instant her skin made contact with his, a blaze of searing heat shot up her arm. Taken off guard, she yanked her hand away, shoved up her sleeve and checked her skin for burns. She saw nothing, not even the slightest tint of pink but she sure felt something. Waves of heat were fanning out from her center like ripples on a pond. Her pussy throbbed as the heat thrust her into near orgasm. "What the heck was that?" She pushed her sleeve back down and tried to silence the rioting crowd inside her by fanning her face. The marching band kicked into high gear, playing a fast staccato. And the chanting girls were doing backflips and carrying on like the football team had just made the winning touchdown.

He answered her question with a couple of raised eyebrows that did nothing to help her suppress the ruckus in her body. Though it did confuse her. If she hadn't been nearly scorched to death by some mysterious electrical charge leaping between his hand and hers, what had that been? And why was she now a throbbing, wet, horny mess?

By his puzzled expression, she guessed it was fair to say he hadn't felt the same thing she did. Not to appear the fool, she pasted on as convincing an "I'm okay honest" smile, fanned her flaming face, and nodded toward his hand. "That's one heck of a grip you've got there, buddy. My, my."

She squirmed as her gaze met his and the heat churning deep in her belly dispersed in another wave. Some of it went down into her groin. Some of it settled at about nipple level in her chest, and the rest rose to her face. She shoved aside the notion of throwing herself on him and instead shed her sweater.

He glanced down at his hand, now resting on his knee instead of where she silently yearned for it to be—on hers, maybe even a little higher. "I didn't . . . did I hurt you?"

"Oh, no. I'm fine. Totally fine. Very fine. Yeppers. Just a little warm." She fanned her face again. "Do you have a thermostat back here? Might want to turn down the heat a few notches. I . . . er, get carsick." She wrinkled her nose, which gained her another brilliant smile from Jestin, which made those adorable dimples deeper, which of course sent the parade into high gear. Marching, cheering, flipping and twirling. "So, um. What did you want to talk to me about?"

He held up an index finger and glanced at his wristwatch again. "Well, what do you know?" His gaze met hers. "It's twelve-oh-one."

"Isn't that something?" she said, trying to sound dry. There wasn't a part of her that was dry, literally or figuratively, except maybe her mouth.

"You'll have a drink with me then." It wasn't so much a question as a demand.

"I have to get to work. I doubt my boss'd be too happy having me come staggering in, reeking of alcohol."

"A small drink." Obviously not the kind to take no for an answer, he poured two glasses of wine and lifted one to her.

She waved it away. "I said, no thanks. Don't take this wrong but I have to ask, what's up with the wine? Do you prefer to talk business with soused women or are you just a control freak?"

"I'm sorry if I seem too pushy. I admit I've been told I have some control issues . . ."

"That's big of you to admit."

". . . but the purchase of this particular artifact means a great deal to me and despite the fact that you were also hoping to buy it, I was thinking you might like to celebrate with me."

"Me? Celebrate with you? You don't even know me. I don't know you either." *But boy, would I like to!*

"If anyone, I assume you know the copperplate's value and might have a measure of respect for the significance of this purchase." He tried to hand her the glass again.

She shook her head, still refusing to accept it. "I'll give you that, but—"

"And as someone who has a great deal of respect for such antiquities, and a person of character," he added, emphasizing the last part. "I appreciate the fact that you have no hard feelings for having lost." With beseeching eyes, he offered her the glass for the third time. "Please?"

Who's saying I don't have hard feelings? "Um . . ." Good grief, he looked so darn sweet, like a little boy begging his mother for a puppy. What woman could resist? "Okay! Okay. Just spare me the puppy dog eyes, would you?" Besides, what would a single taste of wine do to her? A teeny, tiny sip would be safe. And although it broke her "No consuming any drinks she didn't serve herself" rule, she'd watched him pour it right in front of her. He had no reason to do anything crazy, like drug her. Besides, she was a plain-Jane, horse of a girl—so tall and big-boned for a Filipino woman—no way his type. He was just a lonely man, looking for someone to celebrate his victory with. It was kind of sad when she thought about it that way. She accepted the glass and took a sniff. It smelled strong. She wrinkled her nose and told herself it would have to be a very small taste.

Looking very pleased, he lifted his glass in a toast. "To Filipino copperplates."

"Yeah. Copperplates." She touched her glass to his, drank a small sip, surprised by the fact that she actually enjoyed the spicy but incredibly smooth flavor of the wine. Usually, she hated wine.

He watched her drink over the rim of his glass.

Oh, that was good. She smacked her lips, and just to make sure it tasted as good as she thought it had, she took a second sip before handing him the still half-full glass. "Okay. That's enough wine for me. So, if you'd like to get on with things, explain why you dragged me in here, I'd be mighty grateful." Before he set down her glass, she snatched it from him. "You know what? Think I'll take one more sip." She faked a cough and added in a raspy voice, "The dry air in the car's making me thirsty."

"Yes. Dry air." He watched her drink with laughing eyes then took it from her when she finished. "Are you sure you don't want more? This is an extraordinary vintage. I save it for special occasions."

"No, no. I'd better not. Despite my size, I'm a total lightweight when it comes to alcohol. If I drink any more, I'll be boring you with sob stories about my high-school days."

"That sounds rather pleasant, actually."

"Oh, don't get me started."

"Very well. Maybe another time."

Another time? There was going to be another time? That thought put the parade into overdrive. Things were getting real festive down below. Most notably, the fast but steady beat of the deep bass drum was thrumming in her pussy. The girls were doing triple backflips.

"I was hoping, since you had a keen interest in bidding on the copperplate, that you might know an individual who would be able to translate it? I can't even tell what language it's in, wouldn't know where to begin looking for someone."

All he wanted her for was her connections? Bummer! The parade came to a screeching halt, that is, all but the drum. That still beat at a steady pace down below.

Whoever was pounding on that drum was obviously not paying attention.

"You know, you didn't have to get me tipsy to ask for some help," she pointed out, trying not to sound as disappointed as she felt. "You should've saved your expensive bottle of wine for someone else. I'm afraid you wasted it. Whether I wanted to or not, I can't help you. At least not directly. I work for a woman who has a store in Birmingham. She's the one with the connections. I'm just the buyer."

"Hmm. What's the name of the store? Perhaps I should pay her a visit."

"You're welcome to go there anytime you like. It's open to the public, especially someone with . . ." *Gobs and gobs of cash.* ". . . an obvious appreciation for rare antiquities. The name of the store is Kim's Uniques. We're on Old Woodward, just north of Fifteen Mile road."

"Okay. I know where that is. I appreciate your help. Thank you."

"Not enough to let me buy that copperplate off you?" she joked.

"No, I'm afraid not." He reached forward and rapped gently on the window separating the driver from the passenger area, and the limousine turned up the auction house's driveway and into the parking lot.

Kaya shot Jestin a quick glance—who wouldn't? He was so fun to look at—then got out, ducking against the rain. Getting more drenched by the second, she fumbled with the door locks, cursing them for not being automatic. Finally, soaked to her skin, but at least back to normal with the exception of a slight tingle down below, she plopped into the driver's seat, started the car and flipped on the wipers.

The limousine, and its sexy passenger, were long gone.

Jestin watched the woman fumble with her door locks through the window, tempted to jump out, grab her again and drag her back to him, back into the car, back into his arms, back into his life.

Patience, he told himself. You must be patient.

That had been no ordinary woman. Human, yes. Common, far from it. He knew from the moment they'd first touched, from the blaze that had burned in his blood at the joining of their energies. She had felt it too. And her reaction to the wine—a formula that would make all women but one cough and sputter with disgust—had only affirmed his suspicions.

Kaya Cordova was his mate.

With mixed feelings, he told Bridgette his driver to take him home. He had preparations to make.

"I'M SORRY I'M late—"

At hardly over four feet, and probably no less than eighty years of age, Kaya's boss, Mrs. Kim, could hardly be described as physically intimidating. But the little frail-looking woman knew how to work with what she had. She could give a person the nastiest glare this side of the Mississippi at the drop of a hat and it was said one of her mean-eyed stares could make grown men twice her size shake in their boots in fear. At the moment Kaya was at the receiving end of one of those stares.

"You know I have appointment every Friday. I had to cancel," Mrs. Kim said in broken English as she polished a tarnished silver picture frame with brisk movements. "To top it off, you come back a mess and empty-handed? What happen?"

"I'm very sorry, Mrs. Kim. It's raining like you wouldn't believe."

"Really?" Mrs. Kim asked, looking doubtful. She glanced out the door then shook her head. "Why you lie to me?"

"It isn't raining now?" Kaya took a look for herself, then, disgusted at the sight of a cloudless, brilliant blue sky that reminded her of a certain set of eyes, said, "I swear it was raining earlier. And regarding the auction, I really tried. I wanted to get one item in particular. A Filipino copperplate I know Mr. Vandenberg would've paid a small fortune for," Kaya said, referring to their best customer, a man whom she'd never met. "But I was outbid."

"Copperplate?" her boss repeated, still scrubbing.

"I couldn't believe my eyes when I saw it. It looked exactly like the one I saw on the net. Same odd-looking inscriptions, everything."

"You did not get it?"

"The price went sky high, higher than the budget you gave me for the entire auction."

Mrs. Kim set down the frame. "I must have it. You must get it for me. You know the one who bought it? Tell me his name. I bet he work for that Mr. Angus."

"No, I know Harry Angus's buyer and that wasn't him. I've never seen this guy before. I chased him down afterward. In fact that's why I was late. I went to him after the auction, tried to talk him into selling the copperplate to me, knowing you'd feel this way." So she was stretching the truth a smidge, but the subject of selling did come up. She had to cover her butt, get herself off Mrs. Kim's shit list. "Unfortunately, even though it seems he has no idea of what he has, he refused my offer."

"Did you get a card? I call him. He listen to me."

"All I have is a name—Jestin . . . something." Kaya anxiously rummaged through her brain, trying to recall his last name. She was bad with names anyway, but with the added distraction of his eyes, and smile, and those dimples, it was a lost cause. Outside of his first name, the rest had gone in one ear and out the other. "I can't remember his last name," she admitted.

Mrs. Kim mumbled something in Korean, something Kaya knew wasn't polite and she took that as her cue to go in the back and get to work on the books. She was less than halfway through the payables when Mrs. Kim came back and parked herself in front of her desk. Kaya mentally prepared herself for a tongue-lashing.

"I give you big reward," her boss said.

"Reward? For what?"

"You get me copperplate. I give you big reward."

"You mean . . . like a bonus?" Mrs. Kim had never given her a bonus. Heck, Mrs. Kim had never given her a raise, not in three years, even though she'd made her craploads of money.

"Yes, bonus. How about . . ." The older woman eyed Kaya shrewdly. "Fifteen thousand?"

Kaya fought he urge to gasp. "Fifteen thousand dollars?" That was a windfall!

Fifteen thousand would pay for her grandmother to stay in the nursing home she loved for almost six months. That was huge, considering just this week Kaya had been trying to come up with a way to explain to Grandma why she had to move. Still lucid, but getting less so every day, Grandma didn't take bad news well. Even learning the evening's dinner menu didn't include chocolate cake caused an uproar. "The plate hasn't been authenticated yet."

"I trust your judgment."

"That's very kind but I'm certainly no expert—"

"I give you fifteen thousand if you can get it from man Jestin."

"I . . . I'll see what I can do. I'll need some time to find him, since I can't remember his name. Although I did mention the shop. He said he might come here—"

"You must not wait. He will sell it as soon as he discovers its worth. And I can't afford for that to happen. You must find him first." She shooed Kaya out from behind the desk, through the back stockroom, and out the shop's back door. "You go. Find him. I pay up to fifty thousand for the copperplate. No more. Make him say yes." She slammed the door before Kaya could respond.

After gaping for a few minutes at the closed door, Kaya turned and muttered, "Okay." She got in her car, shoved the key in the ignition, cranked the engine to life, then said, "What now?"

And just then, a crack of thunder ripped through the sky and another downpour coated her car.

"Great. Just great. I'm on the hunt for a devil with dimples in the midst of a hurricane." Not knowing what else to do, Kaya pulled out of the parking lot and headed back toward the auction house. "I hope this storm's not an omen of what's to come." She flipped the wipers on high speed.

Chapter 2

I'M SORRY BUT THAT INFORMATION IS CONFIDENTIAL," THE WOMAN seated behind the cashier's desk at the auction house said in answer to Kaya's question. "You understand I'd lose my job if I gave out our customer's names and addresses."

"Of course. I'm sorry. But I . . . he . . . Jestin asked me for some information about the copperplate he purchased today. I'd call him but he didn't give me a phone number."

"Yes, well, I'm sorry. I can't help you."

Kaya sighed. "Oh well. Hopefully, he'll be able to find someone to authenticate the plate on his own then. I located the gentleman who'd translated the original copperplate at the National Museum of the Philippines."

The woman looked less than impressed. "Is that so?"

"Couldn't you at least give me his last name? He told me but I'm such a nitwit I forgot."

"I'm sorry. No. If you'll excuse me?" Evidently, trying to get away before Kaya harassed her to death, the woman stood and shuffled out from behind the counter. "I have some work to do."

"That's fine. I'll just be going now. Though, if you would do me a tiny, tiny favor?" She didn't wait for the woman to agree to continue. "If Jestin whatever-his-last-name-is happens to call here, or come in for any reason, will you tell him Kaya Cordova from Kim's Uniques is looking for him?"

"Certainly." The woman disappeared behind a door.

Kaya stood in the lobby, the only things separating her from the information she needed—and possibly fifteen thousand dollars—were a four-foot counter and some nerve. She looked to the right. She looked to the left. She looked up, searching for a security camera.

It was mighty quiet. There wasn't a soul in sight. And no camera either. What luck! What crappy security!

Go for it! a voice inside her head shouted. *Before the screen shuts off and you have to punch in a password. No time to wait. Do it now.*

Before she had time to rethink her options, or second-guess the wisdom of what she was about to do, she ducked behind the counter and knelt almost under the desk as she ran the mouse over the countertop, activating the computer screen.

Bingo! The woman hadn't signed out.

Kaya skimmed the registration list for Jestin's name, found it easily then repeated, "Draig, 1253 Lakeshore Drive," over and over as she hurried from the building. Luckily, no one stopped her as she made her hasty retreat.

Lakeshore Drive was at least an easy road to find. As its name suggested, it ran parallel to the shore of Lake Erie in the affluent town of Grosse Pointe Shores. The homes situated on the road were positively palatial. Owned by some of metro Detroit's more well-known bazillionaires, like business owners, descendants of

Henry Ford and professional athletes, they were giant, beautiful, and intimidating.

Jestin's house was no exception.

A home that had to be the size of Kaya's house times five, it was enough to take her breath away. A redbrick fence enclosed the house and surrounding land, an iron gate the only way onto the property. Naturally, it was locked.

Kaya pulled up to the gate's column and pushed the call button. A man's voice—not Jestin's—answered. "May I help you?"

"Hi. My name is Kaya Cordova," she said into the little metal speaker box. "I'd like to see Mr. Draig."

"One minute please."

Kaya toyed with her key ring as she waited for the man to determine whether or not she warranted a visit to the handsome and obviously extremely wealthy Jestin Draig.

Moments later, the gate swung open. Assuming that was an invitation to enter, Kaya drove up the tree-lined drive to the house, parked and walked the short distance to the front door.

If ever Kaya Cordova—humble buyer who very rarely rubbed shoulders with the rich and famous—felt out of place, it was the moment she stepped into Jestin's foyer.

She swallowed back a sigh of amazement, forced her gaping mouth to close before something unfortunate happened, and nodded as Mr. Gibs, the elderly gentleman who let her in, motioned her to follow him into a dark, cozy study.

She took a seat in a huge leather chair and waited for Jestin to join her, thanking Mr. Gibs before he left.

"What a pleasant surprise." Jestin's deep voice, smooth as satin and warm as hot chocolate, caressed her raw nerves.

Almost feeling at ease, she twisted her body to greet him with a big smile. "I was in the neighborhood and thought I'd stop by."

He had a pleasant smile on his face too. So pleasant, in fact, that her heart did a funny little hop in her chest and her cheeks flamed hot. "Glad you did." He took the chair next to hers, throwing a casual arm over the back. "Would you like a drink? Some more wine perhaps?" he asked, his eyes glittering with challenge and mischief.

"No, no thanks."

"Very well." He sat back and eyed her sharply for a moment. She couldn't help squirming under his assessing gaze. Not only did it make her feel exposed, but also incredibly turned on. Like grab-the-man-and-jump-his-bones turned on. As she struggled with the urge to either give in to the temptation or run like a great big chicken, he asked, "Would you care, then, to tell me the real reason you're here?"

"I have a feeling you know," she practically stuttered.

He leaned forward, looked her dead in the eyes and said, "Indulge me."

Her breath caught in her throat at the double entendre. The more liberal parts of her psyche and anatomy prepared to do just that as her mind screamed, "Whoa, Nelly!"

"I . . . I came to make you an offer on the copperplate," she said.

"Oh, that." He donned a reasonably convincing pout. "I'd hoped your visit was of a . . . more personal nature."

Me too. "I'm sorry to disappoint."

"No, no. Don't be sorry. I'm not. However, I will tell you I am not interested in your offer to purchase the plate. At least not at this time."

"I'm prepared to offer you a great deal of money."

"Which I appreciate."

"Thirty thousand."

He waved the figure away. "You must understand something about me."

"Okay, thirty-five."

"I do not do business with people I don't know personally. It's a practice I inherited from my father. My father was a very successful man," he added, meaningfully.

"I understand. Forty?"

"And so," he said, crossing his thick arms over his chest in a show of iron will. "I'd say you have two choices. Either you can give up trying to purchase the plate from me and leave now, or you can spend the evening with me and get to know me personally."

"Personally? Wait a minute," she drawled, wagging a finger at the suspicious glimmer she saw in his eyes. "Something sounds fishy here. You want me to get to know you personally?" She scooted forward in the chair, planted her hands on her hips and gave him a challenging glare. "Are you sure you're not just trying to get me to sleep with you?"

He had the nerve to laugh at her! "As I said, I do no business with strangers, and I assure you, many of my business associates are men. Would you make the same assumption if you were a male?"

She shrugged, trying not to look worried about the fact that she was rapidly losing control of these negotiations. She couldn't afford to do that. But it was so hard to keep her mind on track with so much wicked temptation staring back at her. Especially when he kept showing off those dimples. "I might. For all I know, you could be homosexual."

"I assure you I'm not homosexual." He gave her one of the most sinful grins this side of Hades.

Her cheeks burned and her knees melted to the consistency of molten marshmallows. Worry stiffened her spine, reinforcing it, but only slightly. There was too much at stake here to be allowing a smile, a set of the cutest dimples on earth and a few naughty suggestions to mess with her mind. *Get it together, girl! You're about to let the charmer wearing designer duds and a pair of killer dimples win round two.* "Then you aren't telling me I have to sleep with you to buy the plate?"

"No. If you decide to sleep with me, it will be because you want to, not because you are coerced," he said in a voice that had her almost ready to throw up the white flag in surrender. "I don't have any respect for a man who must trick or force a woman into sleeping with him."

For some reason, his last comment didn't ease the worst of her worries. She'd learned a long time ago that sex and business didn't mesh. She couldn't afford to blow this deal, yet she wanted to sleep with him like she'd never wanted to sleep with a man before. And he hadn't done anything more than bat his eyelashes, flash an occasional smile and toss a couple of suggestive comments her way. "Even so, this is an extremely unusual request and frankly, I don't think it's—"

"I would like to assure you that whatever we do—or don't do—tonight would not be held against you in our negotiations. Along the same vein, sleeping with me will not make me lower my price. And so, the choice is yours. Spend a pleasant evening with me, and have some chance of buying the plate, or refuse and have none." He sat back and waited, his unwavering gaze on her face making it mighty difficult to think about anything but jumping into the nearest bed with him.

"Let me make sure I've got this straight. You want to spend the evening with me. Yet, anything I do during that time won't help me. Nor will anything I refuse to do hurt me."

"In a nutshell, yes."

"Any catches—er, besides the obvious?"

"None. Oh, that is, unless you have a problem with being honest."

"Oh?" She felt her cheeks flaming for the umpteenth time. She didn't remember ever blushing so often in such a short span of time.

"I value honesty above all else, in both business and personal relationships and I intend to test your integrity tonight. No matter what question I ask, you must answer it truthfully."

"All this to do a single deal?"

"That's right."

"And you expect complete honesty? Always?"

He nodded.

She swallowed a lump the size of a bowling ball in her throat. While she wasn't one to lie constantly, she'd always been a firm believer in the benefits of the occasional white lie. This was especially true when it came to dealing with men, and in business. "I don't know. Like I said, this is highly unusual. I need to think."

"Take all the time you need." He looked down at his watch.

Mrs. Kim's promise of fifteen thousand dollars echoed in her head and she dropped her gaze to the floor to give herself some room to think. Would it be so bad to spend an evening with a rich, handsome man? Maybe even—gasp!—sleep with him just for the fun of it? It had been so long since she'd had sex, she'd almost forgotten what it felt like. And she'd never slept with someone who looked like Jestin, or someone who possessed such an air of restrained power before. There was some kind of invisible force around him. She could practically see it.

She could get around the lying thing, she was pretty sure. Besides, he wouldn't know if she was lying. He couldn't read minds. No one could do that.

She nodded. "Very well. Only one evening?"

"Yes. Tonight. You will have dinner with me." He glanced at his watch again. "I prefer to dine early. Three o'clock."

"That's fine. I didn't have any lunch." She didn't add the reason why she'd missed her lunch break—specifically because he'd insisted on taking her for that little car ride.

"Excellent. Afterward, I always enjoy a spell in the steam room and then a massage. You will join me." Again, that was no question. It was a command.

His tone rankled her a bit but his expression did much to counteract its more unpleasant effects. Once more, she found herself fanning her heated face. Her spine felt soft, her insides flitty and fluttery.

Then, the thought of sitting in a hot steam room with a nude Jestin, the only thing between her body and his a few feet of terrycloth, skipped through her mind and her fluttery insides went all ascurry like leaves blown in a storm. A wave of hot shivers buzzed up and down her spine. Heat pooled in her groin, her empty pussy clenched.

No sooner did the words, "Very well," come out of her mouth

than she was being led, her hand in his, up a flight of grand, sweeping stairs to the most opulent bedroom she'd ever seen.

She looked from their joined hands, to his handsome face, to the mammoth bed and muttered under her breath, "Ho boy. I have a feeling I'm in way over my head here."

"Only if you don't appreciate the more refined pleasures of the flesh," he whispered in her ear, his words and the caress of his hot breath on her neck sending a blanket of goose bumps down the left side of her body. Just before completely melting Kaya into a puddle of goo by whispering any more smoldering words in her ear, he turned, strode across the room and opened the door to a large wardrobe. "I think you'll find everything you need in here. Perhaps you'd like to freshen up before dinner?"

Kaya stepped up behind him to take a look. Hanging on padded pink satin hangers were frilly, lacy garments of every color, some skimpier than others. "I see you've done this before. You're better stocked in lingerie than any woman I know. But my mother always told me not to wear another woman's undies. Ew."

"You'll find that none of the garments have been worn. They all still bear their sales tags. I had to guess your size. I hope they fit—"

"You bought all these for me?" She tugged at a long, white satin gown, ran her fingers down the smooth fabric, measuring its weight. It was pricey, not doubt about it. "After what? A ten-minute ride in your car? Doncha think that was just a smidge premature?"

"I knew you would come."

"My, my, my, aren't we full of ourselves?" she asked, sifting through the other garments. They were all absolutely gorgeous.

"No, I knew you wanted the plate. Besides, the security officer at the auction house called. If you had any aspirations of getting into the spy business, I suggest you consider something a little safer instead, preferably that doesn't involve keeping secrets, stealing information or performing any other covert operations. To put it bluntly, you stink at it."

She dropped her hand and lifted her guilty gaze to his face. "They saw me?" Her cheeks flamed hotter than they already were. "Why didn't they stop me?"

"Because I told them to let you go." He reached into the wardrobe and pulled out an ankle-length, white terrycloth robe. He handed it to her as she stood gape-mouthed, still trying to respond to his answer.

Finally, she opted to just close her mouth and nod.

"Have you ever had a massage?"

Still unable to speak, she shook her head.

"You may keep on your underclothes if it makes you feel more comfortable. And you may choose between a masseur or masseuse."

"I'm easy. Whatever. Just make it someone who's blind, if you could. That way they won't see anything that'll crack them up."

"I assure you anyone in my employ is a professional and would never laugh at any of my guests."

"Okay," she said reluctantly. "I'll take a woman then. A big-boned woman like me who has real boobs . . . and cellulite. I don't want a mannequin with a twenty-two-inch waist and perfect hair."

"I can manage that."

"Good. That makes me feel better." She waited for him to speak, but he simply pointed at the robe. "Oh! Do you want me to undress now? Before dinner?" She stood holding the robe to her chest, not sure if he expected her to shed her clothes right there on the spot, with him watching. She had no intention of doing so, if that was the case. Nor did she intend on wearing any of those sexy numbers he'd had the gall to buy for her. What . . . what nerve!

Nerve like steel. Muscles like steel too. She liked steel.

"You can change now if you like. I will be. I prefer to be comfortable when I eat. Also, I want you to know that even if you wear none of these tonight, I wish to give them to you as a gift. You will take them with you when you leave. I admit, I have a weakness for buying lovely things for women, particularly women who spark my interest as you have."

She sparked his interest? Big-boned Kaya Cordova? "I . . . I . . ."

"I will leave you to your preparations. There are some personal items in the bathroom, if you need them." He motioned toward the nearby door. "I will return in a half hour."

"Okay."

The second he closed the door behind him, she made a mad dash for the bathroom. She stripped nude and turned on the tub's tap then sat on the tiled deck and hung her legs over the side to give them a quick shave. Continuing north, she shaved her way up to her armpits, making sure she left every inch of skin silky smooth. Then she coated herself with the scented body lotion he'd so kindly supplied, put on a pair of clean, black lace undies and the matching bra—the man had guessed her sizes perfectly. She wasn't sure if that was a good thing or not—and shrugged into the robe. After brushing her teeth, fixing her makeup and fooling with her hair, she returned to the bedroom.

He was waiting for her. He greeted her with a quick visual assessment and a smile that left her knees wobbly.

Chapter 3

SITTING IN A CHAIR WITH ONLY A TEENY, TINY TOWEL WRAPPED around his hips, one arm curled over the top of the chair, the other draped over the padded armrest, Jestin was once again living, breathing temptation. Kaya's gaze flitted over his broad shoulders, wide chest and muscled stomach like a butterfly hopping from flower to flower. Finally, after skidding down his smooth-skinned legs, also corded with muscles, it found a resting place on his face.

"I trust everything is to your liking," he said.

"And how."

"I wasn't sure if you preferred any particular brands of lotion, shaving creams or toothpastes."

"Oh, that." Her face heated again with embarrassment. "No, I'm easy. Don't care much what brand it is, as long as it does the job."

"Very good. Are you ready?"

"Yes. But . . ." She let her words trail off. Surely he meant to put some clothes on before they went down to dinner.

He raised his eyebrows in question as he stood his full six-foot-something.

"That's what you call comfortable?" She motioned to his naked torso. "I mean, don't get me wrong, I appreciate comfort as much as the next girl, but most people prefer wearing clothes when they eat."

"I don't. In fact, normally I'd eat completely nude. I'm forgoing that pleasure for you." He offered his arm to her. "Shall we?"

She took a split second to admire the way the thick ropes of muscles of his arm flexed as he moved, before curling her hand around his forearm. "Okay. I just hope you don't spill anything hot on yourself. You could end up with a wicked burn."

"Wouldn't be the first time," he said with a twinkle in his eye. He led her down the main staircase to the ground level of the house, across the humongous foyer and down a hall to a grand dining room with deep burgundy walls and rich swathes of fabric dressing a line of windows along one wall. In the room's dead center stood a massive rectangular table fashioned out of dark wood that had to seat at least thirty people.

It was the most bizarre, most fascinating table she'd ever seen. In the place of legs in the four corners were four wooden sculptures of dragons. Their mouths were open, their hands holding opaline globes the size of softballs. Their tails curled up around their bodies to provide additional support to the tabletop that had to weigh a ton. Along the center of the tabletop ran a deep burgundy runner with a continuous line of unlit candles.

Jestin led her across the room, past the table to a door at the rear. They stepped into a smaller, more intimate room with gold walls, a single window and a round pedestal table. The only light in the room came from the five candles in the candelabra sitting in the table's center. Right away, Kaya spied the two place settings, complete with filled stemmed glasses and plates with those metal covers on them to keep the food warm.

Every cell in her body was aware of Jestin's nearness as he pulled out her chair for her. The sensitive skin at her nape tingled when his breath brushed oh-so softly against it like feathers. Stifling a shudder of cold-heat, she scooted her chair in and watched Jestin sit.

The soft candlelight did amazing things to his hair, turning it into a burnished golden color. It also made his face look harder. Deep shadows slashed under his cheeks, eyes and mouth, making him look mysterious, dangerous, despite the smile pulling at the corners of his lips.

He lifted his glass in a toast, and mesmerized, Kaya mirrored his action. "To new acquaintances," he said, gently tapping his glass to hers.

She nodded in agreement then stole a single sip of the wine. It was very similar to the last one she'd tasted with him, in the limousine.

He set the glass on the table then nodded at someone or something behind her. His gaze was above her head level. Before she could turn around to see who it was, an arm reached around her side.

Startled, she jumped, lunging sideways.

The hand, which was attached to a black suit-bedecked arm, which was attached to Mr. Gibs, lifted the silver cover on her plate. Then he stepped away silently, rounded the table and did the same for Jestin.

After she was relatively sure she wouldn't have another surprise, for at least a little while, she glanced down at her plate.

The strange-looking food, which was totally foreign to her, was arranged in the deliberate manner she'd seen on those food shows on cable television. It looked like a little sculpture rather than something she'd want to eat. Not exactly eager to take a taste—she preferred plain old comfort foods like mashed potatoes and extra-crispy fried chicken—she lowered her head slightly to take a whiff.

Fish. She hated seafood.

"Is something wrong?" Jestin asked.

She jerked upright, blinking innocently. "No, no. Nothing's wrong." She tried on a convincing grin for size. Clearly it didn't fit.

Jestin's brows bunched together over the bridge of his nose. He eyed her speculatively, which made her squirm. "Are you certain? Do you have an objection to something on your plate?"

"No . . ." she said, not wanting to be rude. Her mother had always told her it wasn't polite to complain to your host about the food.

Jestin's eyebrows rose. His gaze followed, lifting to where she assumed Mr. Gibs was standing behind her. "Gibs?" he asked.

Mr. Gibs answered. "I am afraid she is lying, sir."

"As I feared." He gave her a martyred look. "As I said, I expect complete honesty, Kaya, or we are wasting our time."

Kaya twisted her torso to give Mr. Gibs a look. When Gibs responded with nothing but an empty stare, she turned forward again. "What's he? Your lie detector-slash-butler?"

"Among other things. Gibs has been in my employ for a long time. I trust his judgment." He added meaningfully, "A wise man knows who to trust."

"You really have a thing about trust, don't you?"

"I have my reasons. A man in my position must know who he can trust and who he can't."

"A man in your position? Are you like a spy or something? Would you have to kill me if you told me what you do?"

"Maybe." He winked. "No, I'm not a spy. But you could say I'm in the security business."

"Ah." She nodded. "Are you like a personal bodyguard to someone famous or more like a mall rent-a-cop?"

"Neither, actually. My work is a little more complicated than that. So," he said, forking a morsel of green stuff with yellow sauce into his mouth and chewing, "would you care to tell me what your objection is to the food?"

He wasn't going to let it rest, darn it. "I was trying to be polite, you know."

"Which I appreciate."

"And I can appreciate your need to determine who is trustworthy and who is not but I'm of the not-all-lies-are-equal mindset myself. When it comes to something insignificant—like my dislike of seafood—I think there's nothing wrong with telling a little white lie." She turned her body so she could give Mr. Gibs another look. "It certainly doesn't mean I'm not trustworthy, at least not in my book."

"That may be so, but then you would walk away from my table hungry and that is unacceptable." He nodded to Gibs and the butler left the room.

Alone with Jestin at last. That realization gave birth to a flurry of contradicting emotions, along with a few stuttering heartbeats and a smattering of goose bumps. Why had he asked the butler to leave? Was he going to do something good? Or bad? She positioned herself so she was facing Jestin straight on again.

"You do not like sushi?" Jestin asked.

"Oh, for heaven's sake. It's only food. Why are you getting so obsessed?" When he didn't respond, she added, "If I'm not mistaken, sushi's not just fish, but raw fish." She stifled a grimace of outright disgust and tried to paste an impassive expression on her face. "Eating raw meat of any kind is dangerous. I won't touch meat that isn't thoroughly cooked, even steak," she said with a level voice.

"How unfortunate." He slipped another forkful of the icky food between his lips. She watched as he slowly drew the fork's empty tines from his mouth. He chewed slowly, visibly savoring the food's flavor. His tongue darted out to lick away a bead of moisture clinging to the center of his bottom lip. She felt herself unconsciously mirroring his action. She even swallowed when he swallowed. She had to admit, he made raw fish look absolutely sinful. "Have you never tasted a steak cooked to perfection—still pink on the inside, seared and spiced on the outside?" Jestin asked.

"No. I prefer my steak with no pink whatsoever."

"But a rare steak is so tender . . ." he said as he stared into her eyes and she felt a few of her muscles getting soft, ". . . juicy and flavorful."

There went a few more muscles. Pulverized to mush. She whimpered.

Gibs snatched away her plate and replaced it with another one. He silently lifted the lid, revealing a thick filet and baked potato with the works. She looked up at Jestin's face.

He smiled and motioned toward the plate. "Better?"

"Yes. Thank you, but I hope it wasn't too much trouble. I wouldn't have said anything if you hadn't made me."

"No, no. Don't worry. Just enjoy." He watched as she cut a small piece, checked to make sure it was cooked through then put it in her mouth.

A parade of spices marched over her tongue as she chewed. She felt herself smiling. She'd never tasted a steak that delicious. Never. It put her favorite steak house to shame. "Oh. Wow."

"Is that a good wow or bad?" he asked.

She swallowed and cut another piece, quickly filling her mouth again. "Definitely good. Very good," she said around the steak. Swallowing first, she added, "This is the most delicious steak I've ever tasted. I don't suppose you'd give me the recipe?"

"It's a family secret," he said, looking mysterious and amused and sexy. He leaned forward, his gaze riveted to hers, and murmured, "I'm afraid I'd have to kill you if I told you."

She giggled as she finished her dinner. It wasn't easy eating when her innards were tied into knots and her throat felt like it was swollen shut from nerves. But she managed to eat a respectable amount. Gibs took their plates away and replaced them with small bowls of ice cream. Chocolate therapy.

She loved this man, consumer of raw fish or not.

Jestin ate the ice cream in the most provocative way possible— tongue licking, lips smacking—and she swallowed a guffaw, instead wagging her finger at him and shaking her head in a show of disapproval.

"You are bad," she scolded.

"You have no idea how bad I am," he said in a low voice that hummed in her belly and made her feel all girly and soft. He stood and reached for her hand. "Shall I show you?"

She looked up into his sparkling eyes and nearly threw herself at his feet, shouting, *Hell yes!* Instead she gave him a light punch in the gut and stood. "You behave yourself, Mr. Naughty, or I'll tell Gibs to send you to your room for a time-out."

She caught the low rumble of Gibs's laughter and turned her head to look at him. He wore a severe poker face.

"I heard you," she said to Gibs. "You laughed, and before I leave tonight I'll make you pee your pants you'll be laughing so hard."

"I," the butler said with a less than enthused expression on his face, "look forward to seeing you try."

"Ha!" Jestin laughed. His face shone with such boyish delight, her knees nearly gave out. To keep herself erect, she gripped his arm and hung on. Naturally, the skin-to-skin contact only made things worse. A wave of warmth washed over her body as she tried to distract herself with thoughts about Gibs and how she'd make good on her promise. He was clearly a tough nut to crack.

Unfortunately, her efforts didn't help much. Feeling all jittery and girly, she let Jestin lead her up the stairs and down the hall. They passed through what looked like a workout room, but with some gear she'd never seen before, into a smaller area. A glass door on the back wall opened to the cedar-lined sauna room.

It was blazing hot in there, so hot, her face burned after only a few seconds. Knowing she wouldn't be able to stay in there for long, she glanced at Jestin as she took a seat on a towel-covered wooden bench.

He looked as cool as a proverbial cucumber, even as sweat poured from every pore of her body, making her feel slick and slimy. He smiled. "The heat rejuvenates me, gives me energy."

"It's draining mine. I'm afraid if I don't leave in a few seconds you'll be carrying me out."

"Just a minute more. Do you know all the health benefits of dry heat?"

"No."

"Heat helps keep your heart healthy, aids in weight loss—"

"Are you trying to tell me something?"

"Absolutely not!" He gave his head an emphatic shake. "It also helps keep your skin youthful by cleansing toxins."

"Great, so you're telling me I look old and am fat," she teased giving him the eye. "I'm dying here. I think I'd rather carry a few extra pounds and bags under my eyes than sit in this miserable heat for another minute." Barely clinging to consciousness, she watched him close his eyes. He looked so peaceful, so comfortable, so in control. Not even his hair seemed to be touched by the heat. The flirty curls were the same, silky and shiny. His golden skin didn't even look pink. It was as if the heat didn't touch him. "It's not fair. Looks like you haven't even broken a sweat yet while my makeup's melted off my face and my hair is a limp, sticky mess."

When he opened his eyes, she caught a strange violet flash in them, like a bolt of static in a darkened room. Then he stood and pushed open the door, taking her hand in his to lead her from the heat into the chill of the workout room.

"Follow me."

She followed, eyeballing the workout gear as she walked. "What is this stuff? Is it for Pilates or something? I don't see any weights."

"Not exactly," he said with a chuckle.

Now extremely curious, she stopped in front of a tall thing with what looked like Velcro wrist straps dangling from it. "Oh! I get it. They work on some kind of pulley system." To test her theory, she reached out and gave one of the wrist straps a sharp yank. It didn't budge. "Wow. You must be strong. The tension is set awfully high. I can't get it to budge even a little."

"Well, should you decide to put any of this equipment to use, I'd be glad to make some adjustments," he said, laughter making his voice uneven. "However, I think I should explain one thing to you. This equipment isn't for your traditional workout."

"My point, exactly. I'm hardly keen on the latest gym gear. I admit I avoid the gym like the plague, but this stuff doesn't look like anything I've ever seen in a gym before."

"That's because it isn't supposed to be in a gym."

"Huh?"

"This is a dungeon."

"Dungeon?" She took another look at the room and its furnishings. "First of all, didn't those go the way of dragons and princes on white stallions, eons ago? And aren't they supposed to be down in the bowels of the basement? Dark, spooky places where prisoners are kept? Why would you have a dungeon next to your bedroom?"

"It's not the kind of dungeon you're thinking of, though I was fond of those as well. They bring back such pleasant memories." He sighed.

"You've lost me."

"This is where my clan role-plays. This is where we play sexual bondage games."

Kaya felt her jaw drop but lacked the wherewithal to pull it up off the floor. Shock slammed through her body, reaching her brain last. "Bondage games? As in BDSM?" On the wake of shock rode profound fascination.

He nodded.

She felt his gaze on her as she hesitantly approached the same piece of equipment she'd touched earlier. It was tall and reminded her of stocks, or a cross. "What's this one for?" When he touched her shoulder, she shuddered, but not because she was scared. She was far from frightened.

"A slave would stand either facing the wall or this way," he eased her around until she was facing him and her chest was pressed against his solid bulk. "Would you like to try it?" At her silent response, a wide-eyed head-nod, he lifted her right arm and wrapped the strap around it then did the same with her left. "As you see, the slave is now powerless to stop me from giving her any sort of pleasure I might like to. Like this." With no warning whatsoever, he tipped his head and slanted his mouth over hers. His lips feathered soft kisses on each corner of her mouth before hardening, making her heart skip a few beats and stealing her breath. When she opened her mouth to draw in a gulp of much needed air, his tongue dipped inside to stroke hers.

Instantly she found herself dizzy and weak with need. Her pussy throbbed with each pounding beat of her heart. Her knees softened. Her body tensed. And her self-control snapped. Just like that, she realized she would sleep with him. Tonight.

His kiss was hot and demanding and thorough and she quickly lost herself in it, in his flavor, in his spicy, masculine scent, and in the emotions they stirred in her. She felt such joy, such hunger, such need to relinquish all control to him, body and mind. The feelings swirled round and round inside her until they were all mixed up and she couldn't tell what was what anymore.

His tongue stroked hers, twisted, thrust, tasted. Drowning in swelling need, she met his fire with her own heat, silently pleading with him to take her. Her arms still tied out to the sides, leaving her hands useless yet itching to touch him, to pull him closer, she groaned in agony into their joined mouths.

She was going, going, gone. Her heart was pounding so hard, it was bound to leap from her chest. Her lungs were screaming for air she didn't have the ability to draw in. Just when she thought she'd die, he broke the kiss and pulled those wonderful lips, that magical tongue from her.

And she thought she'd known what agony was!

In those seconds, while she struggled to keep herself vertical, she thought back to all the times she'd done the safe thing, stuck her toe in the water to test it rather than just suck it up and dive in. What had her playing-it-safe, take-no-risks attitude gotten her? Had it spared her any pain? Maybe a little. Had it also stolen her chance to find even fleeting bits of happiness? Of experiencing everything life had to offer—both good and bad?

It had! Her fears had been more powerful bindings than anything she'd find in a dungeon. They'd made her a prisoner. They'd caged her more effectively than any cement walls, or bars, or cell ever could.

It was time to break free, take a chance, live life. It was Jestin who had helped her see that.

"We're going to miss our massage," he said.

She puffed up her chest, pushing her breasts forward, and lifted her chin. "To hell with the massage."

The fingertip of his right index finger traced her jaw then slid lower, along her neck to her breastbone. It stopped where the deep V-shaped opening of her robe closed. "Then you wish to be here with me? I will say this again because I want you to be sure. You do not have to sleep with me if you are not certain it's what you want."

"Believe me, there isn't a part of me that isn't certain."

"Very well." Jestin looked as pleased as Kaya felt as he unfastened her wrists. Kaya shook her arms and rubbed her wrists when they were unbound. "We will go into the bedroom now."

"We will?" She took another look around. "But this place has promise and I'm intrigued, thanks to that sneak peek you gave me." When he gave her one of his trademark lifted-eyebrow "really?" looks, she amended her position. "Okay, okay, it's a little scary too. Maybe too scary. You don't get into pain or anything, do you?"

"Nothing you can't handle." He reached forward and raked his fingertips over her right breast through the rough cotton robe. Her nipple tingled and puckered, the reaction making her gasp in surprise. No man had ever stirred such overwhelming wanting in her body before. He smiled at her then caught her arms in his fists and dragged her closer until all her soft curves were pressed against his hard angles. He tipped his head and found the sweet spot on her neck. He nibbled and kissed in between words. "You're not quite ready for the dungeon yet, don't have a respect for what it means to be here with me. But that doesn't mean things won't get hot. In fact, just in case I go a bit overboard, we'll have to come up with a safe word before we start."

"Safe . . . word?" She let her eyelids shutter out the visual distractions and concentrated on the fire he was churning in her body with every touch and kiss. Goose bumps erupted over one side of her body as mind-blowing need pulsed through her veins. Her pussy burned to be filled, her body burned to be possessed, her spirit burned to be complete. Complete with this man, a man she hardly knew.

"Yes," he whispered. His hand slid into the opening of the robe and traced the cup of her lace bra. Her spine arched, pushing her breast into his palm. "Hmmm." His voice rumbled through her body like thunder on a still summer night. "Give me a word you would not normally say during lovemaking, something easy to remember and say."

Say? Talk? Think? How could she do any of those things with his hand closed over her breast, kneading it and grazing her sensitive nipples until she wanted to scream. And his mouth . . . the things he could do with his mouth. She was sure her neck would never be the same. "Like . . . ice cream?"

He unfastened the front clasp of her bra then closed his hand over her bared breast. His touch was like a brand, so fiery it left her reeling. "Yes, like ice cream," he murmured. As if he wanted to illustrate, he dropped to his knees, untied the belt of her robe and parted it. Then he ran his velvet tongue over her nipple as if he was licking an ice cream cone. Over and over until she swore her blood was on fire and her legs shook with the effort of standing. He scooped her up into his arms and carried her toward the door. "If I do something you don't like and you want me to stop, say ice cream and I'll stop."

"Okay," she whispered, wrapping an arm around his neck.

His soft hair tickled her arm as he turned his head to see where he was walking. But that was nothing compared to the other sensations her body was being pummeled with while he carried her.

She felt weightless in his arms. Small and powerless yet safe. There was something, some kind of energy that buzzed around him, humming just slightly in her ear. The sound seemed to seep into her pores and buzz through her bones like a low vibration, making her pussy throb until she thought she'd weep.

How are you doing this to me?

He opened the door to a huge, opulent bedroom with a bed that put a king-size bed to shame. It was giant, the size of a smaller bedroom all in itself. Low, it sat on some type of pedestal she couldn't see. It looked like it was hovering above the floor on air.

He lowered her onto it. The mattress was extremely soft and she sank into it, making her feel like she was lying on a cloud. When he climbed over top of her, she shivered.

Her body tight and ready, her pussy wet, burning for his touch, she didn't want to wait another second for him to fill her. "Please," she whispered. "Take me now."

In response, he silently helped her shed her robe. When she met his gaze, she swore she saw red and gold flames in his eyes, sparking, dancing, whirling.

Who are you? What are you?

She lay on her back, mesmerized by the sight of those flames until he pulled off the towel hiding his erection. Then her focus definitely went south.

His cock was huge, and quite clearly ready. It stood fully erect. Her fingers itched to trace the rim of the head. She ached with the need to take it into her mouth and taste him.

As if he could read her mind, he shook his head and pressed down on her shoulders. Then he scooted back toward her bottom and dropped his fiery gaze to her mound. "Open for me," he commanded, his tone resonating like a gong through her trembling body.

How are you doing this to me?

"You will have your answers soon, my sweet," he murmured. He used both hands to gently pull her bent knees apart until her pussy was open and exposed.

She once again shuttered out the world by closing her eyes, hardly able to sift through the intense sensations he stirred in her body through the other four senses. His touches left her skin aflame. His voice made her insides thrum. His sweet, spicy taste still lingered on her tongue. She drew his scent into her nostrils. It too was sweet and spicy like her favorite Thai food, and she couldn't get enough. She eagerly drank it in, breathing in deeply over and over until she was dizzy.

"I'm going to taste you now," she heard him say. But so lost in the rapture of those overwhelming sensations and the joy they brought, she hardly comprehended them.

She felt him push her knees back farther, until they were so wide apart the muscles of her inner thighs burned with the stretch. His soft curls tickled her skin as he lowered his head. Then he touched her. One fleeting touch to her labia and she was nearly out of her mind with wanting. He parted her swollen lips and found her clit, flicking his tongue over it. She heard herself cry out. Each flick of his tongue was like the lick of flame. Balls of white light danced behind her closed eyelids. She shivered with fever as his tongue danced over her clit, carrying her closer to release with every stroke.

And then she was there, her body coiled tight like a spring, at the pinnacle of orgasm. She writhed under him, her pelvis gyrating with every thump of her racing heart. He stopped his oral onslaught on her pussy, traced a burning path up to her throat with his tongue and positioned himself over top of her, his hips between her thighs.

"This is the test," he whispered in her ear as he pressed the head of his cock against her empty pussy.

"Test?" she said, gasping for her next breath. She blinked her eyes open to stare up into his beautiful face.

"If your spirit is strong enough and you are able to accept what most people believe is impossible, then when we join, you will have your answers. You will see me as I truly am."

Despite being nearly blind with need, she reached up and ran her fingers over the smooth skin of his shoulders. It was cool under her touch. Soft as satin. "I don't understand."

"Whatever you see, you must not be afraid. It is me and I will not hurt you. Not ever. Do you believe me?"

A little scared, curious and overwhelmed, she looked into his eyes, searching their sapphire depths for answers to her doubts.

"Take my strength, draw from it if you must, if you feel yourself being overcome. I want you to." And with that, he pulled back his hips and then drove his cock deep into her pussy.

A primal roar burst up from her chest, shot out her mouth at the raw joy and wonder of their joining. As he thrust in a second time, it felt as though she'd been thrown into a blaze, a giant inferno that licked at her skin but didn't burn her. Words that weren't hers, thoughts she hadn't thought, feelings she didn't have coursed through her, binding themselves to her soul. They echoed in her head and pulled at her heart. Joy, sorrow, pain, elation, hope, fear, they churned inside her, growing stronger with every second that ticked by until hot tears seeped from her closed eyes and burned her cheeks.

"That's it, my love. Accept me. Accept all of me and we will grow together. You must trust me, open yourself up to me," she heard him say as his body drove hers to the edge of bliss. Fingers pulled and pinched at her nipples. Teeth grazed the skin of her neck. His cock filled her completely. She pulled her legs back farther and tipped her hips up, changing the angle of his thrusts until she found just the right position.

She felt his weight lift from her body, felt the chill of the air on her skin. Then felt the pressure of a fingertip on her clit, drawing tight circles over it until her mind was numb and her body screaming for fulfillment.

Once more she was there, on the verge of orgasm. Her chest and stomach warmed, her insides tied into tight knots. Her hands clenched into tight fists, reaching for him. She wanted to feel his weight and heat as she came, needed to feel it pressing against her. Her arms trembling, she reached up, pulled him down until his chest was heavy on hers, and gave herself over to release, letting it sweep through her in a furious blaze.

When the heat eased, she blinked open her eyes.

And sheer terror shot through her body. "Ice cream! Ice cream, ice cream!"

Chapter 4

THE AIR OVER HER BODY SHIMMERED AND FOR A BRIEF SECOND or two, the man who had formerly looked like the epitome of California hunk was now about ten feet tall, red—as in red like the color of an Irish setter—and covered with scales. His—no, *its*—face was like a lizard's, with a long snout and sharp teeth the size of her pinky finger, pointed ears and the most bizarre eyes. They were still blue but instead of round pupils, the centers were oblong and vertical like a cat's. A puff of smoke billowed from its nostrils as Kaya let out a full-blown scream.

The air shimmered again, like she was looking through sparkling water and the monster vanished, replaced by Jestin's scrumptious bod. She shook her head, rubbed her eyes and blinked several times. All that did was clear her vision a smidge, allowing her to watch the image shift back and forth several more times from man to monster, monster to man with crystal clarity. What the hell was going on?

Then, as her pussy spasmed, she realized he was still inside her. That . . . whatever he was. She glanced down, following the wide line of his chest and abdomen to where his body met hers. Even now, his gigantic cock was thrusting in and out of her. For a brief instant, his body was coated in scales. That sight made her scream again. She jerked away from him, crab walking backward.

Look into my eyes, Kaya, his familiar voice echoed in her head. *Remember what I said? It's still me, Jestin. Your spirit is strong if you're seeing me as I truly am. I would like to mark you now, if you will let me.*

She shook her head against the words rumbling through her body. "You're not marking me with anything until I know what the hell is going on. Is this some kind of joke? Because if it is, it's not funny." Her fingers found the edge of the mattress and she spun around on her bottom, flung her feet over the edge and jumped to her feet. She snatched up a throw from the floor, and in a wild sprint for the door, wrapped it around herself. The second she burst out into the hall, she ran smack dab into Gibs, who didn't look surprised to see her.

"Looks like I didn't have to work hard to get that laugh outta you, did I? Joke's on me. Har-de-har-har. I'm outta here. You and Jestin can have your laugh now. Sick bastards!" She shoved her way around Gibs, heading toward the bedroom where she'd left her purse and clothes.

Unfortunately, Jestin followed her. He stood in the doorway, still morphing back and forth from man to beast, watching her gather her things in her arms. The only thing stopping her from leaving was his body blocking the doorway. "No, Kaya. This is no joke. This is real. I am real. Touch me and you will know the truth."

"Nuh-uh! I'm not getting any closer to you than I have to. I'm not strong and this is insanity. I can't be seeing . . . what I think I'm seeing. You can't be— I can't be— Oh hell! Just let me leave."

The man-monster didn't move. It stood very still, still changing back and forth from one form to another, as she slowly backed away. Her heart pounding so hard she could hear it, she checked the room for another exit. But her gaze kept leaping back to Jestin, taking in every detail of its alternating gorgeous and hideous forms. In its latter state, it sported short arms, hook-shaped digits with long claws, powerful rear legs and tail. The only thing that even slightly resembled the man she knew as Jestin was the beautiful golden mane of hair running down his neck and back. And in a blink he was back to being the beautiful man she knew.

"Trust yourself if you cannot trust me. Believe what your heart is telling you," he challenged.

She ran to the window to see if she might risk jumping. She was only two stories up, but couldn't get the window to open. "What the fuck?" she said, her back turned to him while she continued fighting with the window. "Are these windows nailed shut? Shit! If this is what I get for deciding to cut loose a little and take some chances, then I think I was better off hiding in my cave, watching everyone else take all the risks."

"You don't believe that."

"Wanna bet?"

Once again, he changed into the monster. *I would like to ask you a single question. If you answer honestly, you will have no choice but to see the truth.* The monster took one step toward her. Thanks to his huge size, that one step left her cowering in the corner, nose to chest with it.

"If I answer your question, will you let me leave?"

The monster nodded its giant lizard head. A forked tongue jutted out of its mouth, wagged up and down above her head a couple times like a snake's tongue then disappeared back in its mouth. *If that is your wish.*

She shuddered. "Fine. Ask away. I want to get the hell out of here." *Hell* was for sure the operative word, since she figured that thing had to have escaped the very bowels of it somehow.

"Are you lonely? Have you been searching for something—someone—to fill a void in your life?"

"Yes, but I was thinking about getting a dog. Dogs don't break your heart. They don't cheat on you, or act like they can't live without you one minute and then like they couldn't give a shit whether you lived or died the next. Dogs are loyal and trustworthy and love you even if you forget their birthday. You feed them, you take them for a walk and they love you. End of story."

"Are you afraid to trust? Afraid of me?" it asked, its lips curling back, displaying a single row of razorlike teeth. It bent its neck so its face was inches from hers and his hot, sulfur-smelling breath burned her cheeks and nose.

"Heh, yeah. You look like something out of a sci-fi film," she said, her gaze fixed to those teeth. When it wagged its tongue in front of her nose again, like a lizard looking for its next meal, she said, "Are you going to eat me? Please don't eat me. Oh God." She searched the tiny bit of space between it and her, frantically looking for a clear escape route. Her breath sawed in and out of her lungs in quick, shallow pants and her heart thudded in her ears. Her knees turned to marshmallow and she wondered if she'd be able to make it across the room if she tried to run.

"No, I'm not going to eat you. Remember what I said about my strength?"

Hot tears burned at her eyes but she blinked them away. "Yes, but—"

"Take my hand." It lifted a giant claw-tipped paw.

"No." She shook her head. There was absolutely no way she could touch that . . . thing. That monster, uglier than anything she'd ever seen in a horror flick.

"Please." It nodded again. Light shimmered around it like an iridescent cloud, red and gold and blue. "Take my hand and conquer your fear." Slowly, it reached toward her, its digits curling and uncurling as its paw drew closer, closer to her hand.

She stood frozen like a deer caught in headlights, unable to budge from blinding panic. Then his scale-covered skin brushed against hers and instantly she felt a charge of electricity zap through her body like thousands of volts of pure, raw power. It buzzed up her spine, through her head then down to her toes. She briefly thought about yanking her hand away but something stopped her.

Take my strength, draw from it if you must. I will not hurt you.

Her hand shaking, she closed her fingers one at a time around one of his digits and drew in a slow breath. A single eye blink later, a warm sensation seeped up her arm and spread through her body, slowing her racing heart rate. Her trembling stopped. Her knees returned to normal.

"Very good," he said.

As she watched, a mist swirled around the creature like a fog caught in a brisk wind. As the cloud cleared, she saw Jestin, the man, had returned to her and by some miracle she wasn't so anxious to run like a scared ninny from the house. In fact, for some in inexplicable reason, she felt eager to get closer to him.

This is insanity!

Why did it feel like she'd never take another breath if she couldn't take it with him? Why did she want nothing more than to mold her body to his, sink into his embrace and shut her eyes to the monster she'd seen him become? She'd never been so forgiving in the past when it came to men. She'd dumped men for much more trivial matters—like a love of seventies classic rock music. Ozzy Osborne? Gag! Why was she now not only able but willing to accept Jestin, despite the fact that he either had played the nastiest trick on her ever, or was some kind of freak of nature?

Maybe it was because he'd trusted her enough to show his ugly side to her, instead of putting on airs and pretending he was perfect, like people usually did when they started a new relationship. Or maybe it was because of the power she could practically see shimmering around him and the way it made her feel—safe, cared for. Then again, maybe it was because she was mentally unstable.

Blinking back tears of confusion, she reached forward and reluctantly caught a lock of golden hair in her fingertips. "Was it a trick?"

"No."

That almost made her feel better. At least he hadn't tried to scare her on purpose, though that left only one frightening option. It was real. "Which one is really you—the monster or the man?"

"They both are. Although you alone can see me in my true form, and only when we are most open to each other—at the moment of climax."

"I don't understand. How could this be? Giant lizards don't exist. At least not in Michigan." Shaking, she released the curl and wrapped her arms around herself.

"Come to me. Let me explain." He drew her into his arms. She fought him for only a second then gratefully fell into his embrace, thankful for the small measure of comfort she found there. Confused, scared, she pressed her cheek to his chest and listened to the slow, steady thump of his heart and the soft whoosh of his breath. He walked her to the bed, sat and positioned her on his lap, capturing her chin in his hand and forcing her to look into his eyes. "I am from an ancient bloodline, one humans think had gone the way of dinosaurs eons ago. In truth, despite their efforts to kill us off completely, we have survived, and continue to increase in strength and number, because we are superior to humans."

"You speak of humans like you're not one," she said, stating the obvious.

"I'm not. I'm an Immortal. What most humans would call a dragon."

"A dragon," she repeated, not sure if she should check herself into the nearest hospital for some major drugs or accept what she'd seen as something more than a hallucination. If she hadn't seen it with her own eyes, hadn't seen the monster that looked exactly like the dragons in the Asian artwork she'd studied in art school, hadn't smelled the scent of sulfur on his breath, hadn't felt the hard ridges of his scaled skin with her own hands, there was no way she'd believe it. As it was and since her senses had never deceived her, she had no choice but to accept the impossible and believe him.

Those adorable dimples poked into his cheeks as his lips pulled into a warm, encouraging smile. His eyes sparkled. "You have passed the second test, have proven yourself strong enough in spirit and thus worthy to be my mate."

"I have," she said, not sure if she was happy about that or not.

There was something, she supposed, to being married to a powerful dragon-man who was gorgeous, would live forever, knew how to make her melt like an ice cube on asphalt in July, and had enough money to feed a small nation. But . . . but when she imagined her dream man, scales, a forked tongue and a six-foot-long tail had never been among the attributes she'd visualized. "This is very fast. Like I said, I was thinking about buying a puppy, not finding a 'mate'."

He stroked her thigh while he held her. "I understand your ambivalence." He kissed a tingly, tickly trail down her shoulder and arm, making it increasingly hard to remember why she wasn't so sold on the idea of becoming his mate. "I will give you as much time as you need to make your decision."

His promise of patience eased some of her worries but she was still bothered by the truckload of questions rumbling through her brain, not to mention all the tingles and hot flashes his strokes and kisses were birthing. She gently lifted his hand from her thigh. "Thanks. For not pushing me."

"I would never force you to make a decision you're not ready for."

"I appreciate that. In fact, I wish everyone thought that way. I dated a guy once. We were going out for oh, maybe six months and then he threw the 'M' word at me."

"'M' word?"

"Marriage. Then he proceeded to give me a deadline and told me if I didn't have an answer by that deadline, we were done."

"And?"

"I told him I didn't need any more time to think about it. And I left."

He chuckled and she marveled in how deeply she felt the gentle rumbles in her belly, and how the sparkles in his eyes made her all happy and warm inside. Those feelings almost shoved away the lingering doubts, but not entirely. She was never one to make a decision of any kind based on emotion. That was plain foolish.

Facts. She needed facts. Lots of them.

Still, that didn't mean there was anything wrong with having a little innocent fun while she gathered facts, she reminded herself. She could do both concurrently. She was a very adept multitasker. She released his hand, letting it go about its business making her all tingly and hot again. It dutifully carried on.

"I'm not saying I'm agreeing to anything. But I do have some questions," she said. "Like would . . . would we have children? And would they be . . . like . . . you?" she asked, tipping her head back so he could get the sweet spot right below her ear. Oh yeah, that was the one. She shivered, and not because she was scared anymore, and completely forgot what she'd been saying. "This isn't fair," she mumbled, not trying to stop him. "You're using your sex appeal to your advantage. And it's working . . . and here's the kicker, I know you're doing it and I'm letting you because I like it."

"Then I will stop." The hand that had been on her thigh swooped up her body, resting on her tummy while the other one rested at the side of her face. He traced her bottom lip with his thumb. "Yes, you would carry my children. And the pregnancy would be normal, our babies will appear human at birth. There will be only the slightest birthmark to reveal their true nature. Female offspring remain in human form all their lives. The males, however, go through The Change during adolescence, in their late teens."

She was slightly disappointed that he'd taken her half-joking comment about his sex appeal seriously, but also relieved, since she was now a little more capable of thinking, comprehending the facts he was providing to her. "And even though I'm human, the children would be immortal like you?"

"Yes. They are immune to the effects of aging beyond adolescence as well as to all human diseases." He combed his fingers through her hair, capturing a lock and pressing it to his lips. That familiar naughty glimmer sparked in his eyes.

"I see." She squirmed in his lap. Although his words were confusing and her brain felt like it had been scrambled and fried in a pan over high heat, there were other parts of her that seemed to know on a gut level that this was right and that she belonged with Jestin Draig, the dragon-man. "I hate to sound self-involved or shallow or anything but what about me? You and our children would remain young and healthy and I'd become an old hag. I mean, why would you want a stooped old biddy for a wife?"

"With the completion of our Joining, you would become somewhat immortal."

"Somewhat?"

"As long as I remain alive, you would not age. However, you could still die from other causes."

"Interesting. I could live with that, but one last question."

"Go ahead."

"Are there any other Mrs. Jestin Draigs running around the world? I mean, you say you've lived a long time and I'm not so naïve to think you haven't had other women, what with that setup down the hall. But I'm so *not* interested in being a member of a harem. Heck, I can't handle sharing a bathroom with another woman, let alone sharing a man."

He released the tendril of hair and rested both hands on her shoulders. "No. There is no other Mrs. Jestin Draig. Not any longer." His fingers walked up her neck to slide around the back of her head. He traced her lower lip with his thumb. "I was Joined once before. A very long time ago. But my mate died . . . in a tragic accident." Deep pain darkened his eyes.

Wishing she could comfort him but knowing she couldn't, that there was nothing she could say or do that would lift the weight of his sorrow in the slightest, she laced her fingers through his and whispered, "I'm very sorry."

"I wanted to die with Anelise. A part of me did, which was why, up until now, I never considered taking another mate."

Not knowing what to say, wanting to ask him why now and why her but afraid to, she nodded and ran her hands up and down his arms, following them to his shoulders. She leaned into him again, resting her head against his chest.

"I will explain one other thing to you, so that you have all the information necessary to make your decision."

She nodded against him.

"Our people are Guardians. That is our role in the world. Much like in the fairy tales you probably read as a child, we protect things—not usually princesses in high towers—but magical artifacts that would threaten any of the Immortals. There would be some danger—"

"Danger? But you are immortal. What could threaten you?" she asked, suddenly worried for his safety. She straightened up and waited anxiously for his answer.

"Each species has its weakness. They can be destroyed. For the red dragon, my people, it takes the spell spoken by a powerful mage. The spell has been lost to the humans for centuries, so at the moment we are safe."

She wanted to sag against him with relief. The thought of him being destroyed, even if he was scary in his other form, it was simply too much for her to imagine. "That's good to hear. But you said each species. There are other types of immortals?"

"Many different bloodlines, yes. There are the Lamiae, commonly known as the muses, several different clans of vampires including the Ancient Ones and Wissenshaft, and a variety of shapeshifters."

"I thought all those things didn't exist."

"They exist. And as my mate, you will likely meet many of them, which is why I wanted to mention them to you."

"I . . . see," she muttered. She felt like she'd walked into the *Twilight Zone*, or fallen through a hole and landed in a different world, a world she'd never known existed, with strange beings and bizarre rules.

"Of course, the biggest danger to you would come from your own, from humans. And that is if they were to ever learn of my true nature. Even if they could not destroy me, they would try. And their methods would be deadly to you and to any other humans who happened to be in the way."

"Is that what happened to your wife . . . how she . . . ?"

"Yes." He blinked several times then continued in a softer voice, "Fortunately, the only way any human would learn what I am is if you told them." He caught her face between his palms, forcing her to meet his gaze. "So again, I challenge you to search your heart. If you make the wrong decision, a great many lives, including your own, could be at stake. I shouldn't have told you so much and I've put my clan members at risk by putting our secrets in your trust so soon."

"I swear I won't tell a soul. Not even my priest."

"You see now why trust is so important to me?"

"I do. But you will give me time to think about this whole mate thing, right? I mean, this is a lot more complicated than deciding what breed of puppy to buy and that's taken me months. Even now, it's a draw between a cute little cocker spaniel or an Irish setter."

"I vote for the Irish setter," he said with a grin.

"Why did I know you'd say that?" She gave him a soft slug in the belly.

"Seriously now . . ." He let his hands fall away from her. "Take as much time as you need. Also, understand that the process of taking a mate isn't a simple one. There are several stages. If you were to change your mind, you could do so at any point up until the final Joining."

"Okay."

He eased her to her feet, stood and helped her find her clothes, then strode past her. "I will leave you to make your decision." He opened the door and stood in the doorway again. "Gibs will help you carry your clothes to your car."

"Okay. Thanks for the beautiful gifts. I never expected . . ." She paused. "But one thing I was hoping for—" She hesitated for a moment then continued, "I hate to bring this up now, after everything that's happened. Everything we've talked about. What about the plate? You said you would consider selling it, if . . ." She let her words trail off again.

"Yes, I did." He looked pained as he nodded slowly.

"If it means someone or something is threatened by your selling it, you don't have to."

"No, no. I must keep my word. But will you give me the same consideration I have given you? Will you come back tomorrow? Spend another evening with me? Give me a chance to consider my terms for the sale?"

Give him the same consideration? Oh, this guy was good. Nothing like heaping on the guilt to make her walk away empty-handed even though he'd told her he would sell it after only one night. "Sure. I'll play along for one more night. After tonight, I'm anxious to see what other surprises you have in store for me. A little scared, too."

"Thank you." He gave her a gentle kiss on the lips that made her insides melt like warm butter. "'Til tomorrow. Seven?"

"Yes. Seven'll be fine." She left later with a car full of sexy lingerie, a brain full of confusing thoughts and no plate for Mrs. Kim. Yet, she was in good spirits.

Unfortunately, Mrs. Kim didn't share her sunny outlook when Kaya returned to work the next morning and let her know she'd found the buyer and was close to cutting a deal with him for the copperplate. Although Mrs. Kim allowed Kaya to remain at work for the day, she badgered her with a zillion questions about who the buyer was, where he lived, what kind of demands he was making. Kaya kept her answers as vague as possible and kept busy until quitting time. She left, making Mrs. Kim a departing promise that she'd return the next day with the plate in hand or not return at all.

Finally, Mrs. Kim seemed pleased.

Now the pressure was really on. Not only would she lose out on the biggest bonus of her career, but her job as well. She had to do whatever it took to convince Jestin to part with the copperplate. Anything.

Or become his mate tomorrow. A dragon's mate. An Immortal. After having known him for maybe thirty-six hours. Faster than it had taken her to pick out the paint for her living room.

"Forgive me for saying this. You've made a terrible mistake, sir."

Jestin sighed as he ceased pacing for a second before resuming the useless motion again. It wasn't like it would bring her back to him any quicker. Yet he couldn't bear to stand still. And sitting at his desk and concentrating on his work was damn near impossible. "Gibs, you must trust me," he said with confidence he didn't feel.

"As I recall, that's not in my job description."

"Neither is nagging me, but you do that often enough." Jestin gave his servant and dearest friend a smile to soften the blow of his words. "You know I'd be lost without your nagging, my friend. Promise me you'll never stop."

"You have my word. But what will you do if the woman does not come back? You told her a great deal more than—"

"I had to. She was scared senseless. She will be back. I am certain."

"Is that so? You are certain? Then you are pacing to get some exercise? I give you thirty to one odds she doesn't show."

"Thirty to one? You're mad, but who am I to not take advantage of a madman?" Jestin accepted the wager with a handshake. "Don't you see? She is the one. I thought I could keep things casual, not go through with the final Joining. But now . . ."

"Then God help you."

Jestin purposefully ignored his friend's jab. "I didn't want this. I didn't want another mate. You know how I was after Anelise died. Yet now that I have seen Kaya, talked to her, tasted her, I cannot fathom the idea of existing without her. I know I am right. She drank the wine with no ill effects, she saw me in my base form. Two tests passed and the third—"

"She lied," Gibs pointed out.

"About fish. She answered the most important question truthfully, the one about being lonely and needing someone in her life. Thus she has passed the third test and must merely accept my true form to move to step four."

"I do not think you should've told her everything. She knows too much. You gave her too many reasons not to return."

"Which is wise. When she does come to me, I will know she has done so knowing everything."

"Nearly," Gibs corrected.

"Nearly. I only left out a minor detail."

"She may not find it so minor."

"I will deal with it when the time comes. She wasn't ready to hear it. But tonight when she comes to me, she will have passed the fourth test—having embraced my nature freely. That leaves only two tests remaining. She should be more ready by then."

"You are going too quickly. This should take time—weeks, even months. What if she fails to take the final step? You know the risk to yourself, your people, all of the Immortals. She could reveal your secret, lead your enemies to you. Think what would happen if they found the treasures you have locked away here. With the copperplate alone, they could destroy all the Guardians, which would mean the end for all the Immortals."

"I am aware of that. She could destroy us, yes. But she won't. I'm confident she'll keep our secret. Besides, I'm not convinced she knows what mysteries the copperplate holds, or even has the means to have it translated to find out what they are. But if she does, I have faith she'll return it to me."

"The risk is too great. Anelise was a different sort. She was steadfast, loyal from the beginning. And she was strong."

"And so is Kaya. She will prove so tonight."

"I hope you're right."

"I know I'm right."

"How can you know someone you met just over thirty-six hours ago?" Gibs shook his head. "I will go make the final preparations for your dinner."

"Just make sure her steak is cooked well. She will need a full stomach tonight to face what I have in store for her."

"Too much information, sir." Gibs disappeared through a doorway at the end of the hall, leaving Jestin to pace in peace.

When she didn't arrive at seven on the dot, he told himself she was probably being held up in traffic. When she didn't arrive at five after, he told himself there was probably an accident somewhere causing her delay.

When she still hadn't arrived by five-to-eight, he had no choice but to accept the fact that she wasn't coming and when he did that, he realized exactly how disappointed he was. His mood darkened to the shade of coal. Familiar darkness coiled inside of him, snuffing out the small flickers of light Kaya had ignited the night before. The light he had sworn he'd never again enjoy.

At five after eight, Gibs entered the room with a glum expression that suited Jestin's mood perfectly.

"Why would you look so down, my friend?" Jestin asked. "You were right. You won our wager."

"She has arrived. She is waiting for you in the dining room."

Jestin really had to work hard at not giving loose with a mighty whoop that would echo off every floor, wall and ceiling in his massive home. How much respect would his mate have for a man who shouted like a gleeful boy at her arrival? Instead, he cleared his throat, straightened his tie and smoothed his pant legs. "Very well. Thank you, Gibs. I will join her shortly. As soon as I conclude my business here."

Gibs took in the empty room, clear desk and phone resting quietly in its cradle, smiled slightly and said, "As you wish, sir." He left, closing the door behind him.

Jestin made her wait fifteen minutes before he joined her in the main dining room for dinner. It took every one of those minutes to get his racing heart to slow down, his palms to dry and his breathing to find its natural rhythm. She looked uneasy as he entered. When he stepped near, the sharp tang of her fear stung his nose. She was afraid, yet she came back. He respected her for that. It was a sure sign of strength.

Looking very small in the high-backed dining chair, she tilted her head to look him in the eye. The angle made her eyes look enormous, her heart-shaped face adorable, her thick lashes a mile long, her lips full and tempting. "I apologize for being late. I didn't get out of the store until almost six-thirty and then there was an accident on I-94. Traffic was backed up for miles."

"No need to explain." He scooped up her hand in his, lifted it to his mouth and, staring into eyes the shade of ebony, pressed a kiss to the back of her hand.

She blinked and a hint of pink touched her cheeks. When she dropped her gaze to the salad sitting before her, he released her hand and took his seat next to her, at the head of the table.

"I'm afraid your steak is probably as tough as shoe leather by now," he said after forcing himself to take a bite or two of salad. Vegetables were far from his favorite. Not to mention the fact that the food wasn't moving through his system as it should, thanks to his insides being tied into knots. There were so many things he wanted to share with his Kaya. His mate. Would she let him? Would she get over her fear and learn to trust him?

"That's okay. It's my fault for being late. To be honest, I'm not really hungry. I ate a snack at the store before I left."

"Neither am I," he admitted. "Would you like to retire to the study?"

She looked relieved as she nodded. "Yes. That sounds great. But I'm not insulting anyone by not eating, am I?"

He stood, took her hand in his and waited for her. "Absolutely not, as long as you tell me you're not hungry."

"Believe me, eating is the last thing I have on my mind at the moment," she said as he led her down the hall.

"Hmmm. And if I asked what is foremost on your mind, would you answer truthfully?"

"I would if I knew. Can't say my mind's exactly clear at the moment. It's kind of bogged down with a bunch of things."

"That answer is truthful enough for me." He pushed open the study's door and held it for her, following her into the room and closing the door behind him. He went to the small bar at the rear of the room. "Drink?"

"Just water, thanks."

He poured two glasses of ice water and handed her one, joining her on the settee. After he emptied his glass, he took hers and set them both on the side table. His gaze settled on her lips, tinted an iridescent, glossy pink that reminded him of the roses in his garden.

"I'm . . . I couldn't stop thinking about you last night," she said meekly.

His insides did a few somersaults yet he forced himself to maintain a sedate expression. "Is that so?"

She blinked as she lowered her gaze to her hands, which were sitting restlessly in her lap. "I came here yesterday wanting to buy the copperplate, and I still do. But I also want to know more. About you."

"Are you certain?"

"Yes. The whole dragon thing was a little hard to deal with at first but after a few . . . oh, hours or so . . . I think I got over it. Mostly."

"You are still afraid."

"A little." Still looking down, fiddling with the hem of her top, she nodded.

He lifted her chin with an index finger until she met his gaze. He read so many things in her eyes—indecision, fear, curiosity, to name a few. The others were too vague to identify. "Yet you came here tonight."

"I didn't want to. I mean, I was scared poopless, but honestly I had no choice."

"And I have no choice but to do this." He leaned in, molding his body to hers, and kissed her until his cock ached with the need to plunge into her sweet wetness. She kissed him back with equal heat, her tongue meeting his every thrust with one of her own. Her fingers dug into the flesh of his shoulders, the slight sting of her fingernails a welcome addition to the already overwhelming flurry of sensations battering him. Sounds, tastes, scents, touches. Sweet, hot, soft, tantalizing. They swirled around inside him like a maelstrom. He felt his control crumbling, quickly. His cock strained against his pants, his balls tightened until the skin of his upper thighs burned. Flames licked every inch of his body as overwhelming need blasted through him.

No woman had ever done that to him with just a kiss.

His heartbeat an irregular stutter in his ears, his every muscle a tight knot, he broke the kiss and fell backward against cushions almost as soft as Kaya's gentle curves. "If you are to be with me, and I believe you want to be, you will accept me as your Master."

She looked back at him with heavy-lidded eyes. "I don't know what that means. This is all so confusing. I'm not sure I'm ready."

"Would you like me to explain? Would you like to learn?" He waited for her answer, unable to draw in his next breath until she spoke.

"Yes," she whispered.

"I will show you then. We will go as slowly as you need." So happy he swore he might jump up and down and give a mighty whoop, he stroked her cheek with the back of his knuckles. Her skin was like fine silk. "First, you will address me as Master."

"Okay. Master." The words sounded stilted, awkward coming from her mouth. She grimaced slightly.

"Very good. It will take some time to get used to all this, I understand. But I want you to try. I promise, you'll be pleased with the results."

She gave him a weak smile. "Okay."

"And this is important," he continued, encouraged by her response. "I know it'll be hard, but it's vital. When we are in the dungeon, you must promise to respect me, to always be honest with me, and to trust me, from this moment on. Can you make those promises to me?"

"That's a lot. I mean, I can try. I'm not sure . . ." Her gaze darkened then dropped to the floor. "This is so strange . . . complicated."

Wishing to soothe her, to take away every one of her fears, he ran his hands down her arms. "And I promise to protect you, cherish you and trust you with my very life. Always. No matter where we are."

She didn't speak for a long time. Seconds passed with the unsteady thump of his heart. One, two, three. Finally, she lifted her gaze and looked him in the eye. "Please. Teach me. What do I do first?"

"Kneel before me like this." He gently coaxed her to kneel with slight pressure on her shoulders. "This is how you show me you are ready to listen, to do my bidding." She looked up at him with wide eyes for a moment then lowered them in a natural show of subservience that made his heart swell. He would serve this woman, his mate, Kaya Cordova, for the rest of his days. He would show her the joy that came from conquering her fears and make her every fantasy come true.

"That is very good." He scooped her into his arms and carried her to his dungeon. The training would commence. Immediately. "Now you will see what it means to relinquish complete control."

He felt her slight shudder as he entered the dungeon.

"You will trust me," he said, setting her on her feet.

"Okay."

"Master," he said firmly. "Remember, you must address me as Master when we are in the dungeon.

"Yes, Master."

"Obey me and you will receive rewards beyond your wildest dreams."

"I . . . I will?"

He gave her a slow nod. "Undress."

Chapter 5

I WANT YOU TO UNDERSTAND WHAT WILL HAPPEN BEFORE WE get started," Jestin said as his steamy gaze followed her motions.

Getting hotter by the second, despite the couple of reservations that stubbornly refused to release their chokehold on her, she peeled off her top first then pushed her skirt down over her hips. Her heart was beating so fast she swore it was about to explode, and her hands were shaking so bad it was almost impossible to use them.

She'd spent all last night reading, thinking, struggling to understand her feelings. She'd come to a couple of conclusions. First, the easy one. She had to get the plate from him because it was what her boss needed, it was what she'd promised. It would save her job, no matter what happened between them. And second—but somewhat unrelated to the first—she'd explore what it meant to be a dragon's mate. Despite her natural inclination to rebel against another person's attempt to control her, there was something about Jestin, about this, that felt right. Natural. Exciting and fulfilling, too. By the end of the night, and after reading so much, she'd grown bleary-eyed, she'd become convinced she was about to learn a great deal, about Jestin, about dragons, but also more important, about herself. That made her both nervous and excited at the same time.

"I've . . . never done anything like this." She fumbled with her clothes, dropping them on the floor.

"I understand." He swept up the dropped garments and set them aside then closed his warm hands around her upper arms. "I will show you some patience. However, you won't want to push me by being impertinent or mocking. I know how you like to joke and tease. And I adore you for the carefree, joy-filled, independent woman you are. But this isn't the place for auditioning a standup routine or engaging in a battle of wills. To do so would bring terrible consequences. You would be mocking my feelings for you, my affection for you, and commitment to making you happy and keeping you safe. I will not tolerate it." He released one arm so he could unfasten the front hook of her bra. Then he used both hands to slide the shoulder straps down her arms before closing a warm palm over her breast. His gaze still locked to her face, he said heavily, "Remember—a reward is far more enjoyable than punishment."

"I understand, Master." Between her jittery nerves, the promise she caught in his voice and the way his fingers pinched and pulled at her nipple, she was already close to dropping at his feet. She nodded.

"Your panties. Take them off but leave on your stockings and shoes. I am pleased with your choice of thigh-high stockings over those wretched pantyhose. For that, you will receive a reward as well."

Every cell in her body jumped up and down with glee. "Yes, Master." She pushed her panties down over her hips and let them slide down her thighs until they dropped to her feet. She was about to kick them off when he shook his head.

"You will bend over and take them off properly. Knees straight. Feet shoulder-width apart. Your ass this way." He positioned her so her rear end was right in front of him and he had a clear view of her most secret places when she bent over to tug the bit of lace off her ankles. She managed to get them off without falling over—a real feat considering both her position and nerves. Feeling quite proud of herself, she tried to stand up, but he stopped her with a firm hand on her back. "You will remain like this until I return."

"Yes, Master," she said, not particularly comfortable in the position he had left her in—it hardly brought light to her more favorable assets—but not wanting to displease him. A reward sounded a heck of a lot more fun than punishment, although she'd always found the idea of being spanked sexy. She hoped he'd spank her sometime.

She couldn't see him leave but she heard him. She also heard the squeak of door hinges as he opened and closed a door. Had he left the room? Left her bent over like a jogger stretching for a run? A soft shuffle of feet on the wood floor suggested otherwise. And the prickles of awareness skipping up her spine when he returned to his position behind her confirmed her suspicion. Evidently, he'd only opened a closet or bathroom door.

A heartbeat later, two warm, large hands cupped her ass cheeks and kneaded them until her pussy simmered and slickness coated her inner thighs. She heard him inhale deeply. "Very nice. I can smell your desire and that pleases me. You may stand now."

Her head swam a little when she straightened up. She wasn't sure if her dizziness was the result of the position she'd been in or from the pleasure he'd given her already, with only a gentle massage of her ass.

"Turn around, slave," he commanded in a soft but firm voice.

She did as he asked, puzzled by what he was holding. It looked like a gold, bejeweled collar, like the kind the rich and famous in Hollywood might buy for their little froufy dogs from some over-priced specialty shop. While the collar was pretty—the thing had to have a bazillion diamonds and rubies on it, along with several little silver rings—she wasn't sure what the heck she was supposed to do with it.

Was it for her future pet? That had to be it. A collar for her soon-to-buy Irish setter. How thoughtful! Although it was quite large around for a puppy and certainly a bit glitzy for a setter. They were more sporty dogs than fussy in her opinion.

"This is for you." Looking quite pleased with his gift, he unfastened the buckle and dodged her lifted hands to wrap the collar around her neck. "You will wear it whenever we are in the dungeon." He fastened the buckle.

"Oh! It's for me? Not a . . . oh, my." She lifted her hands to her neck and fingered the facets of the jewels. "I'm . . . gee, thanks. It's . . . er, lovely."

"You are my slave. We would not want to have any of my fellow clan members mistaking you for a free woman. I will admit, and I don't expect you'd be surprised to know, I've brought free women to my dungeon in the past. But never again."

A twinge of jealousy tied her insides into a knot, even though she knew she had no right to feel that way. What he did in the past was in the past. She knew he was no virgin. "No? Um . . . can I ask? Your clan will be here? In the dungeon?"

"I will explain this only because you are new to being a slave and I care about you enough to want you to understand." He traced the line of the collar then let his finger drop lower to the valley between her breasts. "My fellow clansmen do come here. And they would devour you if they had the chance. Literally."

She shuddered as a half dozen images, each one more bizarre than the next, flashed through her mind. "Oh."

"And now you will show me your gratitude for my gift, which is an outward sign of my love for you."

"Love?" She stood frozen as her mind tried to wrap itself around that word. How could he love her already? After only one day? "Love?" she repeated again.

"Love is not a feeling. It is a decision, a commitment. And I have decided I will love you as my slave, my mate," he explained, pushing gently on her knees until she was facing him, kneeling. "With my love comes the promise that I will always put your needs and feelings before my own, to always treat you with respect and caring, to be faithful and kind.

Her kneecaps ground into the hard wood floor and she grimaced slightly.

"What is the matter, slave?"

"Sorry, Master. Floor's hard on the knees. I have bad knees."

"This way." He took her hands and pulled until she was standing then led her to a thing with two low, narrow pads close to the ground and a higher one in between. "This is a prayer bench," he explained. "Kneel here." He pointed at one of the low pads. "Facing me."

"Um . . . like this? I'm not joking. Is it time to pray? Now . . . er, Master?" Although it was awkward getting into position, because her feet tended to hit the other low pad, she was surprised by how soft the cushions were. She clasped her hands together in front of her chest.

"Better?" he asked.

"Yes. Much better. Thank you, Master. Will you be leading the prayer or me?"

"Neither." He pulled off his shirt and she watched, marveling at the beauty of his body, the lines of developed muscles coating his shoulders, arms and chest. When he moved, those scrumptious muscles bunched and stretched. What a lovely sight! It certainly inspired her to say a few words to whatever god had created him. "Would you like to serve your master and receive great rewards in return?"

Great rewards? He'd made a lot of promises of rewards today. She was sure ready to see what that was all about. Tingles skittered up her spine. She imagined him parting her legs wide and pushing his cock deep inside her pussy. A lump completely closed off her throat.

"Kaya, have you ever wanted to be tied up? Forced by a dark stranger?"

"I don't know. I never thought about it."

"What are your darkest fantasies?" His fingertip traced the line of her throat then continued lower. He pinched her left nipple and gave it a sharp tug that made her gasp. Her empty pussy clenched, warm juices dripping down her inner thighs. "You will know, the beauty of being a slave is in both the giving and in the receiving." His other hand cupped her chin and lifted it. Her gaze snapped to his eyes and froze there for a moment then slid south to rest on his broad, smooth chest. She ached to reach out and trace the lines of his pecs, to feel his satin-smooth skin under her fingertips. "Like I said before, when you please your master, you receive pleasure beyond your wildest dreams. I will make your darkest fantasies come true." When he didn't continue, she glanced up. His smile was more wicked now than it had ever been. She trembled, her whole body tense with expectation. He licked his lips then continued, "I'm guessing you'd like to be bent over and fucked from behind. That way, you can touch yourself and come over and over. Is that true, Kaya? Would you like me to bend you over and fuck you from behind?"

"Yes," she whispered.

"And just before you come, would you like me to push my finger into your ass?"

"Oh, yes." Almost ready to come before he'd done more than pull on her nipple, she trembled. "Please."

"You will show me your gratitude first." He unbuckled his belt and unzipped his pants. "You will take my cock in your mouth."

"Yes."

"Would you like to do that?"

"Oh, yes, Master." She could barely remain upright thanks to the trembling his naughty talk was causing. Knowing herself, she'd always held the notion that her mind had as much to do with good sex as her body. Jestin was clearly a master of brain-stroking. She'd never been so ready with so little actual foreplay.

He removed both his pants and underwear, standing before her in all his glory. His skin was deeply tanned all over and smooth-shaven like a swimmer's. His cock was very large, erect. His balls hung heavily behind it.

He gripped his cock in his fist and gave it a couple of strokes and she nearly crumpled over, boneless and weak. Did he have any idea of what he was doing to her? "Open your mouth, slave. Take my cock in your mouth and show me how grateful you are for my gift."

She thrust her tongue out first and took several shy swipes across the head as Jestin held it to her mouth, his hand still wrapped around the base, sliding up and back. She licked round and round then opened wide to take him into her mouth. His flesh felt hot against her tongue. It tasted sweet and spicy, wonderful. As he pulled out, she caught a droplet of pre-come seeping out with the tip of her tongue. Then he plunged back in, fucking her mouth with shallow in-and-out thrusts.

"Touch yourself," he commanded. One of his hands was in her hair, holding her head still as he pumped his delicious cock in and out of her mouth. The other slid up and down the shaft of his cock. "Damn it, you feel good. Touch yourself."

She reached between her legs with one hand and found her clit. It was supersensitive and she gasped at the first stroke. She reached up and laid her other hand on Jestin's lower belly, just above his cock. She felt the muscles under his skin trembling and moaned around a mouthful of cock. She quickened the pace of the circles she drew around her clit until her stomach coiled into a tight knot, too.

Jestin abruptly pulled his cock from her mouth and demanded gruffly, "Turn around."

She stood up and knelt back down, resting her stomach on the high cushion. She felt the heat of his thighs against the back of her legs, even though his skin didn't touch hers. She moaned as he parted her labia with his fingers and pressed two inside. His knuckles scraped against the sensitive upper wall of her canal as his other hand alternatively slapped and kneaded her ass.

"You are such a good slave, Kaya. You are learning so quickly. You deserve a lifetime of rewards, each one greater than the last. I know you will serve me faithfully, and you have my promise that I will live my life dedicated to giving you every pleasure you desire." With his sweet words still echoing in the room, he thrust his cock deep inside her.

The first stroke sent bliss sweeping through her body. Her pussy stretched to accommodate his size then gripped him tightly, increasing her pleasure. The second stroke took her breath away. The third sent her careening toward release. She groaned and tossed her head from side to side.

"Have you ever let a lover push you to your threshold then pull you back, over and over until you couldn't take it anymore? Let him take complete control?"

"No," her answer was a pleading whisper. "Please." She shook all over, so close to orgasm she could feel the grip of release tightening deep in her belly.

He stopped moving inside her but didn't pull out. His hands stroked her back. Sweet butterfly kisses coated her shoulders, giving birth to a flock of goose bumps. She was shivering cold and hot at the same time and ready to lose complete control, to hand it over to Jestin, the man whose words caressed her mind with as much tenderness and raw sensuality as his hands did her body.

She was there with him, not a single cell in her body wanting anything more than to share this bliss with him, to join him in an intense release that she suspected would shake her to her very soul. Her fear was gone. Her reservations burned away by the blaze consuming her body. "I will give you your release in a moment," his rough voice shook as he spoke, suggesting he was as close as she was to losing control. "Trust me."

"I do. In all ways."

"You are not afraid anymore?"

"Not of you."

He pulled his cock from her and pulled on her shoulders, easing her around to face him. "I know I promised you I would fuck you the other way, but I will give you the choice. Would you rather face away from me, or toward me? As before, when I climax, you will see me as I truly am."

"I will see the dragon?"

"Yes."

"I wish to face you."

His smile was so brilliant it brought tears to her eyes. He led her to another piece of furniture that looked a lot like a weight bench and lowered her onto her back. "Kaya, you make it so easy to love you." He eased her knees apart and with his fiery, heavy-lidded gaze fixed to hers, buried his cock deep inside her again. His lips parted slightly as a soft sigh slipped between them. Overcome with joy, she smiled and let her eyelids shutter out the distraction of sight, wanting to relish every touch, every sound, every scent until they found release and the dragon reappeared. He left her there in the dark world filled with the soft thwack, thwack of his groin striking her with every inward thrust, with the combined scents of man, dragon and desire, with the bliss of his intimate strokes inside her body. "Come for me. Take your release."

Tense pleasure gripped her body, pulling it into tight, shuddering coils. Her heavy breaths sounded hollow in her ears, muffling but not completely drowning out the sweet words Jestin continued to whisper to her. And then she was there again, and before she could say a word, she gave herself over to it, to the climax that pulsed through her body like waves on the sea. She gasped and jerked as the waves battered her, over and over, until they slowly subsided to little ripples. Hot tears streamed down her cheeks. She cried out, "Jestin!"

"I'm here, baby."

When she opened her eyes, the air before her shimmered and the dragon stood before her, mighty and powerful and beautiful. In awe, she stared until a moment later Jestin was back, smiling at her, his face and chest flushed.

"Next time. I promise," he said between heaving breaths.

"Next time?"

"You will have it your way."

"What are you talking about? I just did."

He gathered her into his arms, and their bodies still joined, he held her in a tight embrace that made her feel strong and safe and loved. This was right. She was ready to take the final steps, to become Jestin's mate forever.

AFTER LYING IN bed for hours with Jestin, she eventually looked at the clock. It was late, or rather, early. Early morning. She had little more than an hour to get ready for work.

"I should get going."

"Stay here with me." He hugged her tighter to him.

"I have to go to work. No one's going to pay my bills for me." She unenthusiastically peeled his arm off her and sat up. He watched her dress from the bed, all rumpled and sexy and tempting. It took every ounce of willpower she possessed not to jump back into bed with him and go for round three, or was it four for the night?

Once she was fully dressed, she reluctantly brought up the one subject she'd avoided all night. "I need to ask you about the copperplate."

"Yes, I said I would consider my terms and I have. I will sell it to you for what I paid, not a penny more."

"You will?" Kaya couldn't believe her ears. She hadn't even told him yet that she had made her decision, that she would be his mate forever.

Would there be a hitch? There was always a hitch. Would he tell her she couldn't give it to Mrs. Kim? Would he ask her to hide it? "You'll give it to me and I can do what I like with it?"

"Yes," he said, sounding slightly defeated. "In fact, I trust you to make the payment later and will have Gibs bring it down to your car. You may do whatever you like with it."

"That's it?" she repeated, wanting to make sure she understood. "You're going to give it to me just like that?"

"Yes, you expected me not to?"

"I expected something, some terms. A word of caution, maybe."

"I will ask for only one thing—you deliver the payment to me personally tomorrow. Those are my terms."

"Those are terms I can agree to." She didn't know whether to shake his hand or hug him. She opted for a hug and was extremely glad she did the moment he pulled her to him.

Bazillion-year-old fire-breathing dragon or not, the man knew how to hold a woman.

Chapter 6

KAYA WASTED NO TIME GETTING THE COPPERPLATE BACK TO THE store, and to the relative safety of Mrs. Kim's built-in safe. The case tucked under her arm, she raced into the building, shut and locked the back door and shuffled down the back hall toward the front of the store. She heard Mrs. Kim's voice up ahead and the rumble of a man's voice. Just before she reached the back entry to the store, she halted when she heard Mrs. Kim say the word "plate."

"You must get it, no matter the cost. Have you no idea what it holds?" The man's voice rose slightly with anger. "It holds the key to the most powerful spell on the planet."

"Yes, I know. I sent Kaya with offer. I expect her to return with the copperplate today. She promise."

"You should have taken care of this yourself. It is too important and if the gentleman knows what he has, he will not part with it easily."

"But if he is not mage, what could it do for him?"

"If he is one of the red dragons, he will protect it with his life.

The spell would strip all his people of their human disguises and they could then be easily destroyed. In their dragon forms, they are easily killed."

Kaya gasped and looked down at the black case snugged under her arm. Why would Jestin hand over the one thing that could mean the destruction of his entire race? Was the man wrong? He had to be.

Still, she wasn't about to take that chance. She whirled around on her heel. Unfortunately, she bumped into the swinging door as she turned. A quick look over her shoulder told her both Mrs. Kim and the man had heard her.

And a man running toward her at full speed told her he'd seen her, too.

Not taking the time to think, she did what came naturally—she ran. Zigged and zagged around boxes of antiques lining both sides of the narrow hallway to the back door. The man was on her heels within seconds.

Then the deadbolt on the back door did her in. It stuck, as usual. And before she could get it to twist open, the man snatched the case out from under her arm.

"Why were you running?" he asked in a powerful voice that suggested he knew the answer.

Still trying to disengage the lock, she shrugged her shoulders. "I just remembered I'd left my lights on. Don't want the battery to go dead."

"So it had nothing to do with this?" He held up the case.

She finally unfastened the lock and turned to face him. "Oh no. Not at all." She aimed for nonchalance in her expression. "Thanks for holding it for me so I could get the lock."

There were a lot of things Kaya had done in her life, like go to college, buy her own home and pay her taxes. But there were a lot more things she'd never done. She'd never risked life and limb for anyone. She'd never gone parasailing, bungee jumping or white-water rafting and she'd never broken the law.

She figured she was about to do at least a couple of those in the near future. Kaya Cordova would play it safe no more!

When Mrs. Kim lumbered up and spoke to the man she called Mr. Vandenberg, Kaya took advantage of his shift in attention, snatched the case which still rightfully belonged to Jestin and barreled through the door. With a shouting, furious, very large and intimidating man on her heels, she dashed to her car, locked the doors, started it and burned rubber out of there.

She even ran a red light to make sure she wouldn't be followed, and thus she did at least two things on that list in the span of only a few minutes.

There was only one place to go—back to Jestin's house.

Thanks to her nerves being wound tighter than a coiled spring that was ready to snap, it was hell driving the speed limit. But because she couldn't be sure whether Mrs. Kim had called the police or not, Kaya didn't want to take any chances at being pulled over. As a result, it took her over an hour to get to Jestin's. By the time she was sitting at the gate, buzzing to be let in, she was shaking from head to toe. After being let inside, she parked the car, clutched the case to her chest and ran to the front door. It opened before she reached it. Mr. Gibs gave her a friendly smile and said, "This way, please. Mr. Draig is in a meeting. He wasn't expecting you quite so soon."

"Could you please tell him it's urgent? I need to talk to him."

"Very well." He motioned for her to take a seat in the library. She felt very warm and safe in the huge leather chair. "Can I get you something to drink while you're waiting?"

"No. Thanks. But if you could, please tell him it's important."

"Yes, miss." Mr. Gibs left, leaving her to shake and panic all by herself, not a good thing. Her mind jumped from one horrific thought to another: What if that man did something to Mrs. Kim? What if they called the police and reported her as a thief? What if she went home and was greeted by a SWAT team?

By the time Jestin strolled into the room, looking cool as a cucumber, she was an absolute mess.

She couldn't wait for him to wander his way across the room and so she jumped up and ran to him, the case still in her arms and thrust it at him. "I can't believe you gave this thing to me! Why? Why'd you do that? Are you suicidal? I don't get it." She resisted the urge to clobber him with it when he didn't take it from her.

In answer, he lifted both eyebrows.

"That's it? You're just going to look at me like I'm nuts?"

"Why have you returned this to me? Isn't it what you wanted?"

"It was until I found out what the copperplate says."

"You found that out already? From whom? What did you learn?"

"There was a man at the store, talking to Mrs. Kim when I came in. He said it had some kind of spell on it, a spell that would mean the destruction of the red dragons. That's you. That's your people. Was he right or did I just do something stupid that probably cost me my job, maybe even my freedom?"

"He was right. Was his name Vandenberg?"

"Yes. I've never met him before but he's purchased a lot of things from us."

"Yes, I know. He is becoming something of a threat to the Immortals although this is as close as he'd gotten to gaining possession of something that could've done some serious damage."

"Well, aren't you going to stop him? What if he comes after me? What if he gets the plate?"

"There's still no guarantee he has the power to invoke the spell. As a Guardian, I must do my job but I must do it quietly—under the radar, so to speak. I will continue to watch him but I will not do anything covert to stop him. As far as I know, he merely has a collection of relatively powerless trinkets. Nothing of real value."

"But you almost handed over something that could've caused real harm. You don't know how powerful the man is."

"True."

"Why then? Why did you do it?"

"I had no choice. I had to put my faith—and my life—in your hands. It is the next step."

"Yeah well, here. Glad I passed. But now I have some madman collector after me and I am probably jobless. Do those count as steps of some kind?"

He smiled.

"Don't tell me. Losing one's livelihood is step, what? Six? Seven? I've lost count."

He gave her a few innocent blinks. "We do seem to be clocking a new record. Only one step remains." He pulled her into the kind of embrace she'd come to expect from him. Warm, protective, gentle but firm.

Her knees turned to marshmallow and her fiery rage cooled.

She tipped her head up to give him a half-hearted dose of mean eyes. "Will you at least tell me what the final one is so I'm not caught by surprise again? And what will I do about my job? My bills? My criminal record? My grandmother! The poor woman'll be out on the street faster than the jury can say, 'Guilty'."

His laughter rumbled through her body making her insides tingle. "I will consider telling you. However, I believe you are overreacting. You won't have a criminal record because you didn't break any laws—at least none that I know of." He kissed her nose. "Did you?"

"I ran a few lights."

"That's nothing."

"Nothing! I've never gotten so much as a parking ticket before."

"Ah, but you're no longer that fearful—"

"Law abiding."

"—overly cautious woman you once were. I'd say you are uniquely qualified to work for me. The next items I need to buy are being auctioned in Chicago. A spear and a harp that can be used to destroy the Lamiae. What do you say?" His hands slid down her sides until they rested on her hips. He pulled until her mound was pressed firmly against his leg. "I cannot possibly attend all the auctions throughout the world. Will you be my representative? Help me locate artifacts and attend auctions on my behalf? I promise the pay's good—at least double what you were making at your last position." He moved his leg so it rubbed her pussy through her clothes, making her all weak and warm.

Double? Double! That would give her plenty to live on plus pay her grandmother's nursing home bills. Thrilled beyond words, she said, "Wow! I don't know what to say. That's a very generous offer." She added, meaningfully, "Will I get benefits?"

"Absolutely. But I warn you, you must learn your place in my organization. I will not tolerate your stepping out of ranks." He winked. "At least not during business hours." He glanced at his watch, twisted the itty-bitty knob on the side. "Gee, look at that. It's exactly six-oh-one. Quitting time already."

"Wow, where did the day go?" she teased.

He took her hand in his and led her up the stairs and down the main hallway. He opened the door to the dungeon and said, "I don't have to tell you the consequences of insubordination."

She clapped her hands in delight then sobered her expression. "Oh dear. I suppose calling you my hunky, spunky dragon-boy would be considered stepping out of ranks?"

"It certainly would."

"And the punishment?"

His grin literally reached from one ear to the other, bringing back the California-boy beauty she'd admired so much the first time she'd met him, at the auction. Two deep dimples poked into his cheeks, making her all warm and weak in the knees. "Well, since we're still on this side of the doorway it'll be slight. How do you feel about . . . floggers?"

"Never met one personally, but I have an open mind, my widdle dragon-poo."

He gave her an exaggerated sigh and martyred look. "And thus your training continues. First rule, which you seemed to have forgotten already, you will call me Master."

"We're not in the dungeon yet," she pointed out with a smile.

He led her into the room and straight to the kneeling thingy, eased her down until she was on her knees and bent over, her stomach and chest resting on the raised part, her rear end up in the air. "Naturally, for your insolence, you will feel the sting of my flogger on your bare flesh."

"Yes, Master," she said, not bothering to hide the shudder of delight rippling through her body.

He reached up her dress, flipped the skirt over her back, and yanked down her panties. He tugged her knees wide apart so that her bottom was exposed, her pussy open wide. Her breathing came fast and ragged as her spine tensed in anticipation of the first strike. He walked away, strolling slowly toward a cabinet in the far corner of the room, and she tipped her shoulders to watch him.

"You will remain in position, head down, Kaya, or you will taste the sting of my wrath." His tone was firm but far from terrifying.

"Yes, Master," she said, lowering her shoulders.

He returned a moment later. She felt him near her, even though in her position she couldn't see him. It was the way the air crackled, like static electricity, all around him. The little snaps made her skin tingle and gave her goose bumps, too, both very delightful effects.

"Did I hear mocking in your voice?" he whispered.

"Oh, no, Master. Not mocking. I remember what you said. I would never dare to mock you. Not in here."

"Good." In reward, she received a light smack from the flogger. The fringes struck her bare bottom with a slightly stinging whap that made her yip in surprise. Oh, she had no idea how sexy and exciting being spanked could be. Her pussy was already burning with the need to be filled. She arched her back, thrusting her rear end up as high as she could, hoping he'd do it again.

The second strike was slightly harder than the first but equally pleasurable. And the third and fourth made her whimper with need.

"What you do to me," he murmured.

The kisses that followed were soft, gentle and incredibly erotic.

They cooled each of her burning cheeks. Then, she felt his fingertips as he pulled her ass cheeks apart. One finger delved into her crack, sliding slick up and down until just the tip pressed into her tight hole while another slid down to her pussy. Barely able to remain kneeling, thanks to her trembling muscles, she groaned.

"Shall we go for the final step tonight, love? Will you join with me for eternity?"

Thanks to his intimate strokes, the kisses he trailed down her spine, the heat he stirred in her body, it was easy to tell him she'd made her decision. "Yes, oh yes."

She wanted to be his, in all ways, to learn to submit to him sexually, to fall asleep in his powerful arms at night, to stand by his side as Guardian, to live life as she'd never done before.

"Show me how to please you, to make you as happy as you've made me," she begged.

"It will take time, my sweet. I will show you as you are ready. For today, learn this—I will always do what is best for you because I cannot do anything else. I wish for you to trust me, always." As he spoke the last word, he pushed two fingers into her pussy and one into her ass simultaneously, making her see stars. With increasingly swift strokes, he brought her to a swift but mind-blowing climax that left her breathless and dizzy and aching for his cock.

He gently helped her up and led her to what looked like a chair suspended from the ceiling. After gently securing her legs and arms in position, he removed his pants and wedged his hips between her thighs.

"After tonight, we will become one in every way. We will breathe for each other, laugh for each other, cry for each other and live for each other. Your body will become mine, mine will become yours and you will know no more loneliness, no more fear, no more doubt. But it is painful."

"You never mentioned pain. Pain like a little spanking or pain like shoving bamboo under my fingernails?"

"You must surrender your soul to me. You must die."

Her heart skipped one, two, three beats. "Die? But I thought I would become immortal."

"Yes, you will. But immortality comes with a price. You pay with your mortality, with your life. But as I've said before, nothing will happen until you are ready. I will wait for your word. Until then, we will learn about each other, share in each other's bliss. It is as it should be." And then in a single thrust, he drove into her, stealing her breath and mind. All that existed was him. His cock moving within her, his fingertips digging into her thighs, his breath warming her chest, the sound of his breathing and gentle words in her ears.

This time, as she climaxed, she opened her eyes and marveled in the sight of him shifting back and forth from man to beast. He awed her. Such a powerful, beautiful creature. And he had chosen her, the woman who had, until she'd met him, lived as a slave to her fears.

The woman who had been afraid to take any risk now had the courage of ten women. As she was swept away on the waves of passion, she cried out without the slightest bit of fear, "Yes, my love! Yes! I am yours. Join with me."

"And so you will be." Jestin tipped his head and pressed a hot kiss on her chest, several inches above her left nipple. Instantly white-hot flames seared her flesh, leaping and churning through her whole body. She trembled and cried out against jagged blades of pain scissoring along her spine, making her weak. Her senses dimmed until there was nothing but silent, empty blackness. And then an explosion of colors blasted at her eyes. Scents so strong her nose burned shot up her nostrils, and touches so intense they felt like punches battered her skin. Her lungs burned for air and she dragged in a deep breath, blinked her tearing eyes and cried out, "Oh God!" The taste of sulfur soured her mouth.

It is done. You are mine now, and I am yours. We are bound by the soul. His thoughts echoed in her head.

Slowly, she found her way out from under the mountain of sensations to look at him. Although the colors, scents and touches didn't return to their normal state, they eased to at least the point of no longer being excruciating. She still heard even the smallest sound as clear as can be. And her vision was sharper, colors brighter. Scents pummeled her nose and she inhaled, trying to sort them out. And as her body adjusted, she realized with joy that something else had happened in that moment when they'd fused.

She could feel him inside. Could hear his thoughts as he worried about her. Could feel his emotions as he struggled with guilt, fear and bliss. He was a very real part of her now, and she him. The best part yet—she would have an eternity to share his joy and pain. And he hers.

She'd made a deal with one golden-haired devil and would never again face anything alone, not fear, nor joy, nor sorrow.

Her very own devil with dimples.

TAMING HIM

Michelle M. Pillow

AUTHOR NOTE

The world of the Dragoonas, while captivating and erotic, is quite a departure from my normal fictitious endeavors. I hope that you enjoy reading it as much as I've enjoyed writing it.

DEDICATION

To Mandy for your support and humor, no matter what I do. Actually, thanks for making me pasta and . . . for making me pasta . . . Oh yeah, and for the support thing, but mostly for the pasta.

Chapter 1

ALIEN ABDUCTION.

Maggie Stewart shook her head in disbelief as she tried to rationalize the sight before her. Things like that just did not happen in the real world, or if they did, they happened to strange, uneducated people who just wanted attention. Come on. A bunch of intelligent life forms flying around space just bent on sticking things up other aliens' asses? Hum, yeah. Sure. Whatever. Aliens come to Earth to probe the human anus. Not bloody likely.

Nope. There is no such thing as an alien abduction.

No such thing as extraterrestrials.

No such thing as this flying saucer landing right in front of my suddenly dead car in the middle of nowhere.

Maggie gripped the wheel tighter, her knuckles white. She was a sane, logical person. Things like this didn't happen to sane, logical people. If she just reasoned it out enough, the flying saucer would just go away.

Just wait . . .

Waiting . . .

Waiting . . .

It didn't go away.

Her headlights dimmed, flickering until they turned off completely. There were no streetlights on the mountain pass road and she should've been left in utter darkness. However, the light shining down from the ship lit up the entire country road and she could see just fine. This was insane. In a second she'd wake up and it would just disappear.

Wake up, Maggie. Wake up.

Maggie couldn't force herself to move. She was too stunned. It was like a bad fifties movie. The bright lights flashed around the center base of the oval ship. All was silent, except the sound of her heartbeat reverberating in her head. She expected to see dirt and debris flying around her as the craft kicked out its exhaust—or whatever it was these things did. How was she supposed to know what it was called? It wasn't like she worked for NASA. She was just a writer.

Oh, that's it. It's not an alien craft. My imagination is getting away with me. It's just some government ship. Some secret testing thing I've stumbled upon, and soon the military is going to come marching out.

The idea that she'd driven in on some government test facility did little to calm her nerves. She wasn't sure what was worse—aliens or government military. Both could be dangerous. The ship finally stopped moving, and a bright light illuminated in an arch around the section facing her car.

Oh, great, they're coming out to say hi.

Maggie tried to move, but she was still petrified. It was like the simple task of breathing was taking all her energy. Even with her body numbed with fear, her mind was coherent, still trying to rationalize the impossible.

There is no such thing as aliens. There is no such thing as extraterrestrials. There is no such thing as that incredibly built giant humanoid creature walking down the metal docking plank thingy surrounded by bright lights.

She found enough strength to hit the power lock button and was slightly amazed when it worked. The locks slid down and she felt an insane moment of relief—like when she was a kid and was sure a blanket would protect her from the bogey man. The relief was short-lived. The locks only popped back up. She hit them again, glancing to the man as he made his way slowly down from the ship.

The sound of the locks latching only to immediately unlatch seemed to echo in the car. Hitting the button repeatedly, she finally gave up and slammed her hand down on the lock to manually set it. Again, it popped up.

Okay, the locks could easily be attributed to a faulty electrical system in her brand-new rental car. That she could accept. It didn't mean alien forces were at play or anything.

Great. One mystery solved. Now, about this man coming at her.

Could you call an alien a man?

Light silhouetted the stranger as he walked closer to her car. A whimper passed her lips. There was something seductive to the sway of his hips, the way the light caressed him as he moved. His arms hung at his sides, as he walked with authority. Maggie wasn't sure if it was just her impressions of him, but somehow she knew this man had some sort of power in whatever he did. He was powerful, strong, in charge. She was so frightened that she couldn't even tremble in fear.

I didn't even want to come to the Ozarks anyway. Oh, wait, yes I did. I wanted to get away from the latest cheating boyfriend. Damned bastard was having sex with everything but me.

Think, Maggie. Reason it out.

Maybe this man wasn't an alien at all. He looked human in form—two muscular legs, two strong arms. Perhaps he was military. Some secret project she just happened to run across. His body was definitely male and in splendid shape. She saw the tapered outline of his waist, the large breadth of his shoulders. He even moved in that authoritative way those types of guys had.

Yeah, this guy could definitely be military. Special Ops.

The man came closer. Maggie gripped the wheel, as if that simple action could stop him from coming closer, as if her sheer will would keep him at bay. What did the military want with her? She was just passing through. Maybe if she closed her eyes tight, they would think she didn't see them.

Not likely.

Wake up, Maggie. Wake up.

A hand touched the hood of her car, rubbing over it as he walked closer to her window. She watched his fingers as he petted the rental as if it were a wild beast. A chill worked over her body, making her nipples so hard she thought they would burst. There was something soothing yet frightening about the gliding motion of his hand. Her body tingled with desire so hot her panties became instantly moist.

This was just like her dreams, only it felt more real. Maybe if she just stayed still, she'd wake up. If this was her dream, she knew what this man wanted. He wanted her—all of her. And he wouldn't stop until he got it.

No, the dreams were just a psychological reaction to being cheated on by a supposedly impotent boyfriend. They stemmed from the self-worth issues she'd been having lately. If a man didn't want her, her mind gave her an alien who did—one with a hard cock and boundless desire. That's what the shrink had said anyway before suggesting she take this trip to clear her head. Maggie was a rational, smart person. The old shrink was right, wasn't he?

This was *not* an alien.

This was *not* happening!

Her foot twitched, the first sign of movement in her body since she first saw the hand gliding over her hood. She pressed down on the gas pedal, hard. Nothing happened. The car didn't even sputter in response. Regardless, she tried again and again, pumping the gas pedal by frantically jerking her leg.

The man's fingers skimmed along her window, gliding up to the roof. The ship's light momentarily blinded her and she couldn't see his face as he passed by. His clothes were tight, dark. Slowly she turned her head to watch him. His hips and stomach were next to the car window. She gripped the wheel tighter. Her mouth gaped open, sucking in long, hard breaths. A tap sounded on the roof, as if he were drumming his fingers in thought.

Go away. Go away. Wake up, Maggie.

His movements were leisurely as he bent over to the side. Maggie stared at the window, watching, tense, breathing so hard she felt faint. Time slowed in the agony of waiting for the unknown. What did he want? What would he do? Who? Why?

It's just a man. A Special Ops, military man. Just a man. Just a man. Just a . . .

His face came into view. The darkness hid him, but then he turned, looking into her window. For the most part his features were human-like in placement, but a narrow, hard ridge came down over his forehead, blending into his nose. His eyes glinted silver, completely filled in with the almost liquid silver color. She saw her pale reflection in those eyes.

That is not just a man.

A weak scream left her, so soft it would do no good. A tear fell over her cheek. She shook with fright as she slapped her hand over the door lock, forcing it down. It popped right back up. She hit it again and again and each time it unlocked.

Stupid locks. Stupid locks!

He easily shifted his weight, and his muscles rippled beneath his clothing. The man tilted his head. With his eyes so strange a color, she couldn't see what he looked at. Before she knew it, the door was opening and he reached inside. The hand came for her, and she screamed, loud and long, finally finding her voice. It was too late. Besides, she was sure there would be no one to hear her cries, no one to come to her rescue.

The alien man didn't flinch. Maggie tried to move, but fear kept her immobile for the most part. His hand came for her. She screamed louder, weakly hitting at his arm, a feeble defense to his obviously superior strength.

Then he touched her and a euphoric pleasure shot through her at the contact. All fear left her, replaced by longing and hope. She basked in the feelings, wanting them, needing them. Everything was going to be just fine. She was happy, at peace. Growing weak, she moaned softly right before her whole world went black.

SHE WAS IN the dream again. The mist, the voice, the feelings inside her—they were all part of the dream. Maggie couldn't make out everything around her, but she knew she was safe in her bedroom and her thoughts were lucid. In the morning she wouldn't remember what happened, at least not all of it, but when she was dreaming, it was all so clear to her.

She was waiting.

Seeing a shadowed figure towering over her bed, Maggie smiled. This was what she was waiting for and this was what she wanted.

Maggie's skin tingled, and she looked down. Her clothes dissolved from her body, leaving her naked. It was as if hands undressed her, yet she didn't see them. Maybe it was the-man-at-the-end-of-the-bed's will.

Her flushed skin glowed with an eerie blue light, caressing her in a way that made her appreciate her own body. She'd never been one to stare at herself naked as she hurriedly dressed each morning, but in the dreams she was empowered by her own naked allure. It was as if her being naked controlled the man waiting to be called forward.

It was up to her whether he'd come to her or not. At first, when the dreams came, she'd just lay there night after night, keeping him away. Then, unable to take just staring at him, she beckoned him closer. He knew, without her speaking, that she allowed him that much. Maggie somehow just understood him, what he thought, what he wanted. The following night, she'd allowed him to sit on the bed. Things progressed like that for about a week, and each night, the more pieces of his clothing were stripped from him, the closer he got, until he was naked and ready to please her.

Maggie shivered, her body rippling with pleasure as he looked at her dream man now. The man was hot. No, not just hot, but H-O-T hot. He was the kind of man women only imagined in their best fantasies.

By the time he sat on the bed, his boots were gone, as was his shirt. She couldn't make out his face, but she saw his chest shadowed by the blue light—his hard nipples, the ridges of endless muscles. When he moved it was with a liquid grace, as if he knew how to work his body, was used to all kinds of physical activity.

Only when she'd been ready did he bring his tight body above hers. His pants melted from him, and suddenly she was on her hands and knees. At that point was when the blurring started in her mind, leaving her with only sensations. She could feel the impression of a thick, hard cock coming up behind her. Her pussy would drip a seemingly impossible amount of cream, and she was ready to be taken.

Maggie was always frustrated that she couldn't turn around to see him when he fucked her. The dream never let her have the pleasure of seeing his face as he slid deep into her wet pussy. She could never see his cock, never touch him, as she kneeled before him, gripping the coverlet on her bed. It didn't matter. The man knew how to work his hips and her body was always ready to receive him with little foreplay.

Deep in her soul, she had the faint impression that he was frustrated as well, as if he wanted to caress her, take his time loving her. She also sensed that he couldn't, not yet. It was as if his time in her dreams was limited to a few moments and he had to take her right then and there or not at all.

Everything was starting the same as before in this particular dream, only as she turned away from him to offer her pussy, the bedroom melted until she was in a cloud of mist and impressions of hard, cold metal. She waited on her hands and knees, her ass thrust out in invitation. Her pussy clenched in anticipation, even as her body yearned for more than just the thrust of his giant cock inside her. She couldn't seem to cry out, as she wanted to.

How pathetic was she that her best sex came from dreaming?

Maggie waited, her body poised, her legs spread. Despite the limitations, the sex always brought her to climax. Her stomach tightened and she gripped the blankets hidden in the cloudy mist. She couldn't see her hands, could barely see her own breasts. Maybe this time he'd touch more than her hips.

Time seemed to hold still, until even her ass was clenching in anticipation of the first thrust. Hands glided onto her flesh, finding hold on her hips. His cock head was hot, practically searing her as it touched her from behind. Her body was immobile. She wanted to touch her breasts, thumb her nipples. She wanted to lean up and feel his muscled chest against her back.

Even without looking, she knew it was him. It was her dream, wasn't it? Why would she let anyone else take her but the man in her dream? Besides, it was his masculine smell that wafted over her. It was his low voice whispering in her head. She couldn't make out the words, just a subtle tone to the way he talked.

He didn't take her right away this time as his cock stroked up and down her wet slit. She trembled. Why was he holding back? Why was he waiting to take her? He never teased her, not like this. Sure, during the day her senses were tormented with the anticipation of going to bed, hoping he'd come, but he never sexually toyed with her.

What was going on?

Before she could question, he gripped her hips and thrust forward. His hard cock impaled her, fitting so deep she thought he'd rip her apart. Damn, she forgot how big he was. It was like he was stretching her more and more, as if his cock grew bigger each time they had sex. Now it was practically ripping her apart.

Maggie knew it was just a dream. Nothing that large would fit in her body. She didn't care that it was a only a dream, she wanted to be fucked. Even as his cock was in her, she wanted more of him. She wanted his hands on her body. She wanted his finger rimming her ass—something no man had ever done for her, but suddenly she wanted it from him. Hell, she wanted his cock in her ass.

Maggie wanted his giant dick in her mouth, choking her with its size as she sucked him off and drank his cum. She wanted his mouth on her clit, his face smothered in her pussy as she straddled his face. She wanted him to fuck her in every position, every way. Every so-called depraved sexual act—that was what she wanted from him.

Maggie felt a prickling and knew that the watchers were back. That's what she called them in her head—the watchers. They hadn't been there at first and she always forgot about them until they were there. She felt their eyes, even as they were hidden in the mist. Her dream lover knew they were there as well. As soon as they appeared, he began to thrust, moving his large cock inside her, pounding her with it.

The sexual energy in the room intensified until the place smelled of sex. Instantly, she got the impression of males stroking their cocks as they watched her. Maggie tensed, the erotic thoughts just too much. Climaxing hard, her whole body jerked, her mouth opening with a silent cry.

That's when she remembered something else as well. The man behind her never came, never was fulfilled. It dampened the sensations of her release slightly to know he hadn't reached his peak. Then suddenly, his hands were gone and she was alone in her room. The dream was over.

Chapter 2

MAGGIE GASPED, SITTING UP IN BED. HER ROOM WAS DARK, JUST like she liked it. She'd had this strange dream so many times, only now it was more real. She touched her chest, feeling how hard her nipples were beneath her clothing. Her thighs were sticky and a light sheen of sweat glistened over her flesh.

Throwing the covers off her body, she swung her legs around. Her bare feet hit the cool, smooth floor. She started to stand.

Wait. Cold? Smooth? Her room was carpeted. Hotels were carpeted. Where was she?

Maggie screamed at the top of her lungs, drawing her knees toward her chest and hugging them tight. The room instantly lit up at the sound. Everything around her was silver metal, except for the strange, squishy mattress underneath her. It was like a gel pack of some sort. The room looked just like in the science fiction movies she saw on television. With a lump forming in her throat, she remembered the strange ship landing in front of her car.

A ship? An actual alien spaceship? Or was it just a human aircraft landing at a secret military base?

No. No. No. This isn't happening.

"Wake up," she whispered to herself. "Wake up, Maggie."

Maggie rocked on the bed. Her hair was pulled back in a messy bun. She still wore her clothes—the old gray T-shirt, her jeans. Only her sandals were missing. She did a mental examination of her body. Nope. No anal probing. That was something at least.

"Think, Maggie. Think." She bit her lip and closed her eyes, remembering. "Okay. Country road. Car dies. Strange light from above. Military man. He comes for the car. Eyes."

She remembered the most brilliant liquid silver eyes she'd ever seen. Genetic experiment? Government implants? Alien? Somehow, deep inside, she knew it was an alien.

Something deep inside her told her she was on an alien spaceship. She wasn't sure how she knew. It could've been fear wreaking havoc on her mind or it could've been intuition.

After the car, everything was a blur. Darkness. Light. Darkness. Light. She'd been carried. She felt arms on her—euphoria-inducing arms, very muscular euphoria-inducing arms. Feeling her body twitch with desire, she frowned. Great, she needed sex so bad that she was getting aroused just thinking about a kidnapping alien.

So much for the dream being fulfilling.

There was more, but she couldn't decipher between dreams and reality. For all she knew this place was a dream. Had she become so delusional that she was now living inside her mind? Maggie looked around, waiting to see if the dream lover would appear to her.

When he didn't, she tried to figure out what to do next. The thin blanket beside her was so lightweight that she wouldn't draw much comfort from hiding beneath it. Regardless, she pulled it tight to her chest, rocking slightly back and forth. She glanced around the room.

A row of metal drawers lined a wall, at least she thought they were drawers. They didn't have any handles and the surfaces were smooth. Next to the drawers was a small closet door. Maggie leaned over, trying to peek in. Maybe it wasn't a closet but a bathroom of some sort. Across from the bed, on the far side of the room, a closed door was smooth and metal like the rest of the room. A bunch of buttons and sensors were next to it, along with a black computer screen. She could only assume that was the way out. There were no windows so she couldn't look outside, but it didn't feel like the room was moving.

"If you're messing with me, Jeff, so help me I'm going to kill you," she whispered. Jefferson Clarkson III was her ex-boyfriend who had been blessed with money, influence, and a wandering penis. It would be just like him to hire someone to kidnap her. He wasn't happy that she left him.

"You're leaving *me?*" had been his exact words of disbelief. "You are seriously leaving me?"

Maggie could still see the look on his bewildered face. His constant phone calls were one of the reasons she'd been in the Ozarks in the first place. Despite herself, she chuckled weakly and said, "What a jerk wad."

Maggie looked around again, trying to take stock of her situation. She was dressed. She didn't feel violated. Her stomach growled and she frowned. She was starving. The large cappuccino and convenience store hot dog she'd had the day before just wasn't lasting.

It was just the day before right? How long had she been asleep?

"Hello?" she asked. All too vividly she again remembered the man with the liquid silver eyes. If they had merely been mirrored or gray, she would've thought he wore contacts. As it was, they moved and swirled like liquid pools of mercury. She bit her lip, feeling oddly aroused by the memory. It was almost as if she knew him, but that was impossible. He wasn't even human. There was no way Jeff hired a man to look like that. "Can anyone hear me?"

Maggie didn't receive an answer. Slowly, she forced herself to get off the bed. She really needed to use the bathroom. The cool floor made her shiver. She went to the opened door. There was no toilet, just something that looked like a shower stall.

"Hello? Somebody?" she called. "I need some help here."

The door on the far side of the room opened. Maggie gasped. It was him. It was the man who'd taken her from her car.

Except for his face, her kidnapper looked very human. She liked his darker flesh and the way his muscles bulged in all the right places. Thick black hair fell in sexy waves down his shoulders, and she seemed to recall that he'd had it pulled back the night before. In the brighter light his silver eyes didn't seem to glow so eerily, but they were still not human. The brown ridge over his brow was the same and he didn't have eyebrows. It made him look menacing, as if he was glaring at her.

Maggie forgot all about her personal discomforts as she backed up against the wall. The man was positively huge. His broad shoulders stretched the shiny black material of his clothes. Those silver eyes stared at her, making her feel both wanton and scared. He threw off an absolutely intoxicating sexual energy and power, and she couldn't help but feel its effect.

Confident. Strong. Big.

"U du tah ma de." His voice was low, rich, authoritative. The sound surrounded her.

Maggie pulled her arms around her waist, pressing into the wall. If this had been any other situation, she'd have been attracted to him. His firm mouth pulled slightly as he stared at her. He felt familiar, but that didn't make sense. How could an alien feel familiar?

It wasn't like he was her dream lover. He couldn't be. The shrink said that was all in her mind. He said sexual dreams happened to almost everyone.

"Teanastellen?"

Maggie realized he was trying to talk to her. She shook her head, having no clue what he was saying.

"Maakey?"

Maggie again shook her head. The man stepped forward, and the door automatically closed behind him. She made a weak noise and closed her eyes, willing him to go away.

"I ni bara?"

He'd come closer. Maggie opened her eyes. For all his size, his stance wasn't overly aggressive. He lifted a gentle hand to her.

"G'day?" He stepped closer and Maggie stiffened. *"Hallo? Bon die? Olá? Konnichi wa? Daw daw? Buon giorno? Salut? Buenos dias? Hello, how are you?"*

Maggie took a deep breath at the last one. He was going through different Earth languages and various greetings. She recognized a few of them.

"You understand this language?" he asked, speaking perfect English though there was a slight bristled accent to his words. It was damned sexy.

Maggie nodded.

"Ah, good." He smiled, letting the side of his lip curl up. "There are over four hundred and eighty Blue Planet languages, not too many, but I was worried I'd have to go through them all."

"You speak them all?" she asked, her voice a whisper.

"They are not so hard," he answered.

Maggie would've laughed if the situation wasn't so surreal. Not so hard? "Why am I here? What do you want?"

"To be my . . . you call it wife," the man said bluntly, as if it was the most normal thing in the world. There was definitely something rigid and militant to the way he was standing, feet braced apart, strong arms hanging stiffly at his sides. This was a warrior, to be sure. With a body like that, he had to be. "Did you not get the images projected from our computers? When you slept just now, you should have seen all this. They are to prepare you."

This strangely handsome piece of flesh was her dream man? Maggie froze. She wanted to die. This was the man she'd acted so wanton with? No, it couldn't be. This was just too humiliating. Great, now she was a cosmic slut. It wasn't fair. Dreams were in her head. Her dreams were hers and hers alone. No one was ever supposed to live them with her.

As she looked at him, Maggie vaguely began to recall him in the fog of her mind, but the memory of it was still too hazy and scattered. She'd never actually seen his face. Though, there was one hazy image that stood out—that of a strange blue and red dragon.

"I have waited a year for this." The man looked at her as if this should all mean something to her. The more she watched him in the light, she saw a subtle color shift in his gaze, a slight purpling that made it easy to see where he looked. More often than not, it was at her. "Let me explain. We are . . . you would call it military.

We are on a deep space mission. I wish to have someone in my quarters at all times. Regulation says I have to marry to do so, so I marry. I followed the signs and stopped by your Blue Planet to get you. Do not look so worried. I studied your planet scans and then the . . . you call them gods . . . sent me to you. It is . . . you call it fate."

Stunned, Maggie said a little too sarcastically, "I'd rather you just anal probed me and dropped me back off."

The ridge above his eyes shifted. He glanced down over her body with unmistakable interest. "You wish for me to . . . Already?"

Maggie paled, realizing she'd said the words out loud. "It's just a . . . *oh.*"

Okay, talking about anal probing was the last thing she wanted to do with the alien that had kidnapped her—especially when that alien was so wickedly handsome. If anyone was going to be probing her, she really hoped he'd volunteer. He seemed hesitant as he reached for her. Maggie screamed, sliding along the wall out of his reach.

"It's just a saying," she cried. "Crazy people get abducted by aliens and claim to be . . . Oh gawd, I'm insane. That's it. Jeff slipped me some bad acid or something, and now I'm in a loony bin. You're probably my doctor."

"You need medical attention?" he asked.

"I need . . ." Maggie took a deep breath. Her knees weakened. "I need a stiff drink." She looked him over. Damn, he was sexy. Was it wrong to find aliens sexy? "Make that a whole bottle and some kind of pill—lots and lots of pills."

"I will take you to the doctors. They will help you and find you the bottle you need." When he tried to touch her, she jerked away.

"Who are you?" she asked. "What are you?"

"I am Vladei," he answered. "I am a *Dragoona.*"

"Dragon," she whispered.

He nodded. "Yes, very much linked to what you knew as dragons. It has been awhile since we have visited the Blue Planet, but the dragons you now know of were our pets, I believe. You called us wizards or dragon tamers."

"I want to go home," Maggie said weakly.

Vladei reached down for her, so quick she couldn't jerk away. His hand was warm on her flesh as he pulled on her arm, forcing her to stand before him. Instantly, her body calmed. Her heart slowed and she felt no fear. His smell surrounded her, drawing her in. His scent was intoxicating, almost like a euphoric drug. Her body stirred where he touched her, as if he injected her blood with a potent ecstasy. Hot desire coursed through her, and her panties became soaked in a way that she'd only read about in erotic novels.

"You are home," he said.

Maggie moaned weakly. If the touch of his hand did this to her, what would the touch of his body be like? Just thinking about it made her nearly orgasm.

"Give me your name, temptress." His mouth drew close to hers, hovering close to her lips.

"Maggie Stewart." Maggie was too far aroused to stop and think.

"Maggie," he repeated, caressing the word with his firm mouth. Then he kissed her. She moaned. His long tongue parted her lips, slipping between her teeth. The euphoria seemed to leak out of him, surging through her from his hand and mouth. Her nipples ached, so hard they seemed to stab at her bra and T-shirt.

When he didn't move to press his delicious body to hers, she moaned louder, wondering how a stranger could turn her on so much. The pleasure was too great and she couldn't force her thoughts to dwell on the fact. If ever she needed to be slammed up against a wall and fucked, now was the time. Alien or not, she wanted this man. It had been too long since she'd been so aroused—not counting the dreams. Jeff had been an adequate lover at best. Vladei, with his thick muscles and strong body would undoubtedly be a fantastic lover. She bet he could lift her off the ground and pound into her with little effort.

She pulled her mouth away, gasping, "What are you doing to me?"

"Joining you to me." He leaned closer, trapping her to the wall with his hand. His voice was low, hoarse. "Is your body enjoying this as much as mine?"

"Ah," she breathed. Her breasts ached. She'd never been so turned on in her life.

"Try to relax. Let my pheromones work inside you. Soon you will know on instinct that which you do not know with your head." Vladei leaned closer, his mouth coming close once more. "You were chosen for me to be my wife. I went to the gods and told them I was ready and they led me to you."

Somehow, she believed his words. They just felt true. She couldn't explain it.

"This is crazy," she whispered. "I can't be your wife."

"No, you are not yet," he agreed. His voice dipped into a sultry growl. "But as soon as you tame the dragon you will be."

At his words, a surge of sexual power and excitement hit her. "Tame the dragon?"

"My cock is hard for you. Will you accept it?"

What? She gasped, climaxing so hard her back arched and she gasped for air. Maggie could speak.

"Ah," Vladei panted. He bit his lip and ripped his hand away. He grabbed his wrist, as if his hand was burnt. Maggie sank to the floor, feeling as if she'd just had a marathon with her vibrator. Her whole body was numb. Breathing heavily, he said, "I did not expect such a connection."

Maggie glanced up over his tight body. A large bulge pressed against his snug fitting pants. She was no untried virgin, but she also wasn't a porn star. The unmistakable girth of his cock, still hard and wanting, caused her to pull back ever so slightly. She could make out its rod-like shape contoured beneath the material. It was a virtual battering ram waiting to break through the barrier of tight clothing. Just like in her dreams, he hadn't gotten release from their contact. She swallowed nervously, staring at the massive weapon he wielded between his thighs. The thing was huge!

"Come." His voice was hoarse. "I will bring you to the doctors. I should not be selfish if you have need of medical attention. We can finish this bonding later."

"I might need a doctor to examine my head, Vladei," Maggie said, "but I really need a drink more."

Chapter 3

MAGGIE NUMBLY FOLLOWED VLADEI THOUGH THE HALLS. AFTER she insisted she was completely fine and didn't want to see a doctor, he agreed to give her a tour of the ship. Several hours passed in his amiable company.

Vladei was kind and acted like a gentleman for the most part, though he didn't say much. Pressing his hand to the door scanners, he let her pass through the doorways first. And when she walked, he would hold her elbow in an automatic, if not unnecessary, gesture of helping.

If not for the reminder of the weakening potency of his touch, she'd have thought the long metal corridors with their intermittent rows of lights belonged on a Hollywood movie set. It was strange but she wasn't scared, not really anymore. Instinctively, she knew she could trust him, that everything would turn out fine, even if she was still a little mentally wary.

The other Dragoonas she met were polite, if not a little distant. All of them were men—strong, large, military type men with the type of physique only reached with years of hard training.

It made sense because according to Vladei, they were military. Their tight uniforms pulled against their hard frames, outlining each fine specimen to perfection. It was hard, but she tried not to stare, not wanting to admit that the sight of so much male beauty was stirring her desire for Vladei. She might like looking at the soldiers, but she wanted to touch the man who led her through the halls. She watched the men's faces, wondering if they were the ones who'd watched her sleeping with Vladei in her dreams. If they were, they gave nothing away—no knowing looks, no small smiles.

She was still barefoot, but no one seemed to notice. It amused her to catch a few of them staring at her boobs like they'd never seen a pair before. It was obvious that when it came to breasts men were the same—no matter the species. They bowed low to her, speaking in a language she didn't really understand. Vladei informed her that not everyone on the ship spoke Blue Planet languages, but now that she was on board most of them would willingly learn hers so that they could communicate with her. According to him, it should only take a few days for that to happen.

As they walked, it was hard not to stare at Vladei's perfect body. This was all so surreal. She didn't have family back home, or even a wonderful job—she was a writer, often sending stuff to magazines and publishing houses, hoping to get a decent paying job. But staying on a spaceship with an alien husband didn't really fit into the category of acceptable life plans.

Why wasn't she freaking out right now? Glancing at Vladei's firm ass, she sighed. He'd done something to her. There was no fear, barely any worry—at least not about where she was. The more she walked around, the more ingrained ideas began to surface. Was she under a spell? Could this be real? Why did she suddenly know what to do with the little box next to a round window?

"Here, look," he said softly. She blinked at the softness of his voice, instantly following his hand. He motioned to the small, round window as he pressed the box. A veil lifted, shimmering away into nothingness so they could look outside. Maggie stepped closer to the window. Stars spread out over the sky. If she doubted any of this, the spectacular view instantly changed her mind.

"Why me?" she asked.

Valdei stopped. "Why not you?"

"What if I were married already?" she asked. "I mean, how do you know anything about me? What makes you think I'm the one?"

He actually looked like she'd slapped him. His large body tensed. "You are . . . already . . . taken?"

Maggie didn't answer.

"I did not feel this when I bonded you," Vladei continued. He looked at his hand, the one he'd touched her with. Slowly he bent his fingers, studying them intently. Maggie felt her body heating anew with the memory of his euphoric touch.

Seeing the weakness, she lied, believing it was the logical thing to do. "Well, I am married, so you should take me back."

Vladei eyed her. He lifted his chin. Very stiffly, he nodded. "I apologize. I did not mean to offend. I do not know how this happened. The signs were clear. I was called to you, but . . . I am sorry."

Maggie wondered at her disappointment. He must not want her too badly if he was willing to give her up so easily. Maybe the Dragoonas would take her home now. She could go find a hotel, get a good night's sleep, and then spend the rest of her life convinced this was a dream. Looking at Vladei, she wondered if perhaps this could be an erotic dream.

Why was she even contemplating such a thing? Glancing over his tight body, she thought, *Oh, yeah, 'cause he is built like a Greek god.*

"You will be returned, of course," Vladei said, appearing pained by the admission. "It will take five of your days to get back."

"Five days?" she repeated, shocked. "But we just left."

"You slept so that the computer could prepare you for me," he said simply. When he turned it seemed like some of the energy was taken out of his steps. A strange sorrow came over her, as if she could feel it in him. "Come. I will take you back to the room. There you will be fed and your needs attended to."

Vladei turned and led the way down the hall to her room. Pushing a button on the door, he stepped aside to let her pass.

"Where will you be?" she asked, wondering why she suddenly wanted him to share the room with her. She stepped passed him, torn between logic and the desire to invite him in.

"I will report for my punishment." Vladei nodded, ran his hand over the scanner. The door slid down between them.

"Wait. Punishment?" What did he mean by that? Maggie touched the door, wondering why it felt like her heart was being ripped out. Eyeing the sensor, she pushed at it, hoping to open the door. It wasn't like the window control Vladei had showed her and it wasn't like the door sensors she'd seen others using in the hall. She kept pushing at it, hoping to get it to do what she wanted. The lights dimmed and brightened, a tray slid out from the wall, the bed made itself, but the door didn't open. She couldn't instinctively figure it out. Slamming her palm against the metal she yelled, "Vladei, wait! Come back!"

* * *

VLADEI COULD NOT believe he could make such a mistake. He'd been so enraptured with the woman's beauty—her soft brown hair, her round hazel eyes, and her large breasts—that he hadn't felt she was taken. Naturally, he should have seen that she wasn't available and it was his fault that he'd messed up so badly.

Still when he thought of her, his cock was hard with desire. Being out in deep space with the Dragoona military made it difficult to find female companionship. Though they did dock at various humanoid ports to find sexual pleasures with whores, it wasn't often enough to suit his tastes.

Vladei was tired of being alone. He wanted a woman in his bed and in his heart. So, he'd offered his blood to the gods, prayed for a companion, and then waited for a sign. The gods sent him a vision of the Blue Planet and he knew that his wife would be there. That was a year ago. He'd studied all Dragoona military records on the Blue Planet, learning the languages.

Truthfully, it had only taken a couple months to do all that. His kind had been to the Blue Planet long ago, but there wasn't much in the military records about its modern day culture. It was said some of the humans had called them wizards and witches, accusing the Dragoona of bespelling humankind when in truth they were merely bonding with their mates. That fear was one of the reasons he'd brought Maggie to his ship and not stayed with her on her own ground. He didn't want to cause trouble with the locals and since the Blue Planet did not acknowledge alien races, he couldn't just land his ship in broad daylight. Law forbade it.

Most of the time, he lay awake in bed, fantasizing of the night when the woman would someday be his. Once married, he could take his wife with him wherever he went. Dragoona law made them the same person. They shared everything equally. Though they did different things, all consequences were shared. Her good deeds would be his, her crimes would be his crimes, and vice versa. Her life was his, his life was hers.

He'd have someone in his bed, available for all his sexual fantasies. It had been so long since he'd had sex. Sure he pleasured himself. He was Dragoona, after all. He had to. But, after pleading to the gods for a wife, he had to save himself for her. If he found release with another, the gods would forever deny his request.

Why did the gods allow him to assess her dreams if she was taken? It made no sense. He'd gone to her night after night, giving her pleasure and denying himself. He'd stretched her body to fit him. He'd done everything he was supposed to. Then, why did the gods curse him? Had he done something wrong?

It wasn't just sexual pleasure he craved. There would be more between them. He would be connected to his wife, close. Vladei desired that intimacy with her as well. He would give his life to make her happy, to give her everything she wanted and needed.

Vladei took a deep breath. He'd bonded to a taken woman and the laws were clear. He would have to be punished for it, and Maggie would be the one to do it. The loss he felt was so great it nearly stopped his heart from beating. He took a deep breath. It was time to begin the preparations.

MAGGIE WAS FED and given a change of clothes. The tight black outfit was much like Vladei's. He didn't come back to her, but sent others like promised. She was shown how to bathe in a laser shower. The food had a strange texture to it, but tasted like a mixture of oranges and chicken. The men who came to her didn't readily speak, except for the most basic of phrases.

"Hello."

"Good day."

"Nice to meet you."

They wore tight black clothes that molded to their fit bodies and they had, more or less, the same ridge along their brows and the same liquid silver-colored eyes. The only difference she saw in the outfits was in the cut of the neckline. Some were squared, some v-necked, and like Vladei's some were rounded. She wondered if this indicated rank. Vladei had said they were in deep space on a mission.

Maggie couldn't help but smile, as the men practically tripped over themselves to serve her. It was surreal, seeing a bunch of fierce dragonlike warrior men scurrying to pick up the hair tie she dropped while combing her fingers through her hair. The man who handed it up to her did so from his knees. She took it and he actually bowed to her, getting on all fours at her feet.

"Thank you," he said to her before standing.

He was thanking her for allowing him to pick up her hair tie? Maggie suppressed a wide grin. She got the feeling that these men would do anything she asked of them—even if she were to demand they strip from their clothing and stroke each other to completion for her viewing pleasure. In fact, by the way all of their pants bulged at her nearness, she was sure they'd happily comply. But, for some strange reason, even with all their heated stares, she got the impression they would never touch her—at least not without Vladei present.

Okay, being treated like a queen was tempting, especially when her subjects were such hunky specimens of male beauty. It was fun to watch them bend over and pick things up off the floor. Maggie would never admit it, but she'd dropped a few things on purpose.

There was one who especially caught her attention, though it was mostly on a sexual, primitive level. He had stunningly beautiful black hair, thin strands of silk gliding over his shoulders. She didn't ache for him as she did Vladei, but she liked looking at him, liked watching his body move.

But, for all the Dragoonas' gorgeousness, she found herself missing Vladei. He was a stranger—an extraordinary stranger at that—and yet she felt as if she knew him. Her body ached for him in a way it had never ached for anyone. Fear unfurled in her chest—not fear of the ship or the Dragoona people, but fear that she would never feel such desire again once they took her back to Earth.

Maggie lay down in the small bed. The lights turned off almost immediately. She was tired from her long day, but she couldn't fall asleep. Now that she was alone in the dark, wickedly delightful thoughts of Vladei plagued her mind. Her body ached for him.

No matter how horny she was, or how wet her pussy seemed to get with just the thought of his hand touching her, staying was not an option. She knew nothing of Vladei's world. Sure, they appeared like they would treat her nice now and they said they were taking her home—but did she really know any of that for certain? What would happen in a month? After the wedding vows were spoken? She knew nothing of their culture. Well, that wasn't true. She knew a few things—the things they had imbedded in her mind for her to know. But, what were they keeping from her?

"Do you ever know anything for sure?" she asked herself. She'd thought she'd known Jeff. Hell, she'd even put up with him when he claimed to be impotent for those many months. What she couldn't get was how exactly an impotent man could spent the entire time banging his father's secretary and everything else that walked. Now that man had issues. He'd actually told her that the things he wanted in bed were things he could not sully her with—his future bride. Yeah, like she'd ever agree to marry him with a proposal like that. Maggie snorted sarcastically. Somehow, her mouth was just too precious to wrap around Jeff's cock. He'd only ever had sex with her missionary style, and it was mediocre sex at that.

It stank, too, because all her friends were Jeff's friends. Damned, superficial bastards had taken his side. He was the one with the money, after all.

Turning on her side, she sighed. Maggie had always been kind of a loner. She didn't make friends easily and preferred to stay home instead of going out to clubs. She really was pathetic, wasn't she? She had more pleasure reading books than she got in the real world. Maybe that's why she'd become a writer. Maggie wasn't even sure she was a good writer. She wasn't famous, wasn't well known, but she did make a fairly decent living doing it. Hell, she was too timid to be a good fiction writer. Take erotica, for instance. She'd always wanted to try writing it, but had never had the nerve to put pen to paper and start a story.

Sighing, she closed her eyes. If she was going to figure anything out, she needed to get some sleep. Vladei's face came to mind, and she smiled softly. Now there was a man who'd want more than just missionary from her. She wondered if he'd come to her in her dreams. Her body stung, really hoping he would. Maggie couldn't fall asleep fast enough.

* * *

THE NEXT MORNING, or what she assumed to be the next morning, the lights turned on as she sat up in bed. She'd slept like a rock, but didn't feel rested. Vladei hadn't come for her, though she'd waited for him. Her body was taut with unfulfilled desires.

Stumbling to the bathroom and into the laser shower, Maggie instantly reached between her thighs to hopefully ease some of the pain of her arousal. The green lights ran all over her body, warming her flesh. Her finger slid along her slick pussy, tweaking the hidden pearl there. She pinched her nipples, thrust at her hand. Nothing worked. When she finally came, it was a mediocre release that left her wanting.

Pulling on the tight black clothing they'd given her, Maggie was surprised to see the dark-haired man waiting in her room when she came out. So surprised, that she stubbed her toe on the door frame. Instantly, the man set his tray down on the bed and moved to grab her foot. Maggie held onto the wall and he began to rub her toe.

Desire shot through her—a completely wicked and carnal sensation. She looked down. The man's cock was hard, thrust against this tight pants. What was wrong with her? She spent all this time dreaming of Vladei and now she was ready to beg this man to fuck her, to end the ache she felt. Maggie trembled. He looked up and his liquid silver eyes narrowed. She wondered if he knew what she was thinking. Vladei popped into her mind. She wanted him there as well. She wanted both of these men at the same time.

Wicked, wicked thoughts!

Maggie shook her head. What was wrong with her? She wasn't wanton or wicked. She was average. She didn't dream of having ménages. Then, thinking of the men who'd watched her fuck

Vladei in her dreams, she tensed. The man continued to rub her foot, working up her ankle.

"Ah, really, I'm good, thank you," Maggie said, trying to extract her foot from his very capable hands. He glanced up at her, almost looking disappointed that she pulled away from him. His touch didn't send hot waves of pleasure through her like Vladei's had, but there was a primitive sexual call to his touch.

"Thank you," he said, rising to his feet. His voice was gruff as he nodded. When he walked away, his body was stiff. The man picked the tray off the bed and hit a button on the wall. A small platform came out, and he sat the platter of food on it. Nodding his head, the man left.

Maggie sighed, wondering, if she threw her whole body on the floor, if Vladei would show up and give her a full body massage. Her body pulsed to life at the thought. Great. Just great. She was horny again. Her foot tingled as she made her way to the food.

Standing by the platform, she ate in silence. Afterward, she stuck her head in the laser shower and washed her teeth. Hearing footsteps, she sighed and again went to see who was in the room.

To her disappointment, it wasn't Vladei. The stranger nodded, took her empty tray and left. She caught her eyes drifting to his tight ass as he walked. The man gave her a slight smile as he caught her doing it. She was so aroused, that for a moment she considered pinning him to the bed and having her way with him. The man nodded once as the door closed between them.

What was happening to her? It was like she was suddenly insatiable.

Soon, another man came. He handed her a silver dish with what looked like a small pebble on it. Maggie frowned at it, rolling it between her fingers. Seeing her confusion, he motioned for her to put it back on the tray. She did and he slid it into the sensor panel by the door without touching it and left.

"Okay," Maggie drawled to herself. "That was just weird."

The day passed with more visitors, all of them polite, but none of them were Vladei. They brought her food, more clothes, showed her how to open the drawers. One took her around the ship. His English was broken, but she was able to understand a lot of what he said. He pointed out parts of the ship—the cockpit, mess hall, control rooms. When she asked about Vladei the man paled and said nothing, shaking his head in denial.

Oddly, she became more comfortable with being on the ship. A few times, staring out the round portholes at space, her stomach would lurch and she'd feel a little sick—worried about the atmosphere breaching the hull. The fear was unfounded and basically the influence of too many Hollywood movies.

Later that evening, she was dropped off at her room. She sighed, worried about Vladei. He'd mentioned punishment, and she wondered if something bad had happened to him. Going to bed, she again dreamed of waiting for him, her body longing for him, wanting him, desiring him.

The next morning, the process started all over again. Still, no Vladei and everyone refused to speak of it to her. By the third night, she couldn't eat. There was no denying it. She missed him.

Chapter 4

D AY FOUR ON THE SHIP, SHE GOT UP, READY FOR MUCH OF THE same. Someone brought her food and she ate. She took a laser shower and put on the tight black uniform. Hearing the door, she sighed, pretty sure it was the man who came to take the tray away. She came out of the bathroom and froze.

Vladei stood before her. His face was pale, drawn. His hair was pulled back to the nape of his neck. "You are ready?"

"Ready?" she asked, thinking he meant to go back to Earth. Her mind screamed, *No!* How could she go back? Her body was aching for sex, for sex with this handsome alien before her. "Yes, I think so."

"Very well."

Before Maggie could ask for clarification, Vladei turned and ran his hand over the door. It soundlessly slid up. Three Dragoonas stood on the other side. She shivered to see the black-haired man was amongst them. She'd fantasized about him in bed with her and Vladei. In fact, her mind had wandered to such things often. What else was she supposed to do with so much time on her hands and only hot, built men roaming around to serve her? Her body was so tight with longing that not a minute passed when she wasn't thinking of ways to ease the aching in her thighs. Being fucked by several men at once was only one of those many ways.

One man pushed in a cart, distracting her attention. On top of it was a long black whip, a thin knife, and a long rope. She instantly pulled back, wondering what they were going to do to her. Her eyes flew to Vladei. He wouldn't look at her.

"Choose one," the man who pushed the cart ordered. The two others, both with rounded necklines stood behind Vladei.

Maggie lightly touched a whip and drew her hand back. "For what?"

The man picked up the whip and lifted it to her. Maggie cringed.

"Take it," Vladei said, his jaw clenched.

Maggie obeyed, compelled to listen to him. She gripped the leather in her trembling hands. At least they gave her the weapon, instead of taking it for themselves.

Vladei nodded. The man with the cart left the room, taking the rest of his torture devices with him. Maggie gripped the whip, sighing with relief to have them gone.

Vladei lifted up his arms, and the two men stripped him of his shirt. Maggie gasped. Dark flesh covered his chest, every inch of it hard, perfect muscle. The harder texture of his two small nipples matched the ridged flesh of his forehead. Glancing down over his stomach, she saw two small blue points coming up from his pants. It looked like a tattoo of sorts on both hips. When he turned, his back facing her, she saw a small ridge running down the back of his neck, stopping between his shoulder blades. Other than that, he looked completely human.

"For bonding a taken woman," the black-haired man announced. Two shackles came down from the ceiling as he pushed a button. "You will be whipped one hundred times. Each lash to draw blood."

Valdei didn't move as the two men handcuffed his wrists. In fact, he all but helped them. The man with lighter coloring pushed a button, and the shackles drew his arms up.

Muscles rippled beneath Vladei's flesh. His head fell forward and he braced his feet. The two men stepped back, looking expectantly at her.

Maggie watched them as if they put on a strange play. When they motioned for her to come forward to Vladei, she realized they meant for her to whip him.

"Uh," Maggie said, shaking her head in instant denial. "I can't . . . You can't possibly think that I would . . . No."

Vladei glanced over his shoulder at her before turning around to face her. His hands were still trapped over his head. Damn, but he was gorgeous like that. Why in the world had she said she was married? Could she take it back and end this? What would happen? Would she get in trouble for lying to them? Would they still return her to Earth? Did she really want to go home to Earth? Did it matter what happened to her when they were about to whip Vladei for her lie?

She knew she was being selfish, worrying about herself when Vladei needed her to speak up. Fear made her tremble as she looked at him. Part of her really wanted to stay on the ship, to live the exciting life traveling the stars would bring. A bigger part of her wanted to stay as Vladei's wife, to take the leap of faith and trust in his gods that she would not regret it.

"You must," Vladei said. "I have wronged you, disrespected you. It is our law that I be punished for it."

"I can't whip you," Maggie said, dropping the weapon on the ground. She refused to hold it. "I just can't."

His jaw tightened. "If you refuse, I die."

Maggie didn't move. What did she do? She couldn't beat him. She couldn't hurt him like that.

You have to tell the truth. You have to tell them you're not married. You have to tell them that Vladei didn't dishonor you, that you were just a scaredy cat.

Maggie frowned. Dare she risk it? What would happen if she did? Each day the burden of her lie had welled within her until she almost told the truth. But she hadn't dared. She'd been too scared. Somehow, in her heart, she'd felt Vladei's sadness and knew he was technically all right. Just as now, she felt that he told the truth. If she didn't whip him, he'd be killed for this supposed insult. He'd be unjustly punished.

"I am sorry. I didn't know I offended you so deeply," Vladei said when she didn't speak, didn't move to pick up the whip. The two men beside him looked shocked.

"He did not claim your body," the lighter man said. "You wish death for—"

The black-haired man next to him shook his head, silently telling the other one not to interfere.

"I have no fear of death," Vladei said bravely. He lifted his chin, glaring at her. "If it is your will and the will of the gods, I am ready."

"Okay," Maggie interrupted. She lifted her hand and shook her head. Closing her eyes, she asked, "Don't you think this is all going a little too far?"

When she peeked at them, the three men's looks said otherwise.

"I'm not whipping him for touching my arm and he shouldn't be killed for it either," Maggie said.

"But, the bonding . . . ?" the dark man asked. His firm lips pressed tightly together. "He had disrespected you, a woman, giver of life."

Maggie bit her lip. This was insanity. What was she doing? Weakly, she closed her eyes and said, "He didn't disrespect me. I'm not married. I'm not bonded elsewhere. I lied."

The men gasped at her confession.

"What?" Vladei demanded. "What did you just say?"

"I said I'm not married," Maggie repeated, louder. She pulled her arms protectively around her chest. "I lied to you so you would take me home. I didn't know you'd be whipped and killed for it. I just wanted to go home."

Vladei's body stiffened. The men looked horrified. His voice rose, as he said, "You were given the dreams and surely feel it as I do and yet you lie to me? Why? I feel the connection between us. I was sure of it before I brought you here and yet you——"

"Hey, buddy, back off!" Maggie answered. Vladei's nostrils flared. Before he could yell at her, she said, "This isn't exactly easy for me. Where I come from a man asks you out on a date and, if things go well, maybe you talk marriage after a year or so. You can't expect me to discover there are aliens flying around outer space, that you have some gods who tell you who to marry, and then just accept that I'm that someone, no questions asked, all in one day. What did you expect me to say?"

"The dreams should have come to you. If it is true that you are not taken elsewhere, then you must feel me as I feel you. We bonded," Vladei insisted. His eyes narrowed, and she saw the passion he had for her. She felt it as if it was her own. Still, she was scared.

"Where I come from, dreams are just random thoughts that you have when you're asleep. They don't mean a thing!" Maggie wanted to make him understand, but she also wanted to convince herself of it. Things like this just didn't happen. Logical, sane people were not abducted by handsome aliens and they certainly didn't fall in love with those handsome aliens. It just didn't happen!

"Why are you being so stubborn?" he yelled, straining against his ties.

Me? Stubborn?

"Why are you being so unreasonable?" she countered, her voice just as harsh as his. Maggie was glad his friends didn't release him. She wasn't sure she could handle him if he were free.

The two men glanced at each other. The lighter one nodded and left the room. The dark-haired one said, "We will leave you two to settle this."

He too walked from the room, leaving Vladei tied up. The door slid shut, leaving them alone. Vladei yelled after them in the rough, throaty language she'd heard them use with each other and kicked toward the door. His body swung back and forth a few times before he stood once more.

"You know what?" Maggie growled. She reached down and grabbed the whip. "I may just whip you for this whole mess. What kind of barbaric race flies down to a planet, clubs the woman over the head, and then tells her they're getting married? Hell, when's the last time you visited us? While there were cavemen running around and clubbing was considered romantic?"

Vladei looked mortified. "I did not club you. It is against the law to hurt women—especially those we are to make Dragoona women. The men on this ship are here to serve you and will do so gladly in hopes of a reward. You are special."

"Gee, thanks," she drawled sarcastically, even as she felt some small measure of delight at his words. No one had ever called her special before, not like that, not so passionately. Even so, it was all too much. How could she be expected to absorb it all and not make a mistake along the way? No one was perfect.

"You are welcome," he said, nodding.

Maggie chuckled. These people really had no concept of sarcasm. She tossed the whip aside. She didn't know how to wield it correctly anyway, not even in play. His eyes followed it. Was that disappointment on his face?

"And I swear I never clubbed you. You blacked out and I carried you."

Maggie didn't answer. Her eyes were caught by the way his chest lifted with each breath. Damn, but the man was full of muscles. Why was she protesting being married to him again? As a physical specimen, she could definitely do worse. Her thighs tightened. She was so wet she could barely breathe without feeling the twinges of her desire.

"How could you lie about this?" Vladei asked, his voice rising passionately. "I have spent every second since we were last together repenting for what I had done to you."

"You did?" Maggie couldn't help it. He looked so darned vulnerable. Judging by his body and the way others looked at him with respect, he was all warrior and here he was hanging before her all cute and defenseless. It was just too sexy to resist. Her body quivered with longing for him.

His eyes narrowed and she knew she'd somehow questioned his manhood by asking. "Yes."

"What did you have to do?" She stepped closer. He smelled good, looked even better.

"I pledged to the gods to not pleasure myself for a week," he said. His face was so serious, it took all her willpower not to laugh. No masturbating for a week? That was such a man thing to pick as a punishment. "And I paid a blood offering."

Maggie tensed. Okay, that one wasn't so funny. "You killed something?"

His mouth quirked. "I offered my blood."

"Oh, well, that's different." Maggie looked over his chest and arms, not seeing any wounds.

Seeming to understand her curiosity, he said, "Inner thigh."

Her eyes moved down to his tight pants. They hugged his sculpted waist. She licked her lips. The tight bulge was there again, straining against the black material. "Can I see?"

"You are not my wife," he countered. The expression on his face said he was teasing.

"I'm not?" Maggie asked, surprised. "But, you said . . ."

"No, we have not consummated the bonding."

Maggie shivered all over. This was crazy. Suddenly, she didn't care how insane the situation was. This is what she wanted.

"If you choose to be my wife, you may do as you wish to me," Vladei said. There was a challenge in his eyes. "Otherwise, it is best if we do not consummate the bond and if you do not tame the dragon."

"Tame the dragon?" Maggie asked. He'd said that once before.

"It is how it translates," he answered.

"How do you tame it?"

"Are you saying you will stay as my wife?" he asked.

"No."

"Then you do not need to know," he answered. Leaning back his head, he closed his eyes. "Will you let me down now? If I am not to be punished, I have duties I must attend to."

When Maggie didn't move to try and get him down, Vladei turned to watch her carefully. He couldn't believe she lied to him about something as important as being married. He could care less about the blood offering or swearing off self pleasure, but the torture he'd felt inside his chest had been horrific. For whatever reason, the gods had chosen to test him with this. Though, now that he knew the truth, he wouldn't be letting her go back to the Blue Planet. He only hoped his men had heard his order to turn back around as they left him alone in his room with the temptress.

He couldn't stay mad at her though, not when her features softened and she looked at him like that. Maggie was ravishing in the tight black uniform of the crew. It hugged to her lush curves like a second skin. Seeing that she wasn't about to unshackle him, he proudly lifted his chin.

"So, you think no self pleasuring for a week is sufficient enough punishment for kidnapping me?" she asked, returning his challenging look with one of her own.

Oh, this one was stubborn. She lit a fire in his blood. He liked that.

"Yes, longer than sufficient." Vladei stiffened. His voice a little hard, he asked, "Why? How long can you go without pleasure?"

Her eyes widened as she got his meaning. Shrugging, she said, "Months. Years."

It was his turn to be shocked. In fact, he was a little horrified that she might wish to spend their marriage taking such long breaks in between lovemaking. Most Dragoonas found release *at least* three times a day. He looked her over. It would be the ultimate torture to have to see her lush curves for months on end and not touch her. The temptation alone was likely to drive him mad. However would he survive it? Perhaps once they bonded his pheromones would increase her sex drive to match his. He swallowed nervously. He could only hope it would. "How is this possible? You must have much self control."

She didn't answer.

"Will you stay here?" he asked, not comforted by her silence. "As my wife?"

Maggie still didn't answer. She just stared at him with her wide eyes, letting them roam over his body, taking in his stiff erection beneath his pants. She licked her lips and he felt his body lurch.

"Vladei, I can't stay here," she said shaking her head. "It's just not logical."

"Logical? What does logic have to go with what is meant to be?"

"Everything."

"Give me five good reasons why you cannot stay."

"Five? Okay," Maggie bit her lip. "I'm human. I don't belong here. I'm human. This is crazy. I'm human."

This was too easy.

"I am Dragoona and my kind is highly compatible to humans, not only in the ways of the flesh, but in our life spans and breeding cycles. In fact, some of my ancestors were human from your Middle Ages. There is no reason for this to be a problem between us. You are fated to be my wife. You belong with me as my wife because the gods have willed it. And, nothing willed by the gods is deemed crazy." Vladei grinned, as his answer took care of all her reservations about being his wife.

"You think to have an answer for everything, don't you?" she grumbled, but he could see the smile she was trying to hide from him.

"Yes," he said, winking audaciously at her. "Any other questions?"

The cream between her thighs stirred when she moved. He caught a whiff of it and nearly broke the metal shackles on his wrists. He forced calmness into his blood. There would be time for that—very soon. He'd let her get comfortable first. It was only fair he answered her questions.

"There is something," she said, cautiously, still unsure about so many of their customs and ways. "One of the men gave me a little pebble and then stuck it in the door. What in the world was that all about?"

Maggie looked so confused that he couldn't help but chuckle. "The ship's computer logs your DNA and other bodily readings—like temperature and biological makeup. You touched it and when you put it in the computer, it read you and logged you into the system. Do not worry, it is harmless. It is so you can be found if you get lost or if you were hurt, the computer would know by your biological levels. We are all logged in such a way."

"All right, then." She nodded slowly. Pursing her lips in a way that drove him mad with lust, she asked, "What is taming the dragon? Are you the dragon? Is it a sexual thing? Do I actually have to fight some beast? You said dragons are pets, so I have to tame a pet for you? What's the deal?"

"It is a pet of sorts, yes," he answered, trying not to laugh. Vladei could tell she was curious beyond measure. "It is up to you to tame it after we bond completely. It is a test of strength and endurance and greatly reflects the honor of our marriage."

"So if I don't then . . . ?"

"We are still married, just cursed with bad luck and hard years."

"Ah." Maggie nodded. Every depiction of a dragon Maggie had ever seen came to mind—fierce talons, sharp teeth, reptilian skin. No, thank you. Somehow she doubted the moves she learned in self-defense class would work against a beast. The thing would probably eat her before she could even get close enough to see if it had balls to kick. If she were to marry Vladei, she'd have to take the bad years. That was something else to consider, wasn't it?

"Tell me, temptress, if you are not going to release me from my ties, what are you going to do with me?" he asked with a twinkle in his eyes.

Temptress? That one word gave her such pleasure. Without thinking, she said, "I'm going to torture you until you explain this dragon thing to me. And then I'm going to demand you take me home to Earth—the Blue Planet."

He grinned. "Demand?"

The word was a challenge, just like everything else about him.

What was she doing? Maggie couldn't believe herself, even as she walked up to him. Somehow, having the big, strong man tied up made her feel brave. She could touch him and if she wanted to stop, he couldn't do a thing about it. Wondering if touching him would bring the same sensations she'd felt from his hand, she reached for his chest. He stiffened as she ran her hands over his muscles.

"Tell me more about this marriage thing."

His held tilted back and his breathing deepened. "What do you want to know?"

"What will be expected of me?"

Vladei frowned. "Expected? I will not force you into my bed if that is what you ask. Though I do hope you will not wish to wait months and years. My body needs to be released often."

Maggie laughed. "I meant marriage-wise, everyday life. What will be expected of me then? Would I have a job? Would I be a housewife? Do I have to pick up after you and cook for you? Do we have servants? Where will we live? Now that you mention it, do I have a say when we have sex or just whenever you feel like it? What—"

"Oh." He interrupted, grinning. Tilting his head to the side, he shrugged. "You can do whatever you wish. Sex will be of mutual consent, though I may try to seduce you often. Actually, I know I will." He gave her a wickedly delicious look, as he meaningfully looked her over. "Oh, and the crew will gladly serve you as they do me."

Sex will be mutually consented to, though I may try to seduce you often. Actually, I know I will. It took all her willpower not to moan at that one.

"When you say serve, do you mean . . ." Maggie couldn't say the words. She was just asking hypothetical questions, wasn't she? And he was talking in absolutes.

I may try to seduce you often.

"What do you ask?" His eyes narrowed, but there was a spar-kling to their liquid silver depths. He was a clever one. That much was clear.

Maggie swallowed nervously. "You . . . ah . . . sleep with the other members of your crew when there are no women around?"

Okay, it had to be wrong that the idea of him being touched by other men was very alluring. What was wrong with her? It wasn't like she wanted to share what was hers. Wait. Was he hers? Maggie was so confused.

"No," he stated. The word brought her back to reality.

"Oh," Maggie blushed, a little disappointed that she wouldn't get her male-male-Maggie fantasy after all.

"What? Did I say something?"

"No, no, I was just thinking." Without knowing why, she ad-mitted, "It's just that you said 'serve' and I thought that maybe you meant, you know, *serve.*"

"We do not touch each other without a woman present, but the men do like to watch the claiming between husband and wife. If you choose to reward them, you may invite some of the others into our room and allow them to find pleasure in watching. And, should you wish it, you may allow them to touch us—but it will always be as you wish, despite what I want. That is the law."

"You'd want . . ." Maggie couldn't finish the question, so instead asked, "The single men don't mind? No one gets jealous over such an arrangement? Not even the husband?"

On Earth there was no way a relationship like that would work—at least not that she'd ever heard of. Sure, in erotic novels it was great, but in "real life" it seemed egos would get in the way. Someone would always get jealous and insecure.

"I do not see why it would be a problem," Vladei said. "Bonded women release pheromones that are quite enjoyable to the single Dragoona male. And the pheromones from them can often enhance the married couple's sexual pleasure. Why would it be a problem if everyone is enjoying themselves? The men would consider it an honor to help you find release."

Maggie's mouth was dry, as she continued to just stand near him without touching. So the watchers in her dream were real. Vladei said it so casually, as if it was no big deal. In fact, by the look on his face, she got the impression he wanted her to "reward" some of the crew in such a way. It was clear these were very sexual creatures. But, could she be like that? Could she release her inhibitions and just go for what she wanted? "You would let another man touch me?"

"Touch? Yes. Put his cock in your pussy? No. Should we decide to bring another man or men into our marriage bed, their cocks will never enter your cunt. That is mine and mine alone. I will honor all other wishes you ask of me, but not that. There are some things that even I will not share. Your pussy is one of them." His hot gaze moved down to stare at her thighs. Cream already gathered there. His nostrils flared slightly, and she knew he smelled her desire for him. A slight grin curled the side of his mouth. "And, truthfully, I would enjoy watching other men touch you. If you are my wife and belong to me, there is no reason for me to be jealous."

"What of other women?" Maggie asked, her throat dry. Knowing it might be somewhat a double standard, a ménage à trois with another female didn't interest her. The idea of Vladei touching another woman made a wave of jealous anger rise in her chest.

"No," Vladei shook his head, not even stopping to consider the idea. "Another woman to pleasure would take away the focus of the first woman. We have found these relationships don't work as well for the women, as it puts the focus on the man. Only rarely do such things occur, but it is not normal for us. I myself do not wish it."

"Doesn't all this make it awkward among the crew?"

"My crew knows their place. They would never dare to make you feel uncomfortable, or else they'd be stripped of their position."

"Your crew?" she asked in surprise.

"Yes." He nodded. "You did not know this? I am . . . you would call it Captain? Admiral? President? Leader? I am not sure which one. This is my ship to command."

"You're the what?" she asked, her eyes wide.

He smiled. "It pleases me to know that you did not know. It removes any concerns I might have had that you would accept me only because of my position of power. I would like greatly to allow the others to gain pleasure as they watch us."

"And you're sure you wouldn't be jealous?" Maggie asked.

"Why would I be? If you are my wife, you would belong to me. They would only be here to add to our pleasure. Besides, I feel bad for the others. Until the gods are ready to give them women of their own, they will not have a steady presence in their bed."

Maggie nodded. Crazy as it sounded, she was drawn to the world he painted for her. She wanted it. And she especially wanted him.

Watching his eyes, she touched his nipples. They were hard, slightly bumpy to the touch. Curious, she ran her hands up to his shoulders, wrapping her fingers around to the back of his neck. Pulling his hair free, she felt the silky texture of it. His body jerked violently and he actually growled when she touched the ridge she found there. When he again looked down, his eyes swirled with glints of purple and blue. His chest heaved with ragged breaths.

"Like that, do you?" she asked, smirking. He didn't answer with words, but the intense look on his face was response enough. She felt her blood stir, pumping fiercely through her veins. Her hands seemed to have minds of their own as they continued to touch him. Walking around him, she explored his naked back and chest. Unable to help herself, she touched the neck ridge again. He jerked so hard his stomach contracted and his feet came off the floor.

She walked back around to his front, shivering when she saw the wild, untamed look on his face. She pushed his dark hair back, rubbing the ridge on his forehead. He moaned, softly.

Maggie glanced down. Seeing the blue tips on his hips, she bit her lip. Her voice husky, she said, "Tell me about consummation. Anything special or we just . . . consummate? I mean, if we do other things, does that count as consummation?"

"You must drink from me," he groaned, his eye closed tight, "and me from you. Once we share essences, it will be done."

Finding hooks along his hip, she slowly parted them, loosening his pants. She touched a blue point. "Is this a tattoo?"

He cleared his throat. "Yes. A marking of my . . . ah . . . rank. It's a tradition of sorts."

Was he blushing? She couldn't resist. Pulling his pants down over his hips, she freed his cock. It bobbed obscenely before her, tempting her, leaving her fighting the urge to demand he take her. He wore no underwear so it was easy to slip his pants down. Grunting slightly as she passed over a thin scar on his upper thigh, his body tensed. Before she knew it, her tongue had darted out and over the scar. His skin tasted divine.

He jerked, almost pulling free of her grasp. Maggie held tight to him, licking him once more. She wanted this too much.

Maggie pulled back and gasped. He was shaved clean, or maybe had no hair to begin with as his chest was also smooth. She was too stunned to see the place where he'd cut himself as a punishment. It didn't look too bad anyway.

Just like she suspected from her dreams, he was largely endowed. But that wasn't what startled her. It was the flesh of his cock. It was completely tattooed like a winged dragon. The blue tips on his hips were the wings and the mushroomed cock head was the dragon's head. It poked out at her like a serpent. Blues and reds created intricate scales from the tip of his shaft down over the balls. A tail wrapped around his upper thigh. The detail involved was amazing.

"It's a dragon," she said for lack of better words. Then it hit her. Wryly, she asked, "Taming the dragon?"

"It likes you," he smirked, grinning widely. "And it really is a man's favorite pet."

Men, she thought, resisting the urge to roll her eyes. Though to be fair, his was a dragon. Her dragon.

"Are you telling me you don't have real dragons?"

"No, we have those as well, but this is the dragon that must be tamed. Believe me, its appetite for you is fierce."

"Hmm." Maggie ignored his joke, reaching forward to touch his cock. It was the strangest thing she'd ever seen and yet it was highly erotic. She petted the dragon's head as if it were real. Running her fingers down the base of his shaft, she smiled. Being an alien's wife really might not be so bad after all.

Vladei groaned, giving a pained chuckle. "That feels nice. Hurry and ask your questions while I can still use my head. If you keep that up, I'll be in no condition to answer you."

Chapter 5

MAGGIE STARED AT VLADEI'S BODY AS HE JERKED. HE USED HIS strong muscles to pull off his shoes before kicking off the pants she'd left around his ankles. When he was done, he was naked before her. It was time to make a decision. She knew what her body wanted, but did she follow instinct and take a leap of faith, or did she play it safe and use logic. She knew the answer, even as logic fought it.

"Did it hurt to get done?" she asked, eyeing the tattoo. It was so detailed, so perfect, so a part of him, just like she wanted to be.

"Not as much as it hurts right now," he grunted, giving her another adorably pained smile. "I've gone many days without release and you are testing my control."

His cock was in her hand, so hard and ready for her, and her body was wet and ready for him. Vladei made small sounds of pleasure as she stroked him. Maggie became mindless in the euphoria of his nearness. His body called to hers and her hands willingly answered that call. Soon her lips followed and she was kissing and licking at his chest.

He tasted good, salty, sweet. Oh, and his smell—potent, raw, male. There was something primal to the way his body moved and tensed against her fingers and mouth. Before she realized it, she was biting at his flesh. He groaned, speaking to her in his rough language. The more she bit, the louder he cried out. She kissed a hard nipple, soon discovering that his darker flesh was the most sensitive. Sucking at his chest, she felt his muscles contract beneath her lips.

Then to her amazement, she felt his body shift as he lifted up. She pulled back, watching his arms come down from above. The chains moved, his wrists pulling at the shackles as he lifted himself up off the floor. The muscles of his arms bulged all the way up his neck and chest.

He glanced down his suspended body and grinned. Maggie panted in amazement. Seeing such a feat of strength was a definite turn-on. Slowly, she came to him, kissing at his stomach, running her hands over his chest. Vladei held the position and she knew that he wanted her to take his cock into her mouth. She kissed the tip, rolling her tongue over the dragon's head. He jerked. His legs wrapped around her, and she gasped in surprise as he thrust himself deep into her mouth.

She pulled back. He let her go. Maggie stumbled away from him. Panting, she said, "That position can't be comfortable. Maybe we should let you down."

Vladei slowly lowered his body in another great show of strength. Then, hopping lightly, he pulled his body into a flip, kicked at the sensor panel on his way around. The shackles were released, and he landed neatly on his feet. Rising up, he said, "I don't mind a little pain, but it will be as you wish. I want nothing more than to have you pleased with me."

She realized he could've done that at any time. Now that he was free, his head lowered, his eyes stalking. Maggie trembled before his predatory grace. His large body loomed closer.

"How do you want me?" Vladei came closer, breathing hard. He looked like a reined beast, fighting for control. When she didn't answer, he backed her up against the bed and urged, "Kneel before me so that you may drink my essence and we may finish the bond."

Drink his essence? Maggie trembled. If his cum tasted anything like his addictive flesh, she would gladly do so. She began to go toward the bed.

"Ah, but first . . ." He glanced at her and, with a mighty rip, tore her shirt apart. She gasped as he freed her breasts. Rubbing them in his euphoria-inducing hands, he sent hot waves through her body. His very touch left her bending to his will, not that she wouldn't have anyway. "Ah, beautiful. Later you will press them around my cock and let me enjoy their softness. I will take pleasure in fucking them."

No man had ever said such bold things to her. It wasn't a request. Vladei just assumed she'd be willing, as if such a thing were an everyday occurrence. These men were defiantly not like human males when it came to lovemaking. Just as they didn't understand sarcasm, they obviously didn't get embarrassed by sexual acts. His bold confidence excited her.

Suddenly, she understood the life he was offering her. She'd be pleasured and waited on by handsome men, without the jealousy of an insecure husband. In fact, her husband would enjoy watching her get pleasure from others, so long as she saved her heart and pussy for him.

Vladei proceeded to strip her of her pants. When she was naked, he urged her down on the bed. She kneeled before him, kissing a trail down his magnificent body. This was what she wanted. He was what she wanted. She felt it in her soul. He encouraged her mouth down so she could suck him. Maggie tried to tease him by lightly licking at the shaft. He groaned, obviously past the point of being teased as he maneuvered his cock into her mouth. She kept her eyes open, watching the erotic tattoo jutting out from his lean hips, as she worked her mouth over him, taking this thick length to the back of her throat only to pull away and do it again. Reaching down, she grabbed his balls, rolling them in her palm.

Maggie didn't mind oral sex but this time was slightly different. His scent, his salty sweet taste, it all took over, causing her to moan and suck wildly. She couldn't get enough. It's like when his hands touched her. His cock, his whole body, seemed to emit pheromones that just drove her body mad with lust. Her breasts tingled. Her pussy ached. She squeezed his balls tight, willing him to come.

Vladei tensed. The sweet essence of him flooded her mouth and she drank eagerly. His primal, warrior growl filled the room. Maggie pulled back, licking her lips, feeling as if she'd just conquered a wild beast. To her surprise, she found his cock was just as hard as before and looked just as eager.

Vladei lowered his chin. His silver eyes swirled with blue and purple streaks. He tossed her back on the bed, instantly crawling over her. "My turn."

His mouth moved over her breasts, sucking and biting her nipples until she was writhing beneath him. Maggie spread her legs, her pussy wet and needy, so ready to be dominated by the fierce dragon he wielded between his thighs. His essence did something to her, taking away any inhibitions. His large size didn't frighten her. She wanted it, wanted him to fuck her good and long.

His cock brushed her thigh and she was so sure he was going to give her body what it wanted. Instead, he moved down her stomach, rimming her navel before dipping between her legs. Vladei bit the flesh of her inner thigh, nibbling his way to the small thatch of curls guarding her pussy. She looked down and he flicked his tongue toward her. She hadn't realized just how long it was.

Gasping, she tensed as he delved down. His long tongue stroked her, working up inside her body only to pull out and twirl around her clit. She leaned up, watching his head between her legs. Damn, the man was gorgeous. He forced her legs further apart. Maggie thrust wildly against him, feeling as if he were her only anchor in the whole universe. Mindless with passion, she heard her own voice pleading with him for more, to never stop. It was too much, felt too good. She squirmed, clamping her legs down tight against his head. He growled, vibrating her with the husky tone of his voice. The tension built, and she came with a jolt. He groaned, noisily lapping up her cream.

Vladei arched back when the tremors subsided, throwing his head back in ecstasy. His voice hoarse, he said, "I feel you in me. We are joined. You are my wife."

She watched him stroke the dragon between his thighs, understanding what he meant. They were joined. Somehow, their bodies had become one. She felt his desire, his every motion—in the way his eyes took her in, the way his mouth curled at the side in contentment. The look on his face was more intimate than sex could ever be. Watching his large fist swallowing the tip of his thick cock, she grinned. Sex definitely had some advantages though.

"Now you must tame the dragon," he said.

Maggie pushed up, not the least embarrassed by her nakedness because she could tell by the heated look in his eyes how it made him feel to look at her. She pushed him on his back, slinking her body along his, caressing him with her whole body as he kissed her mouth. His long tongue teased her lips until she sucked it deep within her mouth.

Pulling back, she asked, "How does the dragon want to be tamed?"

Vladei sat up, pulling her onto his lap so she straddled his thighs. His large cock brushed her slit and she cried out. She'd just come, but her need was more urgent than before.

"This is crazy," she cried, moaning as she lifted up.

Vladei grabbed her hips, keeping her from thrusting down on him. He teased her with his cock, driving her mad with lust. "No, this is fate."

Maggie couldn't take it. Why was he hesitating? Why was he teasing her? She needed him in her. Why wasn't he fucking her?

Vladei growled as if hearing her frantic thoughts. He pulled her down on him. He filled her up, stretching her body wide. She gasped, the sensation more vivid than anything she'd ever experienced.

Is that why he'd hesitated? Is that why he'd been teasing her to the point cream was running down her thighs? Were all these nights of dreaming just to prepare her to fit him, really fit him? Had he been slowly stretching her pussy for him?

Maggie pressed her hands into his chest, working in shallow thrusts as she adjusted to his size. When her body began to loosen, she leaned back. Seeing them join was erotic enough, but the peeks she got of the tattoo only enhanced her visual pleasure. His cock was so deep, sliding in her cream. His hands touched everywhere he could reach, gripping her hips to thrust harder as the tension began to build. Soon he was tense, releasing himself inside her as she hit her zenith. Her whole body strained, until she felt as if her soul was merging to Vladei's. In that perfect moment, they became as one.

Breathing hard, she fell back. Vladei pulled out. She gasped as he again stroked himself. He was still hard.

"How . . . ?" she asked, swallowing nervously. That was twice now that he'd come, and he was still ready for more.

"The dragon wants more," he told her. Maggie shivered. "Turn over."

Maggie bit her lip. Vladei got up from the bed. Going to the wall, he ran his finger over the corner. A secret panel flipped out. She gasped. Bondage toys, masks, feathers, silks, liquids, whips—every sex toy she'd ever imagined and some she hadn't was in the secret cabinet. He grabbed one of the bottles of liquid, slathering it over his cock.

"Hands and knees," he ordered. The commanding, confident tone excited her. "I will try your lush ass now."

Maggie obeyed, tensing as he came behind her. She flipped her hair over her shoulder, leaning back to caress him. He forced her back down with a hand to her back. There was no hesitance in him as he slathered a generous amount of the cool liquid between her cheeks. It tingled and she jerked as he slipped a finger into her.

"Tight," he groaned, approval thick in his voice.

Urgently, he removed his hand. She felt his cock slip back and forth over her rosette before pushing forward. He was gentle with her, taking it slowly. She'd never felt as cherished as she did with Vladei. His emotion poured over her, his pleasure and desire for her. He hadn't stretched her here, but the euphoria she felt took her discomfort away.

Soon, she was bucking against him. The vision of his dragon cock being swallowed by her ass was in her head. Another orgasm tore through her, her muscles contracting and urging him to release his seed. As she fell forward, spent, she was sure he would be done. One glance over her shoulder told her otherwise. He was still hard.

Maggie moaned. Vladei gave her a sheepish grin. His body moved with more energy than should've been possible. It was like he was feeding off the sexual energy in the room.

"Come, we shower," he said, lifting her up. Maggie moaned again as he carried her to the laser shower. The green lights turned on, cleaning the sheen of sweat from their skin. Vladei kissed her, taking it slower as he built her passions to boiling once more.

By the time he lifted her up against the stall wall, she was as eager as he, though her limbs were numb from the previous pleasure. This time, he made love to her slow, taking it easy. His silver eyes stared into hers and Maggie knew she would never be more complete than she was at this moment. It defied all logic, made no earthly sense, but this wasn't Earth and her heart wanted what her heart wanted.

Tremors hit her, racking her to the core with pleasure. His release joined hers. She knew for sure that she wouldn't be able to take any more. Her body was drained.

Chapter 6

I WISH FOR YOU TO LET ME CALL WITNESSES SO OTHERS MAY partake of our pleasure."

Maggie froze on her way to the bed. He'd just come four times and he wasn't finished with her. She glanced down at his still erect cock, having hoped he'd give her a small break.

Then his words hit her. He wanted to call in some of the men. She shivered. A very wicked part of her wanted him to do just that.

"Their energy will replenish you," he assured her, his tone low, his eyes glittering. "You will then be able to keep going. And, when the time comes, that energy will help us to conceive a child."

Maggie felt herself nodding at him, despite her sudden wave of insecurity at the idea of being watched. Vladei grinned and instantly crossed over to the door sensor. He talked into it, using his gruff voice. He pushed the button several times, pushing in codes before giving the same foreign order over and over again.

Glancing at her, he asked, "Is three enough or will you require more?"

Maggie opened her mouth. No sound came out. She merely shrugged. Vladei called two more.

Maggie hid under the covers, much to her new husband's amusement. He stood naked and proud, waiting for their guests. Seeing how he was excited took away part of her apprehension.

"Did you just call anyone?" she asked.

"No, they are men you know. They have been serving you these last days, and it is right that you should choose to reward them with this honor."

Maggie trembled. The same handsome men that had been walking around her room bowing to her for the last several days? Her body heated to think of them.

Vladei instantly sniffed the air. He grinned. "Ah, I see this pleases you. I am glad you approve of my choices. They are my most trusted crew members, and I have known them a long time. When you were receiving the dreams, each of them came to me hoping to be chosen to please you."

Maggie was stunned. What other species of man would hand-choose other men to please their wives? And hunky, Greek-god-type men at that? If such a thing were ever to happen on Earth, the husband would undoubtedly pick those whose attractiveness wouldn't compete with their own. Though, looking at Vladei, she had to say he was the most attractive Dragoona she'd seen so far.

"These men will pleasure us, but they will not come inside you. For that, it is custom for married couples to take what is called a "third." The third is granted freer privileges of our bed until the time when he finds a wife. Often the third will live with us, helping out around the home when needed, protecting you. You will never sleep with him without me, but we could all find pleasure together when it is so desired."

"And when he finds a wife?"

"We find a new third when we are ready," Vladei answered.

The door lifted and five men walked in. Maggie recognized them immediately. Vladei pointed to them in turn, as he introduced them. Obrin and Hasek had brown hair. Fal was blond. The three of them had brought her trays and taken them away. Kadian, another blond, was the man who'd picked up her hair tie. And Saban was the man who'd touched her foot. She stared at him the longest. He had a wickedly delicious look on his face. He nodded once to acknowledge her attention.

Maggie looked at Vladei. He barked an order, and the men instantly started to strip. Vladei came beside her on the bed and began to kiss her neck, drawing her body's attention back to him. The men stopped moving, their eyes swirling with passion as they watched.

A strange vibration worked over her flesh. Maggie could feel the sexual energy in the room, heating her to the point of near explosion. She closed her eyes. Vladei's hands worked beneath the covers onto her flesh, rubbing her body. The men groaned.

Maggie's eyes flew open in surprise at the sound. They all had dragon tattoos covering their erect cocks, though they were different colors. Vladei chuckled and tore the blankets off her. Gasping, she watched the men looking at her. Their breath deepened in approval and their cocks lurched, becoming fuller.

"They're staring," Maggie whispered to Vladei, torn between watching the men and the very arousing feel of her husband kissing her body.

"Would you like them to do more?" he asked, the subtle sound of hope in his voice.

Maggie nodded. Vladei barked an order. She'd meant that maybe one should dim the lights a little more and perhaps they could move or pleasure themselves or something. But, as they eagerly went down on all fours and crawled toward the bed in submission, she realized her husband had something else in mind.

Vladei stretched his body on top of hers, caressing her. He said something in his gruff tongue and Saban instantly went to the cabinet and pulled out ropes and lubricant. Fal went to the door sensors and dimmed the lights to a seductive level. Suddenly, the bed moved, detaching from the wall and rolling to the center of the room before lowering to the floor.

Maggie watched, her body automatically rubbing along Vladei's as they made love on the bed. He kept kissing her, ignoring the men as he sucked her nipples.

Saban bound the other four men's hands behind their backs. Their stiff cocks thrust out, denied. Two kneeled on each side of her. Then, Saban positioned himself above her head. His hands were left unbound. Maggie looked up. His large cock was over her head, the dragon-covered cock nearly as big as her husband's. She wanted to touch it, but held back.

Maggie shivered, surrounded by six very naked, extremely well-built men. All of them had rock-hard bodies and gave off a confidence that was arousing all on its own. She was amazed at how sex was so natural to the Dragoonas that this situation didn't seem odd in the least to them.

The men were all staring at her, wanting her, their cocks hard for her. But her heart belonged to only one of them. It was strange, but she felt it as sure as she felt anything. She loved Vladei.

"I love you," she said, reaching to lift his face to hers. She melted, as she looked into his eyes. For a moment, the others weren't even there. "Is that crazy?"

"Mm, no," he growled, kissing her deeply, so deeply that she had to squirm for breath to get him to stop. He pulled back, grinning. He adjusted his hips and his cock brushed her thighs. She was so wet. The smell of sex and desire was thick around them. The vibrations of arousal surrounded her until the air practically snapped with a life of its own. Unashamed that the others could hear them, he said, "I love you as well. I've loved you since that first vision I had of you."

Leaning up, Maggie kissed him. When she pulled back, her husband's euphoria was swimming in her blood, rushing to every limb, every section of her lust-filled body.

"They await to pleasure us," Vladei said. "It would please me for you to give them permission."

Maggie glanced around and nodded, eager to have them do so.

Saban's hands slid down over her shoulders to her breasts. His callused palms were warm as he squeezed the globes. The man groaned. Maggie studied Vladei, watching for any hint of jealousy. There was no need. Her husband was too busy watching Saban's hands on her breasts. She felt Vladei's hips move against her.

The four bound men leaned forward, straining against their ties as they began kissing her shoulders and thighs. Maggie tensed. All six of them were breathing hard, moaning as they made love to her. There was something naughty and wicked and so very right about the way the tops of their heads brushed Vladei's tight body as they moved their mouths against her.

Vladei groaned. Saban kissed her neck. Maggie enjoyed the feel of the men's mouths, but she wanted more. Needed more. She wanted their hands on her body, on her husband's body.

"Can we untie them?" she asked, moving to bite Vladei's earlobe.

Her husband groaned. "I wasn't sure if you'd like that, but yes. You can do whatever you wish."

Maggie looked up at Saban, seeing first his large cock hovering as he stood. "Untie them."

The four men grinned as Saban left her to do as she ordered. He freed their hands and instantly they reached forward to touch her. Soon the bed was a frenzy of hands and mouths. Fingers glided over her body, squeezing and touching and stroking. Strong hands glided down Vladei's arms and chest. Maggie tried to touch the full length of her husband at once, reserving her hands for him.

Vladei must have sensed her hesitance and took her hand in his, moving it above her head to Saban's thigh. Running her hand up the man's leg, Vladei wrapped her fingers around the man's thick cock. Maggie moaned, as her husband worked her hand over Saban's arousal. She rubbed her hips up, taking her husband's shaft inside her with the same rhythm.

"I should like him to be our third if you so desire it," Vladei said into her ear. Saban groaned, staring down at her with desire.

"Third?" she whispered, glancing up to where her hand cupped Saban's dragon. Remembering what he'd told her, she shivered. Saban's eyes appeared to darken. Maggie found herself nodding. Both Saban and Vladei grinned, sharing a quick look. Saban groaned.

Vladei pulled her hips, jerking her down further on the bed. Saban kneeled, joining them on the mattress. He placed a knee by either side of her head so his cock and balls were directly above her face. The others looked at him with jealousy, but didn't stop their movements as they continued to caress her and Vladei, moving to touch Saban now as well.

Maggie lifted up and licked the root of his shaft from underneath. The clean, intimate smell of Saban assaulted her. He was muskier than her husband, but not bad. Saban jerked, moaning.

He pulled back, looking down at her. "How does my mistress want me?"

Vladei was busy kissing her stomach. He glanced up, his eyes hot as he smiled. "He wishes to know how you'd like him to come in you so we all may join together."

Maggie was still a little lost in how to answer. It was hard to concentrate with all the mouths and hands moving over her flesh. Her pussy was so wet, aching to be filled again and again. The four men beside her kept going around her wet slit when she would have them thrusting their fingers into her ass while Vladei took her pussy. The men only touched her, and knowing they wanted her was almost too much.

Maggie pushed up, needing to be fucked and soon. Since she'd just come several times with her husband, the need caught her by surprise. She ached and her pussy wept with cream.

"Should I take Saban in my mouth?" she asked Vladei.

"Ah, yes." Her husband nodded, eager for her to do so.

Maggie turned around. Before she could lean over, Saban kissed her, grabbing the sides of her face. His mouth moved differently and he tasted sweeter than Vladei. There was no love in the kiss, just pure sexual enjoyment, a friendship at best. She groaned, taking the pleasure for what it was.

"I am honored to be your third, mistress. I will make you and your husband proud," Saban swore when he pulled back. "My honor will enhance yours."

Then, gently, he urged her mouth down to his dragon. Maggie glanced around to the four men on the sides. Seeing that they still neglected their own cocks, she said, "Find pleasure."

They readily obeyed, taking themselves with one hand, while still kissing and touching her. Maggie expected Vladei's cock to thrust into her, but instead his mouth was on her ass, kissing and biting her cheeks. Then, spreading her thighs, he maneuvered himself so he was lying beneath her pussy. He pulled her down on his mouth, sucking her clit and fucking her with his fingers and tongue.

Saban maneuvered himself on the bed, working his body until his cock was just the right height for her mouth to take him in. Maggie gasped as Saban thrust forward, rimming her lips with his thick cock head. Her mind reeled, unable to concentrate as it was torn between feeling the all the wonderful sensations of the flesh. Her husband's mouth brought her such pleasure that she didn't stop to think as she instantly sucked Saban between her lips. The man groaned, wiggling back and forth. He tasted as different as he smelled.

Maggie smothered Vladei in her drenched pussy as she rode his face. She watched the erotic thrust of Saban's dragon coming in and out of her mouth. Hands were on everyone—touching Saban, moving along the cleft of her ass, and pinching her nipples, undoubtedly stroking over Vladei if the slight bumps along the backs of her thighs were any indication.

It was all too much. She was close. Her body tensed. Maggie

groaned, sucking Saban harder, wanting him to come with her. She touched his hip. As she came, he jerked back, denying her his release. She gasped, jerking against Vladei's face. The four men groaned, jerking with her, coming heavily.

Vladei said something as he pushed her off his face. For a moment, Maggie was worried that she'd been too wanton. One look at his passionate face soothed the fear. The men bowed to her, smiling and sated as they quickly pulled on their clothes, leaving her alone with Vladei and Saban.

Maggie was still aroused. She no longer questioned her amazing sex drive. It was as Vladei said, the men had replenished her energies. She turned on the bed and Vladei kissed her, moaning into her mouth. Her taste was on his lips, mingling with Saban's. It was all too much. Saban came behind her and the two men instantly stood, drawing her up between them.

"This is better," Vladei said. He glanced at his friend then back at her. "It is good that we spend time alone."

A little worried, she glanced over her shoulder. "You're all right with this?"

Saban frowned, confused.

"I can't explain it, but I love him. You, I . . ." What could she say? She barely knew the man. Vladei was in her body, her blood. He was part of her soul.

Saban laughed. "You have a kind heart, mistress. I know well the place of the third and will enjoy fulfilling that place and serving you both."

Saban grabbed her ass before sinking his cock between her cheeks. Vladei did the same from the front, rubbing against her slit. Both men groaned in pleasure.

"You have sucked me well, mistress," Saban said. "If it pleases you, I wish to find release now."

"My cock is ready for you as well, wife," Vladei said, lifting her up off the bed so she was forced to straddle his waist. When he had her supported, she felt Saban move. She kissed Vladei passionately. When Saban came back he lubed her ass with the tingling liquid. Maggie tensed, realizing they both meant to take her like this.

Vladei thrust into her first. She cried out in pleasure. He was so big that she stretched around him. Before he was completely accommodated, Saban spread her ass cheeks and ran his cock along the moistened cleft. She felt him probe her tight hole as Vladei still filled her.

Strong muscles surrounded her as the men crushed her body between them. She felt their hands hesitate as they both kissed a side of her neck. Pulling Saban's hand from her hip, she drew it to Vladei. Both men groaned in approval. Soon they were thrusting against her, filling her completely.

Maggie whimpered. It felt so good. Then, groaning as she peaked, she felt both of the men jerk simultaneously, filling her up. Maggie dropped against Vladei. Saban was the first to pull out. Vladei grunted, weakened and trembling as he let her slide back down. The men lowered her down to the bed, lying on each side of her.

Saban was the first to move. "I have to report for duty. This time is for you two anyway. I'm just for pleasure, not this aftermath."

Maggie smiled at him before snuggling into Vladei's chest. When she heard the door open and close, she finally looked up at him. A moment's shyness overcame her, but he kissed it away. Then, pulling his head back, he said, "You please me greatly, wife."

"You please me as well." Almost scared, Maggie glanced down the length of his body. Finally Vladei's erection had gone down. She sighed with relief. After that last bout, she'd say she was definitely, completely, totally spent.

"I'd say it's tamed," she said, chuckling softly.

"Yes, unless you would like me to try and revive it?" Vladei offered, grinning tiredly.

"Mm," she moaned. Maggie couldn't open her eyes again. "Later. Sleep first."

He pulled her into his arms and held her tight to his chest. She kissed above his heart before pulling back.

"I love you," she whispered, before she could stop the words. Maggie refused to take them back, as she felt his response before he even said anything.

"And I you," he responded, unashamed. "The gods would not have brought us together if it wasn't to be a match of the hearts. Everything else we will need to know about each other will come with time."

Maggie smiled. He was right. Vladei was her fate.